Looking for You All My Life

Melody Carlson

Bethel Baptist Church
P.O. BOX 167
AUMSVILLE, OR 97325

HARVEST HOUSE PUBLISHERS
Eugene, Oregon 97402

Cover by David Uttley Design, Sisters, Oregon

Map illustration by Jan Cieloha, Springfield, Oregon

LOOKING FOR YOU ALL MY LIFE
Copyright © 2000 by Melody Carlson
Published by Harvest House Publishers
Eugene, Oregon 97402

Library of Congress Cataloging-in-Publication Data
Carlson, Melody.
    Looking for you all my life / Melody Carlson.
        p. cm. — (Whispering pines series)
    ISBN 0-7369-0063-2
    I. Title.
PS3553.A73257 E94 2000
813'.54 21—dc21   99-041914

All rights reserved. No portion of this book may be reproduced in any form
without the written permission of the Publisher.

Printed in the United States of America.

00 01 02 03 04 05 06 07 08 09 / BC / 10 9 8 7 6 5 4 3 2 1

To Gabriel Douglas Carlson
Love always,
Mom

One

During the first week of November, traffic through town had dwindled to a thin trickle. Besides the coming and going of the locals, there were only a few late-season elk hunters cruising down Main Street on their way back home, some with elk heads and large antler racks displayed proudly on their hunting rigs (a habit a city girl found slightly disturbing).

Maggie diverted her attention from the "trophy" tied to the hood of a dust-covered pickup parked along Main Street by watching her breath come out in little white puffs that lingered for a moment on the crisp midday air before they disappeared. The novelty of such a simple thing as frost was not lost on her as she walked toward Galloway's Deli. It was not something she'd seen much of in southern California.

The atmosphere had suddenly changed in Pine Mountain. A quiet hush wrapped itself around the streets of this little town until it seemed that even the normally energetic merchants had become unusually subdued. Maggie waved across the street to Elizabeth Rodgers as the older woman pushed a broom across the sidewalk in front of the bookstore, lethargically sweeping dead leaves over the curb and into the gutter below. In some ways the feeling in town reminded Maggie of last spring when she and Spencer had first arrived to discover a dreary and dying business district. Only now she sensed a real spirit of hope and expectation resting beneath this temporary veneer of quiet. And no one could deny that the town looked better than ever with all its recent renovations and face-lifts.

Still, Maggie wondered how this little slump might affect commerce as she passed by the recently refurbished Pine Mountain Hotel. She peeked in the front window to see a perfectly decorated lobby completely void of guests. Of course Brian and Cindy Jordan, with their high-earning computer software stocks, could easily afford a slow season at the hotel, but few other businessowners in town were so fortunate. Even with last summer's boom and the better-than-usual fall season, an unprofitable winter could be the undoing of some of the more fragile businesses. Maggie knew it was silly to feel so overly protective of the town, but whether she could openly admit it or not, the truth was she felt an almost maternal sort of concern.

"Hey there, Maggie," called Rosa from behind the tiled deli counter. "You're early today."

"Thought I'd beat the rush." Maggie smiled sheepishly at her joke as she glanced around the nearly vacant room.

"Pretty bad, isn't it?" Rosa sighed and gave the already clean countertop a swipe.

"I heard we might get some snow," offered Maggie hopefully.

"That's what Sam said too, but it's only supposed to be a light dusting. It'll take more than that to open up the ski season around here."

"But it's still early. Isn't it pretty rare to open before Thanksgiving?"

Rosa adjusted the straw container and thought for a moment. "I suppose so, but we've seen it open in early November before. I guess because of the strong summer and fall seasons everyone had just hoped..."

"Well, maybe the weatherman is wrong about the dusting part of his forecast. Maybe we're in for a foot or two."

"You're sounding more like us everyday. I suppose this disease is the result of our tourist-based economy. We all live in a slightly delusional world." Rosa grinned. "We survive on optimism and unrealistic hopes—and, of course, we're ever dependent on the weather."

"Not to mention a lot of hard work." Maggie glanced up at the menu board. "I'll have a bowl of your black bean soup, Rosa."

Rosa ladled out the dark, spicy-smelling soup. "So what's cooking at the *Pine Cone* these days? Scott's been so busy with Chloe lately that I haven't heard much about work."

Maggie laughed. "Those two are getting pretty serious. I've actually wondered if Scott might be hearing wedding bells lately. And, selfishly, I wouldn't mind a bit. I'd hate to lose him at the paper."

"With Chloe saying she never wants to leave Pine Mountain, my boy may have to rethink his future as a big-city journalist." Rosa handed Maggie her order, then poured herself a mug of coffee. "Mind if I join you during this little lull?"

"Not at all." The two women sat down and Maggie glanced across the dining room to the couple deep in conversation at a corner table. They were an elderly pair and not locals. "Well, as far as what's going on at the *Pine Cone*..." she lowered her voice slightly. "Actually, I think I'm about to break open a pretty big story—at least for Pine Mountain, that is—but I'm sort of nervous about the whole thing."

Rosa's brows went up. "What is it? Or is it top secret?"

"It's about Greg Snider."

"Oh, our notorious postmaster. What's he up to now?"

"I take it that you haven't heard anything about it then? Nothing from Sam or anyone?"

Rosa shook her head and sipped her coffee. "No, and Sam is usually up on all the latest news. Men say women gossip, but I think that's just their cover-up."

"Well, I suspect that Rick Tanner and Greg Snider have been trying to keep this thing under their hats, but I'm on my way out to interview Mr. Westerly this afternoon—"

"Old Arnold Westerly? I can hardly believe that man is still alive—he must be about a hundred by now."

"I don't know about his age, but I do know he owns a couple hundred acres of prime farmland—"

"Right between the Tanners and the old Snider place," injected Rosa, her brow lifting with suspicion.

Maggie nodded. "Anyway, I've learned that Greg and Rick are buying that property and planning some big real estate development out there."

Rosa slapped her hand on the table and laughed sarcastically. "Now if that doesn't beat all. The antidevelopment boys are out there scheming up their own little land deals and trying to keep everything hush-hush. Well, good for you, Maggie. I hope you blow this thing wide open."

"The only problem is…" Maggie's brow furrowed. "I feel bad about Cherise. She's been so sweet to me at the fitness center, and I just hate to see her get hurt by my story."

"Cherise is a big girl and stronger than many think. Besides, Maggie, the truth is the truth. Right?"

Maggie set down her spoon. "Yes. And I've already sat on this news for too long—mostly to protect Cherise because she's the one who gave me the initial information. But I can't be silent about something like this forever."

Rosa frowned. "I hope Greg and Rick aren't taking advantage of poor Arnold. He's a sweet old guy. And all alone."

"He sounded nice on the phone, and very sharp if he's as old as you say. Plus he seemed eager to talk. But I'm afraid he thinks I'm interviewing him for our *Bit of History* section." She broke off a chunk of crusty bread and dipped it into her soup. "In fact, I think I will schedule Scott to do a history piece on him. No doubt this Mr. Westerly has some interesting stories to tell." The bell on the door jingled and Maggie looked up to see Buckie and Kate walk in. "Looks like you've got customers, Rosa." Maggie waved as the couple approached the counter.

"Thank goodness for the regulars." Rosa stood and straightened her apron. "Nice catching up with you. And good luck with that story."

Maggie finished her soup, then she went over to greet Buckie and Kate on her way out. They seemed such a perfect couple now that it made her wonder how any of them had ever missed that potential from the start. "How's business?" she asked Buckie with a friendly smile.

He frowned. "Actually, it's pretty slow this week."

"But this is a great time to do some long-term planning," piped in the ever-optimistic Kate. "I've been encouraging Buckie to have some of his better prints reproduced into note cards and postcards and such, plus I've been checking into some mail-order outfits that I think he could get into, not to mention setting up a Blue Moose website. You know Northwest art is pretty popular these days."

Buckie reached over and patted Kate's arm with open admiration. "Kate's such a whiz when it comes to ideas and marketing and all that stuff. I don't know what I'd do without her."

With mixed feelings Maggie remembered how invaluable Kate had been to Jed's business with that same sort of perspective—and then how suddenly that had all changed, mostly due to her. She smiled at Kate. "Well, if you ever get bored just working for Buckie, you might consider starting up your own marketing consultation service. I'm sure a lot of businesses in town would find your ideas very helpful."

"Hey, watch it, Maggie!" warned Buckie. "Don't you go luring my right-hand girl away from me."

Kate laughed. "Don't worry, Buckie, I'm not that easy to get rid of. But Maggie does have a good point. A consulting business might be something I could do on the side—and drawing in more customers at other places wouldn't hurt your business a single bit."

"You know, Kate," said Maggie, "I've had some thoughts of my own about how the newspaper could help promote businesses. And you're always so full of great ideas—maybe we should get together and discuss them sometime."

"I'd love to," said Kate with a smile that could've been used for a toothpaste ad.

For the first time since their original conflict over Jed, Maggie wondered if she and Kate might actually become friends one day. "Great," she said. "I'll give you a call soon. With business so slow right now, it might be the perfect time to start making some plans for the tourist traffic that will come with the upcoming ski season."

"You mean, if we ever get any snow," said Buckie sullenly.

"It'll come," Kate reassured him. "It always does sooner or later."

ᴏ᷈

Maggie hadn't planned to stop by Jed's shop today as she knew that Leah had invited him for dinner at the house tonight. But seeing Kate and hearing how Buckie was reaping the benefits of that new relationship made Maggie feel worried for Jed. Leah had mentioned just that morning at breakfast how business had been terribly slow for Whitewater Works this week, and although it seemed sort of silly, Maggie felt responsible.

"Hello?" she called as she entered the familiar shop, sniffing the air for the pungent aroma of cedar. "Anyone here?"

"In the back," called Leah. "I'm coming."

"How's it going?" Maggie asked as Leah emerged from the back room, a cardboard box in one hand and a packing slip in the other.

"Still pretty quiet." Leah brushed a dark strand of hair from her eyes. "You're the first one to walk through the front door all day."

Maggie frowned. "Is Jed around?"

"No, he just left. He's working at home this afternoon."

"Well, that's probably good. How's he doing?"

Leah's brows lifted. "What do you mean?"

"Oh, I guess I was feeling a little concerned about him from a business standpoint. I just ran into Kate, and you know how she's so involved at the Blue Moose now, and she has all these great plans about how to market Buckie's work—and well, I suppose I feel a little guilty, like it's my fault that Kate's not here—"

"But *I'm* here." Leah stuck out her chin defensively.

Maggie smiled. "Of course, I know that. And Jed couldn't be happier—"

"But you don't think that's enough."

"That's not what I meant, Leah."

Leah set the box on the floor and folded her arms. "I'm working really hard for Jed, Maggie. I told him he doesn't even have to come into the shop at all if he needs to work on his projects at home. I know this isn't an easy business, especially this time of year, but I'm here for him. Isn't that enough?"

Maggie placed a soothing hand on Leah's arm. "It's more than enough, honey. Really. Jed wouldn't trade you for a hundred Kates. And I'm sure in time you'll have this whole business completely figured out, and then you and Jed will be the busiest shop in town."

Leah frowned. "I don't think either of us want that."

Maggie blinked, feeling somewhat chastised. "Well, you know what I mean. I'm sure everything's going to be just fine. I'm sorry if what I said didn't come out quite the way I meant it." She looked Leah in the eyes. "Are we still okay?"

Leah's dark eyes looked misty, but she nodded. "Yes, of course. I guess maybe I'm a little worried about Jed's business too. There's so much to learn right now. I want to be a help and not a hindrance, but I hate asking Jed questions all the time. Sometimes I feel like I'm nothing but a nuisance."

"I know Jed doesn't think that at all. He loves having you around, Leah. But if you're worried about the business aspects, maybe you could ask Kate to stop by and give you some tips."

Leah pressed her lips together. "I don't really like Kate very much."

"Oh." Maggie thought a moment. "I used to feel like that too, but I'm trying to be more open. And I'm finding there's more to her than meets the eye."

"Maybe. But I think I'd rather try to figure things out for myself around here. I learned a lot just working for Buckie. In many ways these businesses aren't all that much different."

"You're probably right." Maggie glanced at her watch. "Okay, then, I'll see you tonight. Is Jed still coming for dinner?"

Leah's eyes lit up. "Yes. And I'm still cooking. He gave me a venison roast from a deer he shot on his property. Audrey promised to give me a hand with it."

"I'm looking forward to it."

Maggie walked slowly back to the *Pine Cone* to pick up her briefcase before her interview with Mr. Westerly. Something in the tone of her conversation with Leah bothered her a little. Why was Leah becoming so defensive? Maggie hadn't meant to infer that Leah's help in the shop was inadequate in any way. It was only that she felt worried about Jed's business without Kate's experienced hand. It was no secret that Kate had been an integral ingredient in Jed's past success. But why should that threaten Leah? Good grief, Leah was only eighteen years old—no one expected her to replace Kate. But maybe this wasn't about Kate and Leah, reasoned Maggie. Maybe this was about Maggie and Leah...and Jed.

She'd only returned from California a week ago, yet in that short time it seemed things had changed between her and Leah. But with so much going on, she hadn't given it much thought. Until now. Since last week's harvest party,

Leah, like everyone else, had become well aware that Maggie and Jed might be entering into a new phase of their relationship. But so far, that relationship seemed to be developing slowly, which was perfectly fine with Maggie. She had only seen Jed once since the party, and that was when they'd met for lunch a couple of days ago. Even then, the warm look in his eyes had convinced her that nothing between them had changed a bit. She felt content to allow all the time necessary for them to become better acquainted with each other. Plus, she reasoned, they were both busy people with many responsibilities. There seemed no need to hurry anything along.

"Hey there, Maggie," called Clyde as she approached the front porch of the newspaper office. "I think I can feel snow in my bones."

"Really?" she smiled. "The forecast is for a light dusting."

He adjusted the ear flaps on his plaid wool hunting cap. "Wouldn't be surprised if we got us several inches by tomorrow."

"Well, that'd be welcome, wouldn't it? Say, Clyde, I'm sure you know Arnold Westerly..."

"You bet I do. Arnold and I go way back. But I haven't seen the old guy in a coon's age. Why're you asking?"

"I'm on my way to see him right now. I'm about to blow open what could be a fairly big story."

Clyde rubbed his hands together with enthusiasm. "A big story? About old Arnold? Can't imagine what that could possibly be, Maggie girl."

She glanced around to see if anyone was within earshot, and then quickly explained about Greg and Rick's land scheme. "Want to join me for this interview?"

"Oh boy, would I love to! But I've got to meet an old buddy of mine today. He came over from the valley to spend the weekend at my cabin and do some pheasant hunting. But you better get to the bottom of this, Maggie. Arnold's a good guy, and I don't like the idea of anyone, and especially not

the likes of Greg Snider, taking advantage of the old feller."
Clyde clenched his fists and growled. "And after all that antidevelopment nonsense Snider put us through last summer!
Well, all I can say is you better nail this story good and we'll
blast it all across the front page in next week's edition."

She grinned. "You can count on it. Have a good weekend
hunting with your buddy, Clyde."

"Yep. But I want to hear all about Arnold first thing come
Monday morning."

"Yes, sir." She tossed him a mock salute.

"That's my girl." His face softened. "Sure good to have
you back, Maggie. You had me fretting something fierce
while you were gone off in California all that time. Feared
you might change your mind about us and not come back."

"Don't worry, Clyde. I've finally figured out where my
home is."

"And don't you go off and forget it none, either!"

Two

aggie had never been in the area where the Westerly farm was located. But now she understood why Greg and Rick had been so eager to get their hands on it as she admired the lovely, pastoral piece of land with a stream cutting through the middle. Although much larger than her property, it was similar with its wide-open spaces and ponderosa pine forest along the boundaries. It lacked the full mountain views that she so enjoyed on her place, but all in all it was a gorgeous piece of carefully tended farmland. The rich, dark soil of recently tilled fields and the old-fashioned barn with silo with farm machinery parked nearby indicated it was still a working farm. And there, nestled beneath several old willow trees, was a charmingly old, single-story farmhouse with a wide, if slightly sagging, covered porch. She parked in the gravel driveway and walked up to the front door to be greeted by the friendly barks of a black-and-white dog, its tail wagging happily.

"You must be Maggie Carpenter," called a raspy voice from around the side of the porch. An elderly man in clean but faded overalls removed his felt hat and approached her, extending a work-worn hand in her direction.

"Yes, and you must be Mr. Westerly." She shook his hand and was surprised at the wiry strength beneath the wrinkled exterior.

"Pleased to make your acquaintance." His eyes were warm and friendly and his smile seemed sincere. "I see you've met my Lizzie." He smiled down on the dog. "Good girl, Lizzie."

"Is she a Border collie?" Maggie stroked the dog's smooth head, noticing that one of her eyes was murky and gray, probably the result of age and cataracts.

"Purebred." He grinned proudly. "I owned her mother and grandmother and great-grandmother. But she's the last one for me."

Maggie nodded with understanding, suspecting that Mr. Westerly was afraid he wouldn't last long enough to own another dog. "Well, she seems like a very well-mannered girl."

"That she is. Please excuse me for keeping you waiting on the porch, especially when it's getting so cold outside. I think we've got some snow on the way. Come inside. You'll find I'm not much of a housekeeper—that was always Nellie's territory, God rest her soul." He led her into a dimly lit parlor with furnishings that appeared as if they hadn't been changed or moved for more than fifty years. "Excuse the dust and have a seat," he said. "I've made us some fresh coffee. That is, unless you would rather have tea. My Nellie always preferred tea."

"No, coffee is perfect. And you shouldn't have gone to such trouble—"

"It's no trouble." He waved his hand and left.

Maggie sat on the plum-colored sofa, running her hand along the stiff camel-hair fabric, still scratchy after all these years. On one side of the sofa sat a platform rocker and on the opposite side, a tufted armchair covered in a faded cabbage-rose fabric. In the far corner stood a dark upright piano with a painted porcelain lamp centered on the top, its shade a faded pink with silk tassels all around. Numerous decorative porcelain figures posed on tables and shelves throughout the room. They'd probably belonged to the wife—Nellie. All of the figurines were of children and animals—quite a nice collection actually. Maggie glanced with interest at a tall and completely filled bookshelf by the door. It seemed someone was a reader.

"Here we go," said Mr. Westerly as he set a neatly arranged tray onto the low table in front of the couch. Some of the coffee had sloshed out of the dainty cup and into the saucer, but Maggie discreetly dabbed the excess with a small paper napkin, then sipped her coffee, expecting it to taste like the powdery, tasteless instant her grandmother had always used. To her surprise it wasn't half bad.

"Good coffee," she said, pulling out her notepad and tape recorder in preparation for the interview.

"It's Folgers. I don't drink anything but Folgers. Haven't for years." He looked at the recorder. "What's that little thing?"

"It's a miniature tape recorder. We reporters often use these to get our facts straight. Do you mind if I record our conversation?"

He grinned. "Not at all. Is this like being on the radio or TV?"

She smiled. "Sort of." She turned on the recorder and said the date and location. "Mr. Westerly, for today I'd planned to mostly ask questions about the future of your farm, but it has occurred to me that you might also have some interesting historical stories to tell—"

"Well, after living for ninety-two years, I just might have a tale or two."

She laughed. "That's what I figured. But since Scott Galloway handles our historical column, I'd like him to schedule that interview for another time—if that's okay with you."

"Galloway? Is he one of Jack Galloway's boys?"

"Actually, Jack is Scott's grandfather. Scott's dad is Sam Galloway."

"Young Sam Galloway has a grown-up son?" Mr. Westerly scratched his nearly bald head. "Don't know how so many years went by so fast and I didn't even notice. But sure, I'd like to talk to this young Galloway man."

"Good. You can be thinking about what stories you'd like to tell, and maybe get together some photographs or other memorabilia. Now, I have some questions about your farm. First, how long have you owned it?"

"My pa came out here with my ma in the spring of 1901. He came from a farm family back in Virginia. But there were six sons and not enough land to go around, so my pa, being the most adventuresome of the bunch, decided to come out to Oregon. He bought the land for ten dollars an acre." Mr. Westerly laughed. "I know that sounds dirt cheap now, but back then it was no small thing to come up with $2,000."

"But what a good investment for your father."

"Sure was. I was born a few years later. Then my sister came along, and another brother. All deceased now. Seems a mite strange that I'm the oldest and the only one alive."

"You must be living right." She looked into his eyes. "Do you have any descendants?"

He sipped his coffee, and then nodded. "My son, Wilmar, lives down in New Mexico. He's retired now. Wilmar has two daughters, Jeanette and Linda. They used to come out here every summer to visit. And oh, how my Nellie enjoyed those two. Wilmar's girls are both in their forties now, with nearly grown kids of their own. Jeanette has two boys, both in high school. And Linda has a daughter just starting college. I've only seen Linda's girl a couple times. But Jeanette's been out here with the boys quite a bit, although not for the last year or two—the boys are busy now with sports and whatnot."

"Do you have any other children? Or just the one son."

"We had a daughter. Pretty little thing—looked just like her mother. But we lost her in the winter of '38. Saddest day of my life." He shook his head and set down his cup. "Grief just about killed my Nellie." His gaze swept over the glass figurines. "That's when I started buying her those little glass doo-dads. They seemed to help her get over losing our little Annie somehow..."

"I had been admiring that collection." She glanced to her notes and continued. "You mentioned that you had a brother and sister who've both passed on. Do you have any nieces or nephews?"

"Yep. My brother Howard had three children—two girls and a boy. 'Course they're all about retirement age by now." He chuckled. "Though I never did understand how a man could turn sixty-five and just up and decide to quit working."

"Maybe that's why you've enjoyed such a long life."

"Rightly said, I'm sure. Let's see now. I was telling you about my family. I had a sister too. She never married or had children. Taught school right up until the day she died. Miss Jane Westerly—she was a good woman."

"And I imagine you've got some great-nieces and nephews then." Maggie glanced at her notes. "They'd be Howard's grandchildren."

"I can see you're listening real careful. Yes, Howard's children. I think they live in California still. He had a girl and a boy—Clara and Howie. They both got married and had children, but I can't tell you much about them."

"I'm amazed at how well you can remember what you do, Mr. Westerly."

"Nellie always thought family was important. She used to keep up with everyone with letters and birthday cards and whatnot. I've tried to continue, but other than Christmas cards..." His voice trailed off.

"I think you're doing very well to send out Christmas cards. I never sent a single one last year, myself." She leaned forward and looked into his creased face. "Actually, the main reason I'm curious about your family is because I can't help but wonder if you'd ever considered leaving your farm to any of your relatives."

"I'd sure have liked that, but no one ever seemed real interested. Jeanette and Linda always liked coming out as kids, but then they grew up. And although Jeanette used to bring her boys, they're so busy with their own lives these days..." He reached over and patted Lizzie's head and smiled sadly. "I guess me and Lizzie here are just the last of our breed."

"I suppose that explains your willingness to sell the farm then."

"So the cat's out of the bag now." Mr. Westerly leaned back into the chair and exhaled slowly. "Rick asked me to keep all this under my hat for the time being. I'm not real sure why though. Don't know why anyone would care about an old man selling his farm."

"What made you decide to sell?"

"Well, I never really planned to do that. I figured to keep it in the family. And at one point I'd hoped to leave it to my granddaughter, Jeanette. Of all the children, she seemed the one to understand this land the best. She really loved everything about the farm. Used to get up early and go out and help me all the time. And her youngest son, Bradley, is a lot like that too."

"Then why not leave it to her?"

"I offered, but Jeanette said it wouldn't be fair to the rest of the family."

"But it sounds like no one else was interested."

"They weren't interested in the farm, to be sure. But more'n likely they'd be interested in the money."

"I see..." She nodded, considering all this. "But what about leaving the farm to Jeanette with a stipulation that if she ever sold the property, the proceeds would be divided fairly among the others?"

Mr. Westerly frowned. "That's not a bad idea. Don't know why that never occurred to me before..."

"What made you decide to sell to Rick Tanner and Greg Snider?"

"I'm *not* selling to Greg Snider," he corrected her sharply. "I'm selling to Rick. Those Tanners have been good neighbors the last couple of years. First, the dad began helping me out. Then Bill, Rick's brother, stepped in. After he moved away, Rick started helping me out. Our farms adjoin and young Rick understands and respects the land just like I do. I know he'll keep this farm running in tip-top shape, and that's real important to me."

Maggie was speechless. Did he actually believe that Rick planned to continue farming this land? "Uh, is the sale of your property final yet?" she asked weakly.

"We signed papers last week."

"Is Rick's dad involved in the sale too?"

"Not directly. You see, he's in a nursing home now. He's quite a bit younger than me, but he's got that Alzheimer's sickness where you can't remember anything—poor old feller went walking out in the snow last winter without a single stitch of clothing on, nearly froze himself to death."

"I see. And Rick told you that he plans to continue farming—uh, indefinitely?"

Mr. Westerly nodded. "That's right. You see, Rick's like me in that regard. Can't stand to be away from the dirt for more than a day or so."

"It's strange," she began cautiously, unsure of how to best proceed. "I'd heard that Greg Snider was involved in this transaction too."

Mr. Westerly slapped his knee and laughed. "I don't know where you got that notion. Looks to me like Greg Snider's got enough problems on his hands with his own family's farm. The Snider place is just south of me, but they've let it go to wrack and ruin. Hank Snider's got arthritis real bad, and the youngest son, Billy, was working the farm for a while, but then he just up and left. From what I hear, Greg doesn't lift a finger to help out. Now *there's* a farm that needs to be sold—and soon. I'm just glad Rick is taking my farm over while it's still in good shape. Nothing worse than seeing what you spent your whole life working on going to pot."

"And where will you live, now that the farm is sold?"

"Right here, of course. From the start Rick said there'd be no need for me to move out of my house. I'll just continue on as always, puttering around, helping Rick out when I can. It's no secret that I'm getting on in years. I don't expect to be around too much longer. 'Course you never know..."

Maggie swallowed hard as she imagined huge caterpillar tractors tearing up his beautiful farmland to prepare for cheesy condos and golf courses. But certainly Greg and Rick didn't plan to do all this with poor Mr. Westerly sitting in his little house looking on! She continued to ask more questions. Dates and facts. And she discreetly managed to find out what he'd been paid for the farm and how he planned to divide the sum up between all of his father's descendants.

"That seems very fair of you, Mr. Westerly." She closed her notebook. "Now, are you sure you don't mind me printing up this information—things like the selling price and all that?"

He shook his head. "I don't have any secrets. Nothing to hide."

She sighed. Unfortunately, not everyone in this transaction had been so honest. "Thank you for your time, Mr. Westerly."

He waved his hand in dismissal. "It's been a real pleasure. I should be thanking you. But honestly, I don't see how this makes for much of a story. Don't know why anyone'd care about me selling my farm."

She looked into his faded eyes. The color reminded her of the sky today—pale shades of gray. "Mr. Westerly," she began slowly, glancing to see that the recorder was still running. "I want to be completely honest with you, okay?"

"Of course. I'd expect you to be. Is something wrong?"

"I'm not sure. But I've heard, and maybe this is just a rumor—I plan to check everything out completely before I write my story—but Greg Snider's wife told me that Greg and Rick were purchasing your property together...as partners." She wanted to add "in crime," but controlled herself.

Mr. Westerly's face clouded over. "But why would Greg Snider be interested in my farm? He can't even manage his own."

"Because, from what I heard, their plan is to develop it."

"*Develop it?*" His face grew puzzled. "Develop it into what?"

She drew in a deep breath. "I've heard that Greg and Rick plan to turn all three of these farms into a very large community development with condominiums and maybe even a golf course—"

"*No!*" Mr. Westerly abruptly stood, sending his cup and saucer to the hardwood floor with a loud crash of shattered china.

"Oh, I'm so sorry." Maggie fell to her knees and began picking up the shards of broken porcelain. "And this was such a pretty cup—"

"No," said Mr. Westerly again, only more quietly this time. "What you've heard is not true. It's just some mean rumor concocted up by Greg Snider's wife. To be completely honest, those Sniders aren't the nicest of people. Over the years I've tried to be friendly with Hank, but he was always a cantankerous fellow. Still, I'm certain that what you heard is a falsehood, Mrs. Carpenter. You go and speak directly to Rick Tanner and he'll straighten you out, I'm sure of it."

She forced a stiff smile to her lips as she set the broken cup and saucer onto the tray and stood. "I really do hope you're right, Mr. Westerly. I certainly don't want this to be true. You've created a perfectly beautiful farm here, and the best thing I can imagine is for it to continue for many, many years to come."

He smiled and patted her reassuringly on the arm. "And so it will, my dear. So it will."

"But if I find out anything different, say, than what you've been led to believe—do you mind if I include it in my article?"

"You just print the truth, Mrs. Carpenter. That's all anyone expects."

"But what if the truth doesn't match what you've been told?"

"Then let the chips fall where they may." He frowned. "But don't you worry about that, because Rick is an honorable man. I trust him like my own flesh and blood, and he knows that."

She reached out and shook his hand. "It's been a real pleasure to meet you, Mr. Westerly. Like I said, I'll have Scott schedule another interview with you for our historical column."

"Then I'll get busy and dig up some things. You know, I love to read and I used to be a bit of a writer myself. I wrote in journals and such—'course they wouldn't be of much interest to anyone now except to an old fool like me."

"You never know. I'd like to see them."

"I'll find them for you, Mrs. Carpenter. And I'll look forward to seeing this story in the paper next week. Just write the truth, that's all I ask."

"You have my word, Mr. Westerly."

Three

"Are you sure you don't need any help in the kitchen?" called Maggie from the library as she struck a match to the crumpled newspaper beneath the neatly arranged pile of kindling in the fireplace. She guessed it to be Spencer's work, although he was nowhere in sight just now, but judging by Daniel's orange Volkswagen Bug parked right next to the barn, she suspected they were out there practicing music.

"No, everything's under control in here," replied Audrey. "You just put your feet up and relax a little before Jed gets here."

Maggie sighed contentedly and looked on with satisfaction as the wood began to ignite and crackle into bright orange flames. Then she carefully placed several small aspen logs on top and closed the metal grate. Sitting down on the old leather couch, she leaned her head back and admired how much this room had changed in the last couple of months. No doubt it was her favorite room in the house now. Spencer had eagerly filled the floor-to-ceiling bookshelves he'd so beautifully refinished with her many boxes of books that had been stored out in the barn. Probably just in the nick of time too as Jed had warned her that mice would come in from the cold to nibble and nest in there. Naturally, Spencer hadn't bothered to organize her books, but just seeing them on the shelves brought comfort, and she could rearrange them more carefully later—perhaps on some cold, snowy day. She glanced over to the desk Jed had made for her. It was so perfect for this room with its dark, gleaming wood and clean Craftsman lines. And then Audrey had donated the old mahogany office chair; it had once belonged to Maggie's grandfather, a newspaper man himself. He had used it at his own desk while working for the *San Francisco Herald*. Maggie had added some rich earth-toned pillows and other decorative touches, along with numerous candles, which she now took time to light. The cozy room glowed with warmth and personality. Before closing the wooden shutters, she peered out the window to the darkness outside. She wondered if and when this predicted dusting of snow might actually occur. Like a young child looking forward to Christmas, she anticipated this first snow with an almost juvenile eagerness. She wondered if this was simply part of being the newcomer, or did others feel this way too?

She opened her briefcase and set her notes and tape recorder on her desk. Tempted to begin her work on Arnold Westerly's story, she reminded herself that all the facts were not yet in, and to begin the story too soon would definitely slant her coverage—as if it weren't slanted already! But she could go over her notes and prepare some appropriate questions for Rick, her next interviewee. Rick had sounded reluctant to talk with her on the phone today, but when she reminded him that the *Pine Cone* was online now, and an article about their development would help get the word out to prospective buyers across the state and country, he'd instantly grown quite chatty. Now she wondered if that wasn't just a bit deceptive on her part, though it was true enough. Only yesterday Scott had reported that their *Pine Cone* website was getting an inordinate amount of hits per week—and from all over the country! Some people were even phoning Abigail to get more information on tourist attractions to be found in Pine Mountain. Perhaps it was time for the business association to consider some alternative ways to deal with outside inquiries. Certainly the little *Pine Cone* wouldn't be able to handle all these calls indefinitely.

"Hello," said a deep voice, scattering Maggie's thoughts. She looked up to see Jed standing in the doorway watching her. "Audrey said you were putting your feet up in here, but it looks to me like you're thick in the middle of work."

"Not really. I'm just daydreaming mostly. Come on in." She rose from her desk, suddenly feeling slightly awkward and self-conscious and wishing she'd gone upstairs to freshen up a bit. Jed looked extra handsome in a neatly pressed khaki shirt, topped with a muted-toned woven vest. Although she knew he hadn't a vain bone in his body, he always had such a sense of style about him.

"Nice fire," he commented, sinking down into the couch and sighing with deep satisfaction. "This room's become a very inviting place. Quite a difference from when you first moved in here."

She laughed. "That's for sure. In fact, I was just thinking that it's become my favorite room in the whole house. I suppose that means I better get to work on the others."

"Plenty of time for that." He sat up and looked at her. "Sometimes I think you never give yourself a break."

"You should talk, Mr. Whitewater. You're one of the hardest-working people I know."

He smiled. "Ah, so it seems. But what you don't realize is that I always take time to refresh myself."

"You do?"

He nodded. "Yes, it's something I learned from my father. He always took time to walk in the woods, to enjoy nature and relax. I remember how he'd tell me that life wasn't worth living if all you did was work."

"Your father sounds as if he was a very wise man."

"He was." Jed leaned into the back of the couch, stretching his long legs toward the fireplace, then turned and looked into Maggie's eyes. "So how are you doing?"

She allowed herself to return his gaze, almost becoming lost in the dark pools of his eyes before she answered, "I'm okay, I guess."

His brow lifted. "You guess?"

"Well, I'm working on a story that's troubling me a little." She waved her hand. "But we don't need to talk about work—"

"No, I'd like to hear. What is it?"

She sat up straighter and began to explain about the Westerly property, eager to hear what Jed would think of the whole thing.

He shook his head. "Poor Mr. Westerly."

"I know," she agreed. "And he's such a dear man. I just hate seeing him hurt like this. I wonder if there's anything to be done."

"Perhaps when the old guy hears the truth, he can consult with his attorney and possibly get out of the sale."

Maggie brightened. "Wouldn't that be great—"

"Hello," called Leah tentatively as she entered the room carrying a tray of cheese and crackers. "Am I interrupting?"

Jed rose to his feet and took the tray from her. "Of course not. Come on in and join us."

"Audrey says the roast is going to take another half hour. I guess I set the oven too low."

"That's okay," said Maggie. "That just gives us more time to visit."

Leah turned eagerly to Jed. "Oh, I forgot to tell you that this guy came into the shop this afternoon, and he went absolutely gaw-gaw over that twig-and-birch hutch that's sitting right next to the front door. He wanted to know if he could special order several pieces in that same design."

"Did you get his name?"

Leah smiled. "He gave me his card, and I gave him yours. I assured him that I thought you could make more pieces, and I even asked him to write down what he had in mind."

"Good girl."

Now Leah was beaming. She continued to chat with Jed, sharing various ideas about the business while Maggie leaned back into the couch and relaxed, allowing their words to flow over her like a fountain. Content to sit quietly next to Jed, she enjoyed the warmth of the fire and the sounds of father and daughter happily conversing.

Finally Jed turned to her and put his hand on her shoulder. "Hey, I hope you don't think we're ignoring you as we talk shop here."

Maggie sighed contentedly. "Not at all. I was just taking your father's advice and relaxing a little."

Jed's arm slipped around her shoulder as he gave her a little squeeze. "Good for you."

Leah leaned over and picked up the empty tray. "I better get back to the kitchen. That roast is probably almost done now." She sounded cheerful, but as she left Maggie thought she saw a slight frown crease her young forehead.

Jed's eyes remained warmly on Maggie. "You know, I still can't believe it."

"Believe what?"

"How my life has changed in the past several months. For years and years I've never felt completely at home." His brow grew thoughtful. "I mean, I feel at home up on the mountain and in the woods and everything. But I've never felt completely connected somehow—not since I was a small boy anyway..."

"And do you now?"

He nodded. "Just sitting in here with you and Leah is the closest thing I've felt to being at home since both my parents were alive."

She sighed. "That's a beautiful thing to say, Jed."

"It's a beautiful thing to feel."

"Dinner's ready," called Leah.

After they were all seated and Jed had said a brief blessing, Audrey asked him to carve the roast. "It seems fitting that, as you were the hunter, you should carve the meat."

"I'm not too sure what I think about eating deer meat," said Maggie with wide eyes. "I can't help but think of the beautiful creatures that grace the meadow right next to my house."

"Oh, Mom," said Spencer with exasperation. "Now how do you suppose that would make a cow feel?"

They all laughed, and then Daniel shared a hunting story of his own about the time his nearsighted grandfather nearly mistook a cow for an elk, and how the irate rancher threatened to have both of them locked up. Dinner for the most part was delicious, but Maggie still wasn't sure what she thought about the actual taste of venison. It wasn't bad exactly, but different than beef. Unwilling to offend Jed or Leah, she kept her opinions to herself.

"Say," began Jed as Spencer and Daniel went for seconds. "I had an interesting letter this week. I'm not sure what to make of it."

"Tell us," said Leah with bright eyes.

"Well, back in the late seventies, Steven Harris—this guy who'd been my best childhood friend—went over to be a missionary on some South Pacific island. I can't even remember which one offhand. He used to write to me, but then he suddenly stopped and for several years I heard nothing. Then I learned about five years ago that he'd died while living in that country. I was really saddened to hear of his death, and the news actually had quite an impact on my own life." Jed looked around the table. "But at least Steven died doing something he believed in. Well, anyway, just this week I get this really odd letter from a man by the name of Michael Abundi who lives on the very same island that Steven did. As it turns out, Michael was a good friend of his. He says he owes his salvation to Steven, and as a result he believes that God has called him to come be a missionary in Pine Mountain."

"You're kidding!" exclaimed Audrey. "What an extraordinary story."

"Pretty ironic, isn't it?" said Maggie. "Our country usually sends missionaries to places like that. But he's coming here."

Jed nodded. "And this guy isn't wasting any time either. He plans to arrive next week and wants to know if he can stay with me. Apparently Steven had told him all about me before he died."

"So, is he going to stay with you?" asked Leah.

"Sure. I think it should be interesting to get to know him. He sounds like a very nice person in his letter. He writes well and seems educated."

"A missionary to Pine Mountain," repeated Audrey as if still processing this unusual information.

"I'd like to do a story on him," said Maggie. "Do you think he'll be willing?"

"Don't know why not." Jed heaped another dollop of mashed potatoes onto his plate. "He seems to have a lot to share."

After everyone sufficiently praised Leah for the fine dinner, Maggie offered to clean up, sending everyone else to the library. But before long Jed slipped back into the kitchen. "Thought I'd make myself useful," he offered as he took over rinsing plates and handing them to her as she loaded the dishwasher. Occasionally their fingers brushed each other, sending a happy tingle up her arm. Jed took out the garbage, then lingered on the back porch for a moment. "Hey, Maggie, come here!"

She hurried outside to see what was wrong, then followed his gaze up to the dark sky where hundreds of delicate snowflakes could be seen floating down in the beams of the back porch light.

"Oh, it's absolutely beautiful," she breathed with excitement, stepping out from the protection of the porch overhang to allow the delicate snowflakes to fall directly upon her upturned face.

He joined her, putting an arm around her waist. "Not as beautiful as you!" he whispered as he pulled her close, his face very near hers.

"Where'd you two go?" called Leah from the still-open backdoor.

Maggie felt herself pull away from Jed's embrace, instantly wishing she hadn't. "We're down here, Leah. It's snowing!"

"Snowing?" cried Leah, bounding down the steps and twirling around in the fast-falling flakes. "Oh, isn't it wonderful!"

Soon they were all outside, dancing and rejoicing in the falling snow. Even Daniel joined in, which Maggie thought was sweet since he'd obviously seen many winters in Pine Mountain before. Finally Audrey enticed them all back inside with her famous homemade apple cobbler.

∽

By the next morning the only remnant of last night's snow was wet pavement, and perhaps the mountains were a bit whiter. Maggie went to the fitness center to work out before her interview with Rick. Concerned about what Cherise's reaction might be to running the story about the Westerly property, she broke the news to her as gently as possible, but then quickly realized her worries were for nothing.

"To tell you the truth," began Cherise in an irritated tone, "I don't give a flying fig what you write about my stupid husband."

Maggie blinked and blotted her face with a towel.

"Yeah," continued Cherise in a matter-of-fact voice. "Greg deserves to have his name dragged through the mud a little right now. And if you don't do it, I might just do it myself."

"Sounds like things have gotten worse between you two..."

Cherise rolled her eyes dramatically. "Well, after my uncle straightened out the financial part of my business, he sat me down for a little chat. He strongly recommended that Greg and I see a marriage counselor together."

"That sounds like wise counsel."

Cherise slammed down her bottle of cleaning fluid. "Yeah. That's what I thought too. But will Greg agree to come with me? No way! *He* doesn't have any problems, he says. According to him, *I'm* the one who's all messed up. I just couldn't take it anymore. So I went in and saw the counselor all by my little lonesome. And after just two visits, the counselor ups and says to me that she thinks we have some very serious marital problems!"

"I'm so sorry, Cherise."

Cherise's blue eyes had turned an almost electric shade. "Yeah, well, I'm sorry too. Sorry I ever hooked up with a man like Greg Snider!"

Maggie didn't know what to say. She felt way over her head just now. After silently shooting up a prayer for wisdom, she said in a gentle voice, "You know, Cherise, I don't know that much about how things are between you and Greg. But I do know a little about relationships..." She paused to make sure Cherise was listening.

"Yeah?" Cherise was waiting.

"I don't want to sound preachy or anything, but I've found that if I put my trust in God and not in human relationships, I don't get so disappointed. Plus he gives me the strength and courage to get through some of these difficult things. Does that make any sense?"

"Maybe." Cherise had begun to clean a piece of weight equipment again. "Do you think it would help if I went to church, Maggie?"

She smiled. "Yes, I do. But you probably shouldn't expect that Greg will go with you."

Cherise laughed. "Now that would take a real act of God!"

After a quick shower, Maggie went over to meet Rick at the newspaper office. As it was Saturday, no one else was there and she had to unlock the doors and turn on the lights herself. She puttered around the empty building waiting for him to arrive, and just when she was about ready to give up, she noticed a new shiny black pickup, with its sales stickers still intact, park out in front of the office. And out sauntered Rick. She bit her lip and prayed for grace. This wouldn't be easy.

After settling into her office, she turned on her tape recorder and began. "Mr. Westerly told me that you all signed the sale papers for his property last week, and the sale is final. Is that correct?"

"Yep. We're past the five-day rescission deadline too." He folded his arms across his chest and leaned back in the chair. "So it's all finished and done now."

Maggie glanced toward her window. "Is that a new truck out there?"

He grinned. "Well, a developer's got to look prosperous, if you know what I mean, plus it'll be a tax deduction. We've already ordered some magnetic signs to put on the doors of our trucks, and our name is TS Development. Personally, I wasn't sure if we should be spending too much money just yet, but as Greg says, it takes money to make money."

"Yes, that brings me to another question, if I may. Where did you and Greg come up with enough money to purchase Westerly's land?"

He laughed. "Ever heard of a thing called a loan?"

"I see. And regarding the selling price—do you feel that you offered Mr. Westerly fair market value for his land?"

This made Rick laugh again. "Maggie, this is *business*."

She looked intently at him, searching for any sign of conscience. "I'm sorry, Rick, Mr. Westerly gave me the impression that you were his friend."

Rick's face grew cloudy, but he said nothing.

"I did a little research yesterday and learned that according to local real estate values, the Westerly property was worth about twice what you and Greg paid Mr. Westerly for it."

His brows lifted. "That much, eh? Well, thanks for that information. Might be helpful down the line."

Maggie tried to contain the hostility that now bubbled within her. Turning her gaze downward to her notepad, she continued, "And does Mr. Westerly know of your plans to develop his property?"

"Look," his eyes narrowed. "I know what you're getting at, but the fact is Arnold could do with his property as he wished when it was *his* property. But it's no longer his property now."

"When do you plan to start developing the land?"

"Just as soon as possible. You know what they say, time is money."

"I see. And how long before this project is completed?"

"Well, phase one should be well under way soon—that means we hope to have sewer, water, streets, and utilities installed this winter. Then actual housing construction will start in early spring. But our associate developer will begin promoting and selling lots immediately. Any of your rich California friends interested in a vacation home?"

She ignored that and continued to question him about lot sizes, selling prices, amenities, and any other information that might pertain to those interested in investing in the development. And with congeniality, he carefully answered each question. Then finally she glanced up from her notes and looked him straight in the eye. "And where, may I ask, will Mr. Westerly reside once the bulldozers start tearing up his farm?"

Rick pulled his head back and scowled darkly. "Well, that wouldn't be my problem, now would it?"

"But you've led him to believe that he can continue living there—"

"I don't know where he got that fool notion. His house will be the first thing to go down."

Maggie could stand it no longer. She felt her nostrils flare as she snapped off the recorder and rose to her feet. "I think that's more than enough for my article, Rick!" She moved quickly to the front door, holding it wide open and nodding as if she had suddenly gone mute.

Once on the porch, Rick turned to her and said, "You better not make us look bad in your paper, Maggie. This development has the potential to help this whole sorry town get back on its feet. I don't think the local businesses will take it kindly if you do anything to discourage growth and development of this kind." Then he grinned slyly. "And anyway, we all know that you and the paper are pro-development—you made that real clear last summer. You wouldn't change your stance now, would you?"

She pressed her lips tightly together and, without answering, solidly slammed the door almost in his face. She knew it was childish and rude, but she couldn't help herself. "I've got everything I need now," she said out loud as she marched back into her office and flipped on her computer switch, waiting irritably for the machine to warm up. Then she furiously began writing her story, pounding on the keyboard as if it were personally responsible for this whole horrible affair. Only after nearly an hour did she pause long enough to phone home and let Audrey know that she'd been sidetracked at the office. By the time she finished her piece and was on her way home, she knew that it was one of the finest stories she'd ever written—full of passion and heat and truth. Back at the *Times* it might even have been nominated for an award. But she wanted no accolades for this project. All she wanted was justice!

Four

On Monday Maggie silently presented Clyde with a copy of her TS Development exposé, and then walked grimly back to her office. She wished she could blame her frustration purely on the circumstances of the story, but the truth was she was still getting over her conversation with Leah during their drive into town that morning. It had probably started with Jed taking Maggie out to lunch after church yesterday. He'd invited Spencer and Leah as well, but Spencer had already made plans and Leah had simply shrugged it off, saying she'd "rather not" without offering any explanations. Well, now Maggie suspected that Leah had felt left out after all. And although she'd only hinted at it this morning, and politely enough, Maggie sensed the hurt behind her voice. So she had simply suggested that perhaps in the future, Leah might try to communicate better, for instance if she really wanted to go to lunch with them to *just say so*. But then Leah had become very quiet, pulling into herself as if Maggie's words had hurt her even more. And even after Maggie sincerely apologized, Leah still seemed withdrawn, climbing silently from the car as if mortally wounded. That's when Maggie had recalled her mother's words about how raising teenaged girls was never as simple and straightforward as raising boys. Perhaps this was what she meant. At least Spencer usually came right out and said what he meant, whether or not it sounded pleasant and nice. Just the same, Maggie promised herself she'd try harder to understand Leah. She knew it wasn't easy being eighteen, and it seemed reasonable that Leah could be struggling with all the recent changes in her life—relocating from Arizona, discovering her father for the first time, a new job. It was a lot for anyone to adjust to all at once.

"Maggie!" exclaimed Clyde as he stormed into her office. "This story makes me sick to my stomach!"

She dropped her pencil and stared up at him in horror. "What do you mean, Clyde? I...I thought it was pretty good. I tried really hard to—"

He waved the papers wildly in the air. "Not the writing, you silly ninny! The writing is incredible—brilliant even! I mean what Snider and Tanner have done to poor old Arnold. Why, I'd like to take those two boys out in the middle of Main Street and have them publicly tarred and feathered for the whole town to witness!"

She suppressed a smile. "Now that'd be worth seeing. But I think we have laws prohibiting such things nowadays, Clyde. Aren't there any legal solutions you can think of off-hand?"

His wrinkled features pinched tightly together. "Well, I'll tell you what I *do* plan to do. I'm going to call my lawyer right now and ask his opinion about this whole doggone thing. It just don't seem right."

"But what about the story, Clyde? Do you think it's okay to run it? I've tried to be honest, but I'm sure it comes across as accusatory toward TS Development, if not outright hostile."

"You're the editor, Maggie." He grinned slyly. "And like I've always said, these are your decisions to make. But to my way of thinking, there's no question about whether you should run it or not. Folks deserve to know the truth, even when it's downright stinking and rotten like this dirty bit of business. By the way, have you sent Scott out to get some photos of Arnold's farm?"

"No, but that's a good idea." She made a note. "One thing still troubles me, though."

"What's that?"

"Mr. Westerly still doesn't really know what these boys are up to. I tried to tell him, but he just didn't want to hear it. He doesn't think Greg has anything to do with any of it, and he sincerely believes Rick will continue to farm his land. He even plans to keep living in that sweet little house of his."

Clyde frowned. "Well, it's a nasty chore, but you'll have to set him straight before he reads it in the paper."

"I know." She sighed. "I just hate to see him hurt like this. He's such a nice old guy."

"If it makes you feel any better, I'm phoning my lawyer right now."

Maggie called Scott into her office and asked him to go out to the Westerly farm to take photos.

"What for?"

She thought a moment. "It's for an article. I'll fill you in on the details later. But why don't you give Mr. Westerly a call first and see if you can interview him for our *Bit of History* column while you're out there. He's in his nineties but just as clear as he can be, and I'm sure he has some good stories to share. I promised him you'd come out and he's looking forward to seeing you—he knew your grandfather."

"Sure, I'll see if I can set it up right away."

"And when you see him, please tell him I'll be giving him a call to talk about this upcoming article too."

～

Scott's appointment with Mr. Westerly was set for Tuesday morning, and Maggie decided to wait until the afternoon to give him a call. But when she tried, there was no answer, and as it was a sunny day, she figured he must be working outside. On the following morning as she drove to work, it occurred to her that today's paper was in the process of being printed, and she still hadn't reached Mr. Westerly. Perhaps she would have to simply drive out to see him during her noon hour; then she could actually hand deliver an early edition and gently break the news to him herself. But no sooner did she walk into the door of the *Pine Cone* when Abigail rushed toward her with a frantic expression in her eyes.

"Oh, dear!" she cried. "I've just had a phone call—there's been an accident—"

"*Who?*" Maggie's heart began to pound.

"It's Spencer—"

"*Spencer?* But I just saw him leave the house—just minutes ago. Daniel picked him up—"

"The sheriff just called. Daniel's car hit a truck, Maggie."

She began to sway, her knees growing weak, and Abigail gently but firmly eased her into a foyer chair. "Where is he?" Maggie blurted. "Is he okay? I need to see him right away—"

"Hush now and let me explain. The boys are on their way to the hospital even as we speak. The sheriff said there were no fatalities, but—"

Maggie rose quickly to her feet. "I've got to go—"

"Just hold on. I knew you'd need a ride, and I already called Jed." She peered out the window. "And if that isn't him right now!"

In the same instant, Maggie burst out of the office and ran straight for Jed's truck, jerking open the passenger door even before he could climb out to assist her. "Thanks for coming, Jed," she gasped. "Please, drive *fast!*"

While he drove to Byron, Jed prayed quietly for Spencer and Daniel. Maggie glanced nervously at him as he sped along, passing every vehicle ahead of them, but naturally his eyes were open as he prayed. She attempted to follow his example and focus her mind on praying too, but no matter how hard she tried, it seemed impossible to form any actual sentences—not even in her mind. All she could think was,

"Please, God, no!" She silently prayed those same three words over and over. After what seemed an eternity, Jed finally pulled up in front of the emergency room door, where an ambulance was parked nearby, lights still flashing, engine still rumbling. Maggie leaped from Jed's truck and ran inside the foyer, demanding that the receptionist tell her exactly where Spencer had been taken.

"Goodness, you must've been right behind the ambulance. Here, please fill out these forms—"

"Not yet!" Maggie waved the clipboard in front of the receptionist. "I will fill out nothing until you tell me where my son is!"

The receptionist's eyes grew wide. "He's right there in the ER. You can see him as soon as you—"

"Later!" said Maggie as she pushed through the same door into the same room where she'd been with her mother just a couple of months earlier.

"Hey, Mom," called Spencer from a bed not far from the door as a nurse read his blood pressure.

"Spence!" she cried as tears of thankfulness began to stream down her cheeks. "Are you okay? I was so worried!"

"I think I'm okay, except that my foot might be broken." Then he gingerly touched what looked like a good-sized knot in the center of his forehead. "Oh, and maybe a concussion, the paramedic said." His expression suddenly grew serious. "I think Daniel's in pretty bad shape."

"What happened?"

"Some jerk with no taillights stopped right in the middle of the road for no reason. Daniel hit the brakes, but he still slammed right into him. I guess we were going pretty fast. Daniel got a bunch of cuts on his face from when the windshield broke. And both his legs are hurt, maybe pretty bad. The front of his Bug just smashed right up into the front seat—you know, 'cause there's no engine or anything to stop it. The paramedic said we both could've been killed."

Maggie took in a sharp breath. "Thank God you're okay. Are Daniel's grandparents here yet?"

"I don't think so."

The nurse placed a cold pack on Spencer's swollen left foot, then stuck an electronic thermometer in his mouth. "Daniel's being examined by the doctor right now," she said. "I think the cuts on his face may appear worse than they really are. Most importantly, we need to make certain he suffered no internal injuries where he hit the steering wheel. Spencer seems to be okay in that regard, but we'll run some tests just to be certain. Then we'll get him up to x-ray to see what's wrong with that foot."

Maggie glanced down at Spencer's foot, now puffed up to almost the size of a melon. All things considered, it suddenly didn't seem so bad, although she felt horribly sorry for Daniel and sent up a silent prayer on his behalf. Before long the doctor continued his examination of Spencer, and Maggie apologized to the irritated ER receptionist and sat next to Spencer's bed as she obediently filled in the numerous and repetitive questions on the insurance forms.

Just after the nurse wheeled Spencer up to x-ray, Daniel's grandparents arrived, their faces pale and strained with worry. No medical staff was around to greet them, so Maggie began to explain, trying to gently relay what little information the nurse had given her. "All in all," she finished, trying to sound positive, "it could've been so much worse than it was."

Just then another nurse stepped out and ushered the grandparents back to where Daniel was still being treated and examined.

Once again Maggie prayed for Daniel to be okay, then went out to find Jed sitting patiently in the waiting room. "You must think our family spends a whole lot of time in hospitals." She shook her head.

He stood and took both her hands in his. "How's Spencer?"

"A big lump on the head, maybe a concussion, and what looks like a broken foot. Not much compared to what it could have been." She sighed in deep relief.

"And Daniel?"

"Worse. Hopefully no internal injuries. They're still examining him."

"Let's pray for him."

Right there, standing in the center of the waiting room floor, they prayed together for Daniel's complete recovery. Then they sat down on the hard vinyl chairs to wait. Maggie leaned forward with her elbows on her knees, resting her head in her hands. She felt exhausted and emotionally drained.

"And how are *you* doing?"

She looked over at him. "Of course I'm hugely relieved, but at the same time I feel almost as if I've been run over by a truck myself. No one ever warns you that when you become a parent your heart is no longer your own."

"Hmm." Jed rubbed her shoulders in a gentle and soothing massage. "Does that count for those of us who get our kids late in life—after they're mostly grown up? Or is it only for those who've raised them from babyhood?"

She sat up and looked at him curiously. "I don't really know how it works in that situation. What do you think, Jed?"

He shook his head slowly. "I'm not totally sure yet, but it amazes me how protective I suddenly began to feel toward Leah when I first learned that she's my own daughter. I mean, do you remember how I was so down on her when she wore that little rock star getup at the bonfire? But that was before I realized she was my very own flesh and blood."

Maggie laughed. "Actually, that was probably a very typical fatherly reaction you had back then, even if it was unwitting."

He smiled. "I suppose you're right, now that I think about it. But you know what worries me most, Maggie?" He looked into her eyes, but she just shook her head. "What worries me most is how much Leah seems to expect from me—it's as if she thinks I'm some sort of 'superfather.' And

I find myself trying to be perfect just so I don't disappoint her. I know it must sound silly to you."

"Not at all. It's wonderful to have your child look up to you. I remember how touched Phil used to be when Spence would brag about how his dad was the best cop in all of L.A. County."

"Yeah, I guess I missed out on all that. But even though it feels good now, it's kind of scary and overwhelming some-times...and I'm just not sure I can deliver or live up to her expectations..."

"Don't worry, Jed. You can deliver. Just be yourself. That's all any of us want from you. Some of us believe that simply being Jed Whitewater is pretty special."

His eyes lit up. "Thanks, Magpie. That means a lot, especially coming from you."

∾

Maggie made the appropriate phone calls, first reassuring Audrey, then Abigail, that Spencer was going to be just fine, and then she asked for everyone to pray for him and Daniel. Just as she hung up the phone, Daniel's grandparents came out of the ER and she rushed to meet them. "How is he?"

Suddenly the grandmother began to sob, and the grand-father answered, "He's going to be okay. He may have a cracked rib or two, but they've ruled out any internal injuries for the time being, although they'll keep an eye on him for the next couple of hours. He's on his way to be x-rayed as we speak."

Maggie put a comforting arm around the older woman's shoulders. She'd only met her once, but she understood exactly how she felt. "It really could've been so much worse," she spoke soothingly.

"Yes," she sobbed. "I was just so terribly worried. I guess it's all coming to the surface now. Thank goodness they're both going to be all right."

"And no more little foreign cars for my boy," steamed his grandfather. "When Daniel gets better we'll buy him a tank if need be!"

By three o'clock Spencer was released from the hospital with a cast on his foot. His ankle was broken, but the doctor assured him it would heal faster and more completely than a sprain, and then he told Maggie to keep an eye on him for the remainder of the day in case he exhibited any more signs of concussion. As it turned out, Daniel had only one broken leg; the other was just badly bruised. And the doctor convinced Daniel's grandparents that the facial lacerations were clean cuts that would probably heal up just fine without the aid of any plastic surgery. But they decided to keep him overnight, just to observe him for any possible developments of internal injuries.

Jed drove Maggie and Spencer home. Then, leaving Spencer in his grandmother's diligent care, Maggie went back to town to fill his prescription for pain medication and crutches. At the tiny drugstore, she noticed a copy of today's edition of the *Pine Cone* resting on top of the pharmacy counter. Staring in horror at the front-page exposé about TS Development, she suddenly realized that she'd never had a chance to warn Mr. Westerly about the story yet. After quickly explaining to the kind but curious druggist that Spencer and Daniel were both okay (another reminder to her of how news travels like wildfire in a small town) she called Audrey to quickly explain her further delay.

"Don't worry, honey," Audrey said soothingly. "Spencer doesn't even need any more pain medication until tonight. Take all the time you need to explain everything to that dear old man. Spence is perfectly fine stretched out on the sofa in front of the TV. He's having a bowl of homemade potato soup right now, and he asked me to make chocolate chip cookies."

Maggie smiled. "Thanks so much, Mom. I really appreciate it." Then she grabbed up the prescription and crutches and rushed straight over to Mr. Westerly's farm, praying along the way that his newspaper hadn't been delivered yet, although she knew that was unlikely.

She wondered if he'd read the paper as she hurried up the front porch steps. Perhaps he was one of those people who didn't look at his paper until after supper—she hoped so. She knocked on the door and waited impatiently, then knocked again louder. Lizzie barked sharply from inside, but the door stayed firmly shut. Maybe Mr. Westerly was outside puttering around. She walked around the back of the house, loudly calling out his name, hoping he might be somewhere close by, and willing to search every acre of his property just to find him. But as she called and looked, she continued to hear Lizzie barking frantically from inside the house. Suddenly it occurred to her that if Mr. Westerly was outside, surely he'd have taken the dog with him. So she went around to the backdoor and tried knocking again. She rapped on the window of the door, carefully, for the glass pane rattled loosely. Then she cupped her hands over the reflective surface and peered inside. There, slumped motionless over the kitchen table, was old Mr. Westerly!

Trying the door handle, she discovered it was unlocked and she went inside, her legs shaking as she approached the table. "Mr. Westerly?" she said weakly. "Are you okay?" Lizzie moved nervously around her feet as Maggie reached out to touch his arm. She watched in horror as it slid limply from the table and fell loosely to his side. Her heart pounded louder than Spencer's drum set as she touched her fingers to his old, wrinkled cheek. Cold as marble. She held her hand by his nose and mouth. No breath. No pulse. And there crumpled beneath him was today's newspaper!

"Oh, no!" she cried as she backed away from the dreadful scene. "Oh, dear God, no! Please, no!"

⌒

Maggie never remembered calling 911 or her mother. But somehow Jed's pickup miraculously appeared shortly after the paramedics had entered the house. She was sitting on the wooden porch steps, shivering in the cold and stroking

Lizzie's soft, warm coat, preventing the confused animal from going inside and getting underfoot when Jed walked up, took off his jacket, and hung it over her shoulders. Then he sat down next to her and gathered her into his arms. "Your mom told me everything."

Hot, silent tears rolled down her chilled cheeks as she leaned into his embrace. "I've killed him, Jed."

"No, no, Maggie, you didn't kill him," he spoke softly, his words flowing like a gentle stream. "He was an old, old man. He'd had a good life working on the land that he loved. He was a good man, but he was due to go anytime. You didn't kill him."

"But he was reading the paper."

"I know, I know..." he whispered as he stroked her hair.

"It's been a really bad day, Jed."

She thought she heard him chuckle ever so softly, and she looked up to see, but his face grew serious. "Come on, sweetheart, let's get you home. There's nothing you can do for the old fellow now."

She looked down at the dog. "What about Lizzie?"

"Let's bring her along. She seems to like you."

Maggie brightened just a little. "Yes, she does, doesn't she."

Five

*E*ven after several days and the reassurance of good friends, Maggie still struggled with feelings of guilt over Arnold Westerly's death. Though she knew it would be uncomfortable to attend his funeral, she was determined to do it for his sake. The day following Mr. Westerly's death, Scott had handed her a delicate glass figurine of a young girl in a long blue dress, with dark hair curling around her shoulders. She had a sweet smile and was holding a basket of kittens. "Mr. Westerly asked me to give this to you," Scott explained quietly. "He said it had belonged to his wife, but for some reason he thought you'd like it. I think you made quite an impression on him, Maggie." Of course, this had only started the tears to flowing again, but she placed the figurine on her desk as a reminder of him.

Only a handful of his relatives attended the funeral service, and his granddaughter Jeanette, the one he'd been so fond of, shared some happy memories of her childhood summers spent on the Westerly farm. Afterward, Maggie lingered, taking a moment to speak to Jeanette, telling her of how her grandfather had been remembering his granddaughter only days before.

"Oh, so you're the one who wrote that article?" Jeanette's fine brows arched with what seemed like suspicion.

"Well, yes," stammered Maggie. "I had tried to inform your grandfather about the circumstances of—"

"Rick Tanner says that story was what killed Grandpa."

Maggie's cheeks flushed and she swallowed hard. "But did you read about what—"

"I have no desire to read your small-town trash." The middle-aged woman turned abruptly and walked away, joining Rick Tanner and his family, her back like a stone wall.

Maggie studied the small group of mourners comforting one another. Part of her wanted to rush at Rick and publicly accuse him of being responsible for all this. But another part of her felt guilty, and like a whipped dog she only wished to slip quietly out the backdoor. Just then she felt a nudge at her elbow and turned to see Clyde wearing a clean plaid shirt and bolo tie.

"Hanging in there, old girl?" he asked, a kind warmth lighting his faded blue eyes.

She sighed. "I was just soundly told off by Mr. Westerly's favorite granddaughter."

Clyde scowled. "Hmph. And then off she goes to consort with the enemy. Doesn't she have any idea what Tanner's up to?"

She shrugged. "I guess not. Or maybe she doesn't care. But I thought she was the one who really loved the farm."

"Maybe she loves the money even more."

"I didn't even get a chance to ask her about his dog."

"Arnold's dog?"

"We're keeping his Border collie at the house, but I wondered if someone in the family might want her."

"How about if I go say something?" offered Clyde.

"Good luck," muttered Maggie. She made her way to the door, watching Clyde from the corner of her eye as he approached the group. Words were exchanged, but Jeanette's gaze remained stony and Rick glared at Clyde with open hostility. Then Clyde handed Jeanette a business card, probably for the *Pine Cone,* and walked away, joining Maggie by the door.

"I tried to talk some sense into that woman, but she just won't listen. I think Rick's poisoned her against us. When I mentioned the dog, she said she'd give you a call at the paper on Monday. I don't think she liked the idea of you having her granddad's dog one little bit."

"It figures. And Leah was just getting attached to her." Maggie glanced out to the street as a stiff wind chased some dry leaves across the sidewalk. "Thanks for trying, Clyde. I better go now."

"Don't you go on blaming yourself for Arnold's death," said Clyde quietly as he stepped out the door with her. "We all know he was old as the hills, but if anyone sent him out before his time it was Snider and Tanner."

"Thanks. You're probably right."

"You bet I'm right. And we won't let them off the hook now, will we?"

She unlocked her car door, then turned to face Clyde, noticing how his brow was furrowed with concern. "No, we won't!" The words came out with fresh resolve, and then she nodded firmly. "Somehow, we're going to make them sorry they ever got into this land development business in the first place."

He grinned. "Now that's my girl!"

✦

Jeanette stopped by the newspaper office on Monday and Maggie took her directly to her office and invited her to sit down. She had given this conversation much thought and even more prayer. She began speaking slowly, in a gentle voice. "Jeanette, I know you loved your grandfather very, very much. And just for the record, I think he was a wonderful, dear old man. But I also know that you think my article caused his—"

"I didn't come to talk about that," she snapped back. Then she abruptly stood, switching her purse to her other hand with impatience. "I only came here to discuss Grandpa's dog."

"Yes, Lizzie's a delight. We've enjoyed having her."

Jeanette appeared slightly surprised, almost as if she'd suspected Maggie to be the type of person who might poison or torture a poor, homeless animal whose master had died.

Maggie continued, once again using a calm, gentle voice. "I will understand perfectly if you want to take the dog with you. However, you should know that Lizzie and I hit it off the day I first visited your grandfather. In fact, although I only knew him briefly, I was quite fond of him." She picked up the figurine and turned it around in her hands. "And I felt absolutely horrible to find him like that—"

"*You* found him?" Jeanette's eyes narrowed. "I thought it was Rick."

Maggie looked directly into the woman's eyes. "Look, I have absolutely no reason to lie to you about anything. And if I hadn't come to care so deeply about your grandfather, I wouldn't even bother trying to convince you of the truth." She set down the figurine and picked up an edition of last week's paper, holding it out toward Jeanette. "And if you're half the person your grandfather believed you to be, I'd think you would want to read this article for yourself. He spent a lot of time telling me his side of the story, all of which is included here."

Jeanette reluctantly took the paper. "Rick Tanner says it's just a bunch of lies."

"Why don't you read it, and then judge for yourself? There's nothing in there that can't be easily proven. I'd like your family to know the truth, Jeanette, even if it's too late to change anything."

"What do you mean, too late? To change what?"

"Just read the article—do it for your grandfather. Then we can talk if you want to."

"Fine," she said sharply, her hand reaching for the doorknob. "I'll read it."

∽

Jeanette didn't call back until the following morning. "I was on the phone for most of the afternoon yesterday," she began in what seemed a rather flat and emotionless voice. "I checked out everything you said. I even questioned Rick Tanner for myself." She cleared her throat. "And I want to apologize to you, Maggie. It seems you were right all along."

"I'm so sorry about all this, Jeanette. I know it must be difficult for you to learn all about this right on top of your grandfather's death. But I want you to know that even as I gathered my information, I kept wishing to be wrong." She sighed. "And I had meant to warn your grandfather before he read the article...but I got there too late. You see, my son was in a car wreck that very same day."

"Is your son all right?"

"Yes, thank you. Just a broken foot that he's now playing up for all it's worth."

Jeanette chuckled. "I can understand that. I have two sons, and they always enjoy lots of sympathy for their sports injuries."

"Right. Your grandfather told me about your boys. At one time, he'd hoped that one of them would want to run the farm..."

"Oh, if only I'd known about this development deal, I'd have gladly agreed to have taken on the farm myself. But at the time, I was afraid it would cause a family squabble. I never dreamed anything like this would happen to the land. It just kills me to imagine a bunch of cheap condo units springing up out here—and I had my husband check into the outfit that you wrote about in your article, and they sound like one of the worst sort of developers around."

"Have you considered having a lawyer go over all the paperwork? Maybe there's some kind of a glitch somewhere."

"I already spoke to Grandpa's attorney. And while he's happy to look over the paperwork again, especially after reading your article last week, he thinks the sale is legal and watertight."

"That's what Clyde's lawyer said too."

"Well, I have to return home tomorrow, but I'm not finished with this yet. I don't plan to leave any stone unturned. By the way, do you think you'd like to keep Lizzie after all?"

"We'd love to. She's a very sweet dog."

"I'd take her myself, but my husband's allergic to dog hair. And because I work during the day, she'd be alone much of the time."

"Don't worry a bit about Lizzie. She has lots of room to run where we live, and she gets along well with our Lab. And I'll let you know if I learn anything new around here. I plan to continue following this whole development deal in the newspaper and, believe me, I won't make it easy on those guys."

"Thanks." Jeanette's voice sounded sad and weary. "And we thought the Tanners were our friends."

"So did your grandfather."

There was a long pause and then, "Maggie, if it's any comfort to you, I don't believe your article killed Grandpa—you were only the messenger. Rick Tanner and Greg Snider are responsible for breaking his heart. Let his death be on their heads."

Maggie wrote down Jeanette's home phone number and thanked her for calling before she said goodbye. While she appreciated the kind words, traces of guilt still remained with her as she unwillingly recalled the sad kitchen scene of Mr. Westerly crumpled over his newspaper. More than ever she realized that the printed word was a very powerful thing.

⌒

At noon she met Jed at the deli. They settled into a corner table, and she told him all about her conversation with Jeanette.

"That must make you feel a little better about the whole thing," suggested Jed as he stirred his coffee.

"Of course, but I'm still furious with Rick and Greg."

"That's understandable. I think a lot of us are still pretty upset. But don't let your anger eat away at you, Maggie. It's not worth it."

"I know. Believe me, I know. I guess just hearing the sound of Jeanette's sad voice got to me. And now I'm all riled up again. Of course, I'll continue to cover the story in the paper. I've already started a piece for this week about Mr. Westerly's death—and how he must've died unhappily. But I hate running it in our Thanksgiving edition as it's sort of a downer and we wanted this to be an upbeat issue. But if I wait until next week, it'll be too late."

"Maybe you could give the article a positive slant. Why not celebrate Arnold Westerly's well-lived life and accomplishments, and then refer to the sadness briefly at the end?"

"That's a great idea, Jed. Thanks."

"And I happen to know he was a man of faith. I'll bet he's looking down on all this with some amusement right now."

"Amusement?"

"Yes. Just think how a little farm down here in Pine Mountain must seem a pretty small thing up there amidst all that heavenly splendor."

She smiled. "I never thought of it like that. But I suppose you're right."

"Anyway, getting back to Thanksgiving, I was wondering if we might be able to squeeze in one more guest."

"Of course." Maggie pushed her empty soup bowl to the side of the table. "May I ask whom?"

"Remember the man I told you about who's coming from the South Pacific? Well, he's already in Portland and plans to arrive on the bus tomorrow."

"This should be interesting."

"Yes. He sounded like a real character on the phone. And by the way, let Audrey know that I'll bring the famous sweet potato dish I told her about—the one my mother used to make."

Maggie smacked her lips. "Sounds delicious."

He reached out to take her hand while lowering his voice. "I've missed you."

She sighed softly and nodded. "Me too. Life's been so chaotic the last few days. Maybe it'll slow down a little with the holidays coming..." She glanced out the window to the clear, blue sky. "Do you think it'll *ever* really let loose and snow?"

"I'm sure it will. Just don't know when. But I know everyone in town, including me, could use that ski traffic about now."

"Pretty slow?"

He nodded grimly. "I'm thinking about taking some of my pieces to a big trade show up in Seattle next month. It's kind of last minute, but a friend of mine offered to share his booth with me. It would be a way for me to expand the business—but I'm just not sure if the timing's right."

"It wouldn't hurt to try, would it?"

"I guess not. But it might be a waste of my time and gas."

"Or you could end up with too much work."

"Or possibly miss out on some good business here. The show happens about a week or so before Christmas—that could be a real busy time for the shop, especially if the ski season opens up by then, which it normally would."

"How's Leah doing these days? She seemed a little stressed out last week. She's been trying so hard, but I think her expectations are too high."

"She's getting the hang of it, and I'm trying to be patient with the learning curve. I guess I never quite realized how spoiled I was having Kate with me for these past few years."

"I'm sure she'd come back to you in a heartbeat." Maggie's eyes glinted mischievously, as if she were baiting him.

He frowned. "You know that's not what I meant. Besides, I'm sure you're wrong. She and Buckie seem to be getting along quite happily."

"You're right. I'm sorry, my insecurity must've gotten the best of me for a minute there."

He looked deeply into her eyes. "Tell me what *you* could possibly have to be insecure about, Maggie Carpenter."

She returned his gaze. "Absolutely nothing at the moment."

"Hey, you two," teased Rosa. "You look like a couple of moonstruck puppies. I came over to try to entice you to have some dessert."

"I'll go for some of that cobbler," said Jed, "seeing how you need the business and all."

Rosa rolled her eyes. "Thanks, I needed that reminder a lot right now. But don't forget, it's usually slow like this right before Thanksgiving. But afterward is a different story, at least when there's snow, that is…"

She returned with Jed's cobbler along with an extra spoon for Maggie. Then she refilled their coffee cups. "We're all looking forward to coming out on Thursday, Maggie. Is Audrey still sure she's up for all this? It sounds like it'll be quite a crowd."

"Believe me, Mom's in her element right now. You should see her lists and things. She even made cute little pine cone turkeys for each place setting." She smiled at Jed. "I'll tell her to make one more for your friend."

"We'll see you then," said Rosa. "And in the meantime, you two can be praying we get some snow—and soon."

Jed laughed. "Or maybe we should pray for patience. Sometimes we just need to learn to wait."

Six

*I*t's too bad your brother couldn't make it for Thanksgiving," said Audrey as she checked the turkey once again.

"Well, at least we got him to commit to Christmas," Maggie said as she turned off the mixer. "Hey, that reminds me—Rebecca is coming then too. Maybe we should do some matchmaking..."

"But Rebecca's older than Barry."

"Oh, Mother!" Maggie rolled her eyes. "By only two years. And Rebecca's dated men who were ten years her junior."

"Now that you mention it, I do remember Barry dating a woman quite a bit older than him too—although I don't think it was a very good relationship."

"Well, you just never know. Anyway, it'll be so fun to have more family here for Christmas, I can hardly wait!"

Audrey stopped peeling potatoes for a moment and turned to face her daughter. "I'll bet just a year ago you'd never have guessed you'd be hosting twenty people for Thanksgiving dinner right now."

Maggie laughed as she poured the orange pumpkin batter into the golden pie shell. "That's for sure. Last year Spencer and I stayed home and had grilled chicken and watched TV."

"You told me you were going to be with friends last year," scolded her mother.

"I just didn't want you feeling sorry for us and thinking you had to drive down to L.A. and roast a big turkey." Maggie licked the spicy batter from the wooden spoon before dropping it in the sink. "Looking back now, I can see how depressing our life really was, but back then I never would have dreamed things could change so drastically in just one year. Sometimes I think about how easily I could have missed all this and it almost scares me."

"What scares you?" asked Jed as he poked his head in the kitchen, a large casserole dish in his hands.

"Hey, you're here!" Maggie rinsed off her hands and turned to face him.

"Yeah, I saw Spencer outside hobbling around on his crutches, and he said to go on in. So, anyway, what's this that scares you?"

She leaned against the counter and smiled. "Oh, I was just telling Mom how frightening it is to think how I might not have moved up here, and about all that I would've missed as a result."

He winked. "And the fun's just beginning." He handed the dish to Audrey. "It might need to get warmed up a little." Then he called over his shoulder, "Come on in here, Michael. I want you to meet our lovely hosts."

A short man dressed in multiple layers of clothing stepped into the kitchen doorway. "Hello," he said with one of the brightest smiles Maggie ever recalled seeing. His white teeth gleamed against his coppery skin, and his eyes shone with warmth and light. "I am Michael Abundi and I am very pleased to make your acquaintance." His accent was a blend of British and something else, but it rolled off his tongue with courtesy and grace.

Jed continued the introductions and Michael heartily shook hands with each of them, smiling all the while. "It is very good to be here in Pine Mountain. I have heard stories and seen pictures of your country. Now I must pinch myself to think I am really here."

"May I take your coat?" asked Maggie.

He shuddered slightly. "But it is very cold here."

Jed chuckled. "Michael's having a little difficulty getting acclimated. He comes from a tropical island, you know."

"Oh, of course," said Maggie. "Why don't you both go into the library. Spencer has a nice fire going in there. He and Leah took the dogs out for some exercise, but they'll be back any minute. And there are some snacks in there too."

"Michael seems nice," commented Audrey as she returned to peeling potatoes.

"Yes, he seems very sincere. It's too bad about the climate adjustment. That must be a shock to him."

"That won't be his only adjustment," said Audrey as she plunked a potato into the pot.

"Well, I'm sure he'll have some culture shock too. But he seems like such a happy person, I'm sure he'll adapt quickly."

"I'm not talking about culture shock either, honey. Have you noticed that we have no blacks living in Pine Mountain?"

Maggie stopped chopping nuts for a moment and considered this. "Now that you mention it...although I've seen African-American tourists in town—"

"That's not quite the same. Don't you think this could be a little hard on Michael?"

"I don't know why it should be any harder for him than it is for Jed—or Rosa—for that matter. They're both in a minority."

"And you know they both suffer for it occasionally. But I suspect it could be even worse for Michael. I mean, let's not be naïve—this town has its share, or even more than its share, of bigots tucked here and there. Remember that family—what's their name?"

"You mean the Ebberts?" Maggie laid down her knife. "I think that rumor about their white supremacy group is a little far-fetched."

"But there's no denying their racial prejudice. You told me yourself about the hate-filled letters they regularly send to the *Pine Cone*."

"Letters I *never* publish." She scooped the nuts into a bowl. "I suppose you've got a point, Mom. But then again, I'm sure Jed will prepare Michael for this sort of thing. Besides, I think it's about time this town grew up a little in the area of racial equality. And if necessary, I'll write a big old editorial stating just that."

Audrey laughed. "Who would've thought editing a little paper like the *Pine Cone* could have turned my daughter into such a radical?"

Maggie grinned with a spark in her eye. "Yes, it seems I'm just making new enemies left and right. But it's sort of fun, you know."

"Just watch your backside." Audrey's voice sounded slightly serious.

ᴑ

Soon the house was filled with people. The Galloways came, minus Scott and Chloe as they'd driven to Portland to be with her family up there. Elizabeth Rodgers arrived, freshly coifed and dressed in a purple velvet pantsuit. She ruled over the library like royalty as she quizzed Michael about his homeland. Buckie and Kate came, and Kate surprised Maggie by rolling up her sleeves and providing some much-needed help in the kitchen. Even Clyde showed up, proudly bearing a large smoked salmon, a prize from last fall's deep sea fishing trip. Then there were the Hendersons from the antique shop, the Jordans from the hotel, and Abigail from work. A full house! Maggie couldn't have been happier as she took orders from her mother and bustled around the kitchen. Somehow Audrey managed to fit everyone around the two tables, with all leaves in, and placed end to end with a decorative turkey at each place setting. Maggie's eyes grew misty as Jed said a heartfelt Thanksgiving blessing. She silently thanked God, once again, for bringing her to Pine Mountain and joining her with all these wonderful people who felt as close to her as family.

Even after everyone was stuffed with the delicious dinner and the tapered candles had melted into short flickering stumps, the group continued to linger at the table, visiting and laughing congenially.

"Maggie, that was sure a nice piece in the paper yesterday about old Arnold Westerly's life," commented Al Henderson. "Now, that man was a real part of our Pine Mountain history."

"Yes, and it's such a shame what those boys are going to do to his farm property," said Clara, making a tsk-tsk sound with her teeth. "Poor old Arnold, I'm just sure that's what finished him off."

Maggie nodded sadly. "It's too bad he couldn't have passed quietly without hearing *that* bit of news."

"Oh, I think you people are all getting a little paranoid about this development deal," said Buckie as he leaned back in his chair and contentedly folded his arms. "Growth will be good for this town."

Brian Jordan nodded. "Yes, if it's done right, that development could be a real draw for the tourist traffic. And speaking for the hotel and restaurant, we could use some business."

"Hmph!" Clyde sat down his coffee cup with a loud clink. "*Done right?* I guess you fellows don't read your newspapers very carefully. Don't you remember what Maggie wrote about the establishment that's doing most of the developing? Maybe our editor should refresh your memory. Go on, tell 'em, Maggie."

"Well," she glanced uncomfortably around the table. She didn't like the turn their conversation had suddenly taken. Yet everyone appeared interested. Even Michael Abundi looked at her with open curiosity. "According to my research this developer is notorious for taking beautiful land parcels and turning them into some pretty shoddy developments. 'Cheap and sleazy' is how the *L.A. Times* described them. Also, he's notorious for cutting corners, using cheap or even illegal labor and inferior construction materials. Then he sells most of the units, leaves the place in the hands of bad management, and moves on."

"Oh, my," said Elizabeth. "That sounds horrible."

"How can you be so sure?" injected Buckie. "What if it's all just hearsay? Or suppose this developer's being slandered by his competition? And don't forget how Rick and Greg were so opposed to bad development last summer. Surely they won't let their very own property turn into the kind of mess you just described."

"The only reason those boys ever opposed development last summer was to protect their little scheme with Arnold Westerly," Clyde blurted out. "Everyone knows it was already in the works, and they didn't want anyone coming in here with more money and cutting them out. It's no secret they stole that land from Arnold."

"*They stole land?*" asked Michael with wide eyes.

"Not really," Jed quickly explained. "They just didn't pay the old guy what it was truly worth. In a sense, they cheated him."

"He signed the papers of his own free will," argued Buckie. "No one forced his hand."

Maggie pressed her lips together, slowly stood, and quietly began to clear the plates from the table while the others continued to discuss this controversial topic. Afraid she wouldn't be able to control her tongue if she sat there for another moment, she hoped to make a quick escape to the kitchen.

"We have some wonderful desserts still waiting," announced Audrey loudly so as to be heard above the banter at the table. Maggie silently blessed her mother for her attempt to change the subject.

"Perhaps we should all get up and move around a little," suggested Abigail. "Otherwise I won't have any room for dessert. And I saw some beautiful pumpkin pies cooling on the back porch that I'm dying to sink my teeth into."

Back in the kitchen, Maggie planted herself in front of the sink and began rinsing dishes. "Don't let it get to you," whispered Jed as he placed a stack of plates at her elbow. "You know how Buckie loves to stir up controversy. He's just playing devil's advocate."

She sighed and continued rinsing. "I hope you're right."

Then Leah stepped up. "Jed is right," she said, patting Maggie's back in a comforting way. "You know how Buckie can be when he gets going on something. Sometimes you just have to ignore him."

Maggie looked into Leah's eyes and smiled. "Thanks, Leah, I needed that."

No one mentioned the development plans again. But Maggie felt sad when Buckie and Kate excused themselves early before having any dessert. They said they wanted to catch a new movie in Byron, but she hoped it wasn't because of the earlier disagreement. Before long dessert was served, and after that the teenagers went out to the barn to play some music; then the Hendersons and Elizabeth and Abigail all said their goodbyes. The rest of the party settled into the library to relax and visit.

"So, tell me, Michael," began Clyde as he leaned comfortably back into a club chair next to the fireplace, "what exactly brings you to Pine Mountain?"

Michael smiled broadly, then stood up next to the fireplace as if he was about to deliver a formal speech. "Thank you for asking, Mr. Barnes. It is very good to be here. I do not know if you ever knew my good friend Steven Harris, but he lived in Pine Mountain a long time ago."

Clyde thought for a moment. "Yes, I believe I do remember Steven. His family was quite prominent in town, and I think Steven was about the age of my nephew. Very good in sports as I recall. Then he got all religious and went off to be some sort of missionary, I think I heard. His folks had several businesses in town, but they moved away some years ago, and I haven't really heard anything about any of them since."

"Steven died on the mission field," injected Jed. "He was also a good friend of mine. In fact, it was letters from Steven that first helped me to realize how much I needed God in my life." He looked down at the floor. "I never really got to thank him for that."

"This is all true," said Michael. "My friend Steven came to live in my country, a tiny island of Papua New Guinea called Beni-Beni, when I was just a boy. After my mother died, my father went to the copper mine to work. But he never came back to get me; later I learned he had died in a tragic mining accident. It was Steven who took me in. Steven taught me to speak English. He also taught me about God. Then he sent me to college to learn to be a pastor. Not long after I came back to my village, Steven became very sick with cancer. He wanted to get well so he could return to Pine Mountain and tell the people there about God too. But he did not get well. Before Steven died, I promised him that I would come to his village to be a missionary in the same way that he had come to my village. And for seven years I have worked and prayed and saved money until I had enough to come here."

"Did you ever become a pastor?" asked Maggie with concern.

"Yes." He smiled proudly. "For eight years I was pastor of Yosaba Church. I also worked as a teacher in the primary school."

"Was it hard to leave your church behind?" asked Rosa.

He tapped his chest. "My church is with me—in my heart. I left three good men in charge back in Yosaba. Pastor

James went to the same college as I, and he is a good man who loves God. And now that I am in Pine Mountain, I can keep my promise to Steven."

"So, you are going to be a missionary in Pine Mountain?" asked Clyde, scratching his head with a somewhat skeptical expression.

"I believe it is the will of God." Michael smiled warmly.

Clyde chuckled. "Well, now I've heard everything. But I wish you the best, son."

"I told Michael that I'd ask our church board if he might preach at a service sometime," said Jed, glancing at Sam for approval.

"I can't speak for the whole board," said Sam, "but the pulpit is mine this Sunday, and I'd be happy to offer it to Michael."

Michael beamed. "If your people agree, I would be most honored."

Sam turned to Jed. "I'll call around tomorrow and let you know."

◦

It was already dark when the rest of the visitors began to leave, but Leah managed to coax Jed and Michael to stay a bit longer, discreetly tempting them with promises of leftovers that Maggie later arranged buffet style on the kitchen table. Then everyone returned with loaded plates to eat around the warm fire in the library.

"You are a happy family," observed Michael after setting his now-empty plate aside. "But I don't fully understand." He looked curiously at Jed. "Leah is your daughter, I know. Is Maggie her mother? Does that make Maggie your wife? But you live in different houses."

Jed laughed. "That's not quite right."

"Maggie isn't my mother," said Leah quickly, "but I live here and she's been a good friend to me."

Maggie smiled at this, the second warm thing Leah had said today. Perhaps things weren't as bad as she'd imagined. "Yes. Leah's been living here with us for a while, and we just don't want to let her go. Spencer is my son. His father died two and a half years ago."

Michael looked into Spencer's eyes. "I am very sorry. I know how it feels to lose your parents."

"Thanks," muttered Spencer, obviously feeling self-conscious.

"You must remember that God is your father now," continued Michael with conviction. "And he will never leave you."

"Yeah, sure," said Spencer without looking back up. "Okay."

"And Audrey is my mother," continued Maggie, hoping to relieve Spencer from the limelight. "She moved here permanently about a month ago. She lives in that little house over by the barn—most of the time." She winked at her mother.

"That is good," proclaimed Michael. "Family *is* very good."

"Yes," agreed Maggie. "Family is very good."

Jed's eyes locked with Maggie's from across the room. "But you're right, Michael," he said, "we are a happy family. Even if we're not all directly related, we're still like a family."

"Yes," said Michael. "I think it is a most wonderful thing."

ᕐᒧ

Leah and Jed offered to clean up the supper dishes, and Spencer hobbled around on his crutches, giving Michael a tour of the house and property, returning quickly from being outside on account of Michael's discomfort with the cold. He hovered over the fireplace, soaking in the heat with a contented smile.

"I hope it doesn't take too long for you to get used to the cold here," said Maggie from the couch. "I don't know how long you plan to stay, but it will get even colder when snow comes."

"Who is snow?" he asked curiously.

Maggie chuckled. "Snow isn't a person. It's what the weather does when the rain gets so cold that it freezes and comes down on the ground and makes everything turn all white and sort of frozen."

Michael looked slightly frightened. "Oh, yes, I have forgotten about snow. I have seen photographs of snow before, but never have I touched it or seen it for real with my own eyes. It is *very* cold?"

Audrey nodded. "Yes. And I understand how you feel, Michael, because I used to live in a place where it was warmer too. But I think we'll all get used to it in time."

"Yes," he agreed, "God will help us."

Maggie went to check on the kitchen help and found Jed by himself wiping off the table with a dishcloth. "Hey, you do good work," she said, looking around the kitchen in approval.

"Better give Leah the credit; she took the lead. She just went upstairs for something." He set the rag by the sink and moved closer to Maggie. "I had a wonderful time today. Thank you for everything."

She smiled as he reached to push a stray strand of hair from her cheek. Then his hand lingered on her shoulder, his fingers gently kneading, sending little electrical currents down her arm and up her neck.

"It's like Michael said," she said quietly, "we are like a family..."

His face moved close to hers. "A very happy family," he whispered. Then his lips brushed hers, first lightly, then developing into a full kiss that left her heart fluttering and her legs as limp as spaghetti.

"I found it!" called Leah as she burst into the kitchen, holding a rumpled photo in her hand. But she stopped in her tracks when she saw them together, and then her eyes grew dark and stony. "Sorry. I didn't know you—"

"It's okay," said Maggie, quickly pulling herself from Jed's embrace, her cheeks flushed with embarrassment. "What do you have there?"

"Nothing!" snapped Leah as she turned and left the kitchen, loudly thumping back up the stairs.

"Oh, dear," moaned Maggie. "And just when I thought things were getting so much better."

Except for a trace of sadness, Jed's face was unreadable now. "It's all my fault," he said finally. "I hate hurting her like this. But I don't know what to do about—" He stopped himself and looked down at Maggie. "This is so frustrating. I just need to take some time to figure everything out. It's not fair to anyone."

She didn't know what to say. On one hand, she wanted to say, "Forget about Leah, and kiss me again!" but that would be immature and selfish on her part. And on the other hand, she hated seeing Leah hurt and longed for their relationship to return to normal—and she'd felt so hopeful only minutes ago.

"It's getting late," he said. "I'm sorry about all this, Maggie. It's certainly not what I'd planned..."

"It's okay. It's not your fault," she said automatically. But she wondered which part he was sorry about. Was it the interruption or the kiss?

Seven

$\mathcal{M}$aggie did a double take when she saw Clyde seated all by himself at the back of the church. He wore an old suit jacket that looked like it might have survived the Great Depression, and in his lap his old fingers nervously rotated a black felt hat. Maggie had never seen Clyde in church before, and she smiled warmly as she slipped into the pew next to him, followed by her mother and then Spencer clumping in awkwardly with his crutches rattling against the bench. Meanwhile Leah went off, Maggie felt sure, to search for Jed.

"Thought I'd come hear what this young man has to say," said Clyde, before she had a chance to comment.

"How did you know for sure that he'd be preaching today?"

"I have my ways." Clyde grinned slyly and then added, "Saw Sam in the plumbing section of the hardware store yesterday afternoon. He told me how to fix my leaky faucet too."

She smiled again as she focused her attention on the view outside the tall windows up front. Although the mountains had received another light dusting last night, it was still not nearly enough to open the ski resorts yet. But the snow was beautiful, lit by the morning sun and shimmering white against the clear blue sky. She noticed Jed sitting in the front row, with Michael and Leah flanking him on either side. She quickly averted her eyes back to the mountain scene, determined not to be distracted from today's sermon by Jed's presence or memories of Thursday night's kiss. But it wouldn't be easy.

After what seemed a lengthy prelude of music and announcements, Jed finally stepped up to the podium and introduced Michael Abundi. Instead of looking at Jed, Maggie kept her eyes on Michael, smiling to herself as she noticed his neat white collar and dark tie, barely visible beneath the layers of sweaters that made him look as round as the Michelin Tire Man, his expression a mixture of apprehension and excitement. But when he began to speak, his eyes sparking with joyful exuberance, she quickly forgot his unusually rotund appearance and listened intently to his words.

"I must thank you all for allowing me to speak in your beautiful church today. And I must thank God for bringing me thousands of miles across the great, wide ocean to your United States." He continued naturally and with surprising eloquence and energy, telling them of the great miracles he'd seen God perform back in his island village—how he'd witnessed actual physical healings, miraculous provisions, and even how a woman was delivered from demons. It was like stories from the Bible coming to life. And the way he told these tales, using actual names and vivid description, sounded amazingly believable, while at the same time seeming almost too fantastic to be true. Then he read some portions of Scripture from the New Testament, describing those similar miracles that had happened nearly 2,000 years earlier. He spoke of the miracle of faith and how it could move mighty mountains, using the scene behind him as a very realistic visual aid. And it felt as if everyone in the entire church was sitting at the edge of their pews, perhaps even hoping that he might speak to their mountains and actually make them move. Even Clyde was leaning forward expectantly.

"And now, I ask you, dear people," he implored, turning back to face the congregation. "What miracle would you ask of God today?" He pointed out the window again. "Surely you do not wish to move *these* beautiful mountains! For then what would you see but flat, barren ground?" The congregation laughed.

Mr. Mitchell from the Gas-n-Go stood up just then. "I have a suggestion, young man. How 'bout you pray for snow so our businesses can keep from going broke this winter?" Maggie wasn't sure if he was serious or not, but several others chimed in their agreement. And suddenly she felt worried for Michael. Was this some sort of test for him? Poor Michael, standing bravely before them, all bundled up in his many layers of clothing, his simple faith so full of sincerity. Yet how could he possibly understand the differences in their cultures? How could he know how skeptical most Americans could be about such things as faith and miracles in the modern-day world?

But Michael nodded thoughtfully, as if seriously considering Mr. Mitchell's request. "Snow..." he repeated the word slowly, "to help your village." That's when Maggie remembered how much he disliked the cold and had seemed quite apprehensive on Thanksgiving when she'd described snow to him. Perhaps this wasn't the sort of miracle that he would personally welcome. But Michael closed his eyes and lifted his hands, imploring God to send them snow, "...send lots of snow! So the good people of Pine Mountain might see and know your power and might! That they might give you glory and honor and praise! Amen!"

After the service people continued to talk about the snow. Some peered out at the still-blue sky, seemingly convinced that it was actually coming at any moment now. But most appeared somewhat skeptical, although good-humoredly joking about how they had better be getting out their snow shovels and waxing up their skis. Maggie wasn't even sure what she thought, although the whole thing made her extremely uncomfortable. Just the same, she heartily shook

Michael's hand and thanked him for sharing the good message about faith.

⌒

By noon the following day, a canopy of lead-colored clouds began to hang low and heavy, and a cold wind began to blow from the north. Maggie stood in the newspaper's reception area and stared out the window in wonder. She'd heard no forecast of a weather change on the morning news today—certainly no mention of any possible snow. Perhaps this was just another taste of their unpredictable mountain weather, another tease of snow that would go as quickly as it came.

"By golly, I think I smell snow in the air," said Clyde as he came in the front door and peeled off his wool gloves. He leaned over Abigail's desk and flipped through the mail, chuckling. "Maybe that Michael Abundi has a direct line to the big weatherman in the sky after all."

"What are you going on about now?" asked Abigail, lowering her glasses and peering up at Clyde as if he were going senile.

He briefly explained yesterday's sermon, and Abigail blinked in surprise. Maggie wasn't sure if it was over Michael's sermon or due to the fact that Clyde had actually attended a church service. "And so, Clyde Barnes," began Abigail with a sharp note of cynicism, "are you saying that if it snows today, you think it's a result of this young man's prayers?"

Clyde laughed. "If it snows today, Abigail, it's more'n likely the result of a Canadian air current gone south, combined with some freezing temperatures and high humidity."

"But what about Michael's prayer?" asked Maggie, suddenly feeling defensive of their faithful young visitor.

He shrugged. "Might just be a coincidence."

"Might not," she quipped back. "But coincidence or not, I think it could be newsworthy. In fact, I think I should do an interview with Michael for this week's edition."

"Good idea," said Abigail. "He's such a nice person, and I'm sure he has lots of interesting stories to tell about his homeland."

"Are you guys talking about Jed's island friend?" asked Scott, emerging from his office.

"His name is Michael Abundi," said Maggie. "Have you met him?"

"Not yet. But my parents sure seem to like him."

"Well, I want to schedule an interview with him. And I'd like you to get a photo. Michael's about your age, I'd guess. He'd probably enjoy meeting you."

"Sounds good." Scott started to head back to his office, then stopped. "Hey, I almost forgot. I came up with a little something in my research that might affect *the development*." The way he pronounced "the development" left no doubt as to his reference. And Maggie could tell by the tone of his voice that his news bit might be worthwhile.

"What is it?" she demanded eagerly. "What did you find?"

He smiled slyly. "Ever heard of wetland issues?"

Her eyes lit up. "Of course. But does the Westerly property have wetlands?"

He nodded smugly. "First of all, the back end of Snider's land is a bog for most of the year—a great place for wild ducks and geese. And the creek through Westerly's has a nice natural pond over in the north corner, another attraction for waterfowl and who knows what other kind of possibly endangered species. You know, the humpbacked three-toed frog or something like that."

"That's right." Clyde nodded with interest. "We used to hunt ducks back there as kids."

"Yes," said Scott, rubbing his hands together. "I happen to think we might have some hot wetland issues going here."

Clyde cleared his throat. "As you all know, I cannot abide to see government bureaucrats interfering with anybody's private property rights. But in this case, I just might have to make an exception."

Abigail nodded. "I know just how you feel, Clyde. My husband, God rest his soul, used to go on and on about government sticking its big old nose into every area of our personal lives. But when I think about what those development boys are up to, all I can say is: *sic 'em, Uncle Sam!*"

Maggie laughed, then sobered a little and said, "I just hope we're not becoming a bunch of mean-spirited vigilantes because of all this. It's not like I want to seek revenge or anything like that…"

"Not revenge," said Clyde. "Justice."

"Yeah," agreed Scott, his tone becoming serious. "And don't forget we're doing this in honor of the memory of Mr. Westerly."

"That's right," said Abigail. "For Mr. Westerly."

"So, it looks as if we're all in consensus then," said Maggie with a slow smile. "And I didn't even realize we were having an official meeting today."

Scott started to duck back into his office, then popped his head back out again. "Oh, yeah. There's something else I almost forgot."

They all looked at him again, but this time he said nothing, only grinned foolishly. "Well, what is it?" asked Maggie finally.

"Chloe and I got engaged over Thanksgiving."

Everyone laughed and congratulated him. Clyde even pulled out one of his cigars and stuck it in Scott's pocket.

"When's the big date?" asked Abigail.

"Um…, I know it sounds really crazy, but we're thinking about New Year's Eve."

"*This* New Year's Eve?" asked Maggie incredulously.

Scott nodded. "Yeah, seems kind of sudden, doesn't it?"

"Are you kidding? I would think Chloe's family would need lots of time to plan for a big wedding. Don't they know just about everyone who's anyone up in Portland?"

Scott's smile faded. "Actually, they're not too excited about the whole thing. I guess her dad thought this little stint in Pine Mountain was just a phase for her or something. Or maybe he'd hoped Chloe's old boyfriend, Aaron Jackson, was going to knock me out of the running." He sighed. "The date was Chloe's idea. She has always dreamed of a New Year's Eve wedding, but we didn't know if we wanted to wait for a whole year." Was Scott blushing beneath that smooth olive skin?

"And what does *your* family think about all this?" asked Maggie.

"As you can imagine, they're totally thrilled. You know how much they all love Chloe. Mom keeps bragging that she's the one who discovered her for me in the first place." He laughed.

"So Chloe must be up to her eyebrows in wedding plans," said Maggie. "I cannot imagine how you two are going to pull this thing off so soon."

"Well, it helps that we have both decided we want a small, intimate wedding—right here in Pine Mountain."

"Oh, won't that be nice," gushed Abigail. "If there's anything I can do to help—with flowers or decorations or anything, you just tell Chloe to give me a call."

"Same here," offered Maggie. "And I know my mother would be glad to help too. She's quite fond of you two."

"Thanks," said Scott, seemingly relieved. "Chloe said she wants to keep everything simple. She's been involved in plenty of high society weddings and she thinks they're nothing but a great big show of how much money the parents have. She doesn't want anything like that for us."

"Good for her," said Clyde. "Sounds like that girl's got a good head on her shoulders."

"Yes," agreed Maggie. "I'm sure you two will be very happy together."

⁓

Maggie slipped into Dolly's Diner, quickly scanning the menu board to see "Hearty Vegetable Soup" listed there. She tried to drop in the diner fairly regularly, if only to catch some of the latest local gossip and to visit with Dolly; and if she was lucky, there'd be a good soup of the day.

"Here you go, honey," said Dolly as she plunked the heavy pottery bowl down on the laminate-topped table. Then she leaned into the other side of the booth and quickly pushed back the café curtains to peer out the window. "Lordy, Lordy, if it isn't starting to snow out there!"

Several people in the diner, including Maggie, turned to gape out the windows and after a few seconds Maggie spotted a single flake fluttering down. "You're right, Dolly. I just saw a flake too."

"Well, glory be!" exclaimed Dolly. "We might just make it after all." She turned to Maggie. "Did you hear about that funny little foreign man who came to town to pray for snow? Someone said he thinks he's a prophet or something."

Maggie laughed uneasily. "His name is Michael Abundi. He doesn't think he's a prophet—he only prayed for snow because Al Mitchell asked him to." She glanced out the window again, this time to spy several flakes falling. "And who knows? Maybe he does have a special connection with God."

"Fine by me," said Dolly happily as she headed back toward the kitchen. "Hey, Jinx, look out the window for a minute!"

Maggie slowly ate her soup, continuing to watch with fascination as the flakes grew in both number and size. By the time she left the diner, the street and sidewalk were already coated with a thin veneer of white. Several shop-keepers and businesspeople were standing at their windows or outside their doors exclaiming over this very welcome change of weather.

"Better late than never," called Elizabeth as she waved from the open doorway of the Window Seat bookstore. "Looks like we'll be having some great book-reading weather before long!"

Maggie saw Jed's pickup pulling up in front of his shop, then he and Michael hopped out. Michael, like a young child, excitedly raised his hands and danced about in the falling snow. She zipped her jacket to her chin and hurried over to greet them.

"God has sent snow, Maggie!" cried Michael. "Another miracle!"

"Yes," she agreed. "It's wonderful! Thank you for praying."

His dark eyes grew serious. "No, no—it is not because of me, Maggie. It is God's miracle, not mine."

She nodded. "Yes, I see what you mean. And of course you're absolutely right, Michael. We should thank God for the snow."

"Say, Maggie," said Jed, "do you think I might borrow your car this afternoon to take Michael over to Byron?"

"Sure," she said. She dug into her purse, curious as to why Jed would need her car. "Here are the keys."

"Thanks—"

"Jed!" called Leah from the front door of the shop. "There's someone from that furniture show on the phone who needs to talk with you."

"I'll have your car back by four," called Jed as he ducked into his shop.

Maggie noticed Michael shivering in the cold. "You should go inside and get warm, Michael. But whenever you have time, I'd like you to come by the newspaper office. I want to ask you some questions about your life, and then I'd like to write a story about you to put in the newspaper."

His eyes lit up. "You want to write about *me* in your newspaper?"

"Yes, I think it would interest our readers. Would that be okay?"

He nodded vigorously. "It is wonderful. Praise be to God! I will come tomorrow if that is all right. I am going with Jed to do something special today."

"Yes. Tomorrow is perfect. How about nine o'clock in the morning? That way we can get it into this week's paper with your photo and everything."

"I will come if Jed can bring me, for I do not drive a car."
He grew thoughtful. "But I can paddle a canoe."

She grinned. "I bet you can. See you tomorrow then."

ᴖ

By late afternoon, at least six inches of snow had accumulated. Maggie stepped out of the newspaper office and felt as giddy as a child as she surveyed the town now coated in a clean blanket of white. Shop windows glowed warmly, and the old-fashioned lampposts looked cheerful, their golden light reflected on the freshly fallen snow. It was like a Currier & Ives card—a true winter wonderland! Jed had returned her car only moments ago, and Abigail had encouraged her to go home early so that she could practice her snow driving while it was still light enough outside to see. "Now, take it nice and slow, honey," the older woman had sagely advised her. "No fast moves, gentle braking, gentle steering...and you'll be just fine." Maggie hurried over to her car, relieved that her windows were still cleared of snow as she hopped into the driver's seat, still slightly warm. On the dashboard was a new ice scraper, probably a thank-you gift from Jed for borrowing her car. How thoughtful of him. But something seemed different inside. She sniffed the air curiously—there was a distinct, pungent aroma of rubber. She turned around to see where it was coming from, and there in the back of her station wagon was a set of four tires. How very odd. Then she recalled Jed quizzing her on Thanksgiving about whether she'd gotten snow tires yet. She hopped out of her car to examine her tires—and there, sure enough, she could see shiny, metal studs gleaming in the afternoon light. Jed had taken her car over to Byron to get snow tires put on for her! She smiled happily as she climbed back in and started the engine. Now, if that wasn't love...what indeed was? She carefully navigated Main Street, her confidence growing steadily (and greatly, due to her new tires). She turned off toward home alone. There was no need to pick up Leah today as she'd said this morning that Jed was going to bring her home later—after they'd had dinner at the Pine Mountain Hotel. Maggie hated to admit, even to herself, that she'd felt a keen prick of jealousy about this news, wishing that Jed was taking her instead. But in the same instant she'd been happy for Leah's sake, realizing how the poor girl might actually be feeling the exact same way toward her much of the time. And although it made little sense, Maggie suspected this little threesome wasn't going to be an easy dance to do. At least Spencer seemed to be happily adjusted to sharing his mother with Jed. Then again, boys were different about these things, plus he had a grandmother as well. Perhaps it was an unfair comparison altogether.

❧

Maggie told her family about Scott and Chloe's good news as they sat together at the dinner table. "And I even offered your help, Mom. I hope you don't mind. But I'm sure they'll need all the help they can get trying to do something like this at such short notice."

Audrey beamed. "I don't mind at all. You know how I love weddings. But New Year's Eve, that's awfully soon."

Maggie explained the couple's reasoning and Chloe's desire for a small, simple wedding. "Actually, the more I consider the whole thing, I think it sounds rather sweet and romantic."

Audrey gave Maggie a long, slightly suspicious look, and then changed the subject from weddings. "I have a few leads for a building that might house the town's library," she said as she ladled out the turkey noodles that were, thankfully, the final remnant of their Thanksgiving dinner.

"Great, Mom." Maggie passed the rolls to Spencer. "What are they?"

"Well, I wrote down the addresses of all the vacant buildings in town that seemed like they might work for a library, then I went and looked them up at County Records in Byron. I thought if I could get someone to donate a building, it would give us more funding to use to stock the shelves—not to mention it's a tax write-off for the donor."

"Good thinking, Grandma," said Spencer between bites. "So, did you find anyone willing to give you a building yet?"

"Not yet. But I thought it was interesting that one building belongs to a Steven Harris, Sr. That must be Michael's friend's father, don't you think?"

"I doubt there was more than one Steven Harris family in this tiny town," said Spencer as he buttered another roll.

"But I thought Clyde said the family left town over ten years ago," said Maggie.

"That's probably right." Audrey poured some salad dressing. "There are a number of properties that have sat vacant for years because the real estate value around here has been so deflated."

"But isn't that changing now?" asked Spencer.

Maggie nodded. "Without a doubt. And it should continue to go up."

"Especially now that we're getting snow!" said Spencer with enthusiasm.

"It certainly won't hurt anything," agreed Maggie. "We must've gotten six inches in town already. I wonder how much that makes up at the ski resort?"

"And it's still falling," reminded Audrey.

"I bet those lifts will be opening up by next weekend." Maggie glanced over at Spencer with a smile.

But suddenly he grew sad, and at the same instant she remembered his foot hidden beneath the table, still in its cast. "Doesn't that thing come off in a couple weeks?" she asked hopefully.

"Yeah, the doc said maybe by mid-December, if I'm lucky." He looked glum. "I almost wish the snow hadn't come yet."

"Oh, Spence," said Audrey, "I know how frustrated you must be, but try to be happy for the rest of the town."

"It's just that I've been waiting *forever* for snow, and now this stupid cast will make the next two weeks feel like two years!"

"Well, after seeing your midterm grades, I think you might be smart to use this time to catch up on some of your homework."

Spencer made a face at his mother, and then returned to slurping his soup.

"I think we got sidetracked, Mom," said Maggie. "Now what were you saying about Steve Harris' parents? Do you plan to use that building for the library? And which one is it anyway?"

"It's that great big old warehouse sort of building on the east end of town. It looks like a giant box with blue paint peeling off in big chunks. I think it used to be a grain mill or something like that."

"And you think *that* would make a good library?"

"Well, no. It certainly wouldn't be my first choice, or even my second one for that matter. It would take far more than my lifetime to accumulate enough books to fill that building. Actually, I was thinking of a much smaller scale, but I thought I'd consider all options to start with. Besides, it might be interesting to talk with the Harris family—I bet they'd like to hear about what Michael is doing here."

"Oh, yeah." Spencer pointed his spoon in the air. "Can you believe that the day after Michael prays for snow, it actually happens? Do you think it's a real miracle?"

"I think it's an amazing coincidence," said Audrey as she placidly stirred her coffee.

"I'm not sure what I think," said Maggie honestly. "I think it *could* be a miracle. I have no doubt that God could do something like that—I'm just not sure why he would."

"Maybe it's just like Michael said." Spencer leaned back in his chair. "Maybe it's to show how powerful God is."

"Maybe." Maggie buttered a roll. "But it does make me wonder—why would God choose to answer one particular request for a miracle, say like sending down snow, but not answer another, say like when Michael prayed for Steven Harris to be healed of cancer?"

"Why don't you ask Michael about that?" suggested Audrey.

"Good idea. In fact, I'm interviewing him in the morning. I'll put it on my question list."

"And here's another question," said Spencer with a gleam in his eye. "Why don't you ask him if he can pray for my foot to be completely healed before the slopes open up?"

The two women chuckled over this, and then Maggie grew more serious. "Already there are some strange rumors going on around town about Michael. Some people are making fun of him. I just hope they don't get carried away with all this miracle business. Poor Michael, I'd hate for folks to start treating him like some sort of sideshow freak or something."

"I'd be more worried about those people who might hate him because of the color of his skin," said Audrey. "Just today, Clara Henderson told me that Lou had heard that that Ebbert fellow is up to no good. He wanted to post a flyer at their store about some meeting or something. Of course, Lou refused."

"Yeah, and there are a few kids at my school who're pretty weird when it comes to all that kind of crud," said Spencer. "I can't believe them. They draw swastikas on their hands and walk around with their heads all shaved, wearing these stupid-looking army fatigues. You halfway expect them to click their heels and salute 'Heil Hitler' at any given moment."

"They're probably just going through a phase," suggested Maggie weakly.

"A dangerous phase," said Audrey.

Eight

$\mathcal{M}$aggie grabbed her jacket and went out on the porch as soon as she spotted Jed's headlights pulling into her driveway. The snow had stopped falling now, and she was amazed at how easily she could see with the porch light reflected on the shiny surface of new snow. She waved as Leah hopped out of Jed's pickup. Then Jed stuck his head up over the top of the cab and called out, "Hey, Maggie. This enough snow for you yet?"

"It's totally wonderful!" she called. "I love it! I just wanted to say thank you for getting those snow tires on, and just in the nick of time too!"

"No problem. I was taking Michael over to Byron anyway."

"Come on in and I'll write you a check for them. And we can make some hot cocoa if you have the time."

"Sure!" He climbed down from the truck and walked over. "Cocoa sounds good. But forget about the check, Magpie. The tires are a gift."

"Oh, no, Jed. That's too much—"

"Now, if you keep going on about this, I'll have to forgo the cocoa and go home," he warned.

"Better listen to him," said Leah as she stomped the snow off her lightweight leather shoes. "I guess I'll need to get some real snow boots."

"I have a pair that you can borrow until you get some," offered Maggie.

"Great. I'll go start up the cocoa," said Leah happily.

"How did your dinner go?" Maggie turned to Jed after Leah closed the front door behind her.

"Very nice." He reached for her hand. "We even talked about you some."

"You did?" She looked up into his face and smiled.

"Leah really admires you a lot, Maggie. She said that sometimes she actually wishes you were her mother."

"That's so sweet." She squeezed his hand, enjoying the warmth and strength of his long, sturdy fingers wrapped around hers.

"But she also said that sometimes she feels like she's in competition with you—and she doesn't like that at all."

"Oh..." Maggie's smile faded.

"I tried to explain to her that the way I feel about you doesn't in any way affect or diminish my feelings for her. And I know she's trying hard to be very mature and understanding about all this, but she openly admitted that she doesn't want to share me with anyone else right now."

"Oh..."

"And when you think of all she's been through—I mean, her mom, the stepdads, the live-in boyfriends—well, it's not all that surprising, I suppose."

"No, not at all. I understand it completely." More completely than she cared to admit, for the truth was, she didn't want to share Jed with anyone else right now either. But for Leah's sake, and because she was the adult here, she knew she would have to at least try.

"And so..." He bent his face closer to hers, his strong fingers still wrapped securely around her own. "I told Leah that maybe you and I could sort of...well...put our relationship on hold for the time being, just long enough to give her some time to adjust to everything." He smiled down at her. "It doesn't change how I feel about you a bit."

Maggie felt a lump grow in her throat as she slowly pulled her hand from his. "Okay..." she said weakly. "I guess that makes sense."

"I figured if we set our relationship aside for a short while, Leah will begin to feel more secure and, hopefully, she'll understand how committed I am to her as her father."

"Right." She tried to swallow the tight lump and nodded her head. "I understand, Jed, really I do."

He squeezed her arm with a slight frown. "Believe me, Maggie, this isn't easy for me to do—" Just then the front door opened behind her, and the porch was flooded with light from the house. Jed looked beyond her and smiled.

"Hey, there," called Leah. "The cocoa's almost ready. Want me to bring it out to the porch?"

"No, we'll come inside," said Maggie, quickly turning to enter her house. "It's getting pretty cold out here."

Audrey and Spencer joined them in the kitchen. Everyone talked of the snow and the upcoming ski season with excitement. Even Spencer seemed better now, boasting to Leah that, even with his foot in a cast, he could probably snowboard better than she, as she'd never skied or skateboarded or anything.

"Don't be so sure of yourself," teased Leah, "Sierra promised to give me lessons on opening day, and she thinks I'll be really good. By the time you get up there I'll probably be way ahead of you."

His face grew sober. "Yeah, I'll probably never get to snowboard. I'll probably be permanently crippled when they finally take off this stupid old cast." He thumped his foot loudly on the floor and then grimaced.

Leah placed a comforting hand on his shoulder. "No you won't, Spence. I was just kidding. I'm such a big chicken, I'm sure you're going to be way better at snowboarding than me. I'll probably end up having some big old wipeout on my very first run and end up in a complete bodycast, or at the very least, crutches for the rest of the season."

Spencer laughed, holding his crutches out. "Hey, I'll let you use these if you want!"

"Let's hope no one suffers any more broken bones," said Maggie with a serious tone.

"Here, here," agreed Audrey, holding her cocoa mug up as if in a toast. "And here's to a whole lot of snow and a great winter season for Pine Mountain."

They all held up their mugs. "To a good season," said Jed. "And thanks be to God for sending us snow."

Maggie smiled at him, telling herself that this little delay in their relationship was really for the best and that anything worth having was worth waiting for. Of course, her heart wasn't a hundred percent convinced by her mental pep talk, but at least she could try to be a good sport about the whole thing.

ᵔ

Maggie spent nearly an hour interviewing Michael the next morning, the whole time wondering what possible angle she might take with this story. He made it perfectly clear that his main purpose in coming to Pine Mountain was to be a missionary, or in his own words, "to preach the good news to the lost souls that my good friend Steven cared so deeply for..." How could she write *that* in the newspaper? She could just imagine certain individuals taking strong offense to being Michael Abundi's "mission field," and yet she didn't want to compromise his message either. Finally Scott stopped by to take Michael outside on the porch to shoot some photos, and after that he gave him a tour of the newspaper office. Maggie sat at her desk, going over her notes. Perhaps she'd play up the Steven Harris connection, maybe even contact his parents for a quote—she knew she could get the number from her mom—then she'd show how this unusual friendship had motivated Michael to come over here. She'd already completed her opening paragraph by the time he stopped in to say goodbye.

"Thanks for coming, Michael." She smiled up at him. "I think I'll try to reach Steven Harris' parents for some comments on this story."

"Steven's parents?" His dark eyes grew wide. "I have never met them. Do they live here in Pine Mountain?"

She shook her head. "No, but I think I might be able to reach them."

He frowned slightly. "They did not approve when Steven chose to leave his home to become a missionary. He wrote them often, but they never wrote to him. Not until he became ill ..."

"Oh my. How sad."

"But I would like to speak to them—if you think they would be willing to speak to me—or maybe they will not want to..."

"If I reach them, I'll remember to ask," offered Maggie, suddenly unsure as to whether she wanted to include their quote in her article or not.

"All right. I must go now. Thank you."

"Stay warm!" she called as he left her office.

She returned to her writing until she heard Abigail on the intercom. Her voice sounded stiff and formal as she spoke. "Ms. Carpenter, a *Mr. Ebbert* is in the lobby wishing to see you. I told him you were busy right now. But he demands—"

"That's right!" came a loud male voice, also over the intercom. "I demand to know why you people aren't printing my letters to the editor in your newspaper!"

Maggie thought for a moment. She hated leaving poor Abigail on her own to deal with this troublemaker, but she was just as reluctant to invite him into her office and listen to his ranting and raving. She'd heard he was long-winded and could go on for some time. "Just a moment," she answered. "I'll be right out." Then she quickly saved her story on the computer and braced herself for what she felt sure could turn into an ugly confrontation.

Expecting to find an angry-looking skinhead much like Spencer had described last night, she was surprised to see a large, tall man wearing blue jeans, a dark green parka, and a full head of hair. But it was his facial expression that gave him away. It was as if the hatred had been etched deeply into his features. His mouth turned down at the edges and a deep line furrowed between his brows. She doubted this man had ever laughed much.

"I'm Maggie Carpenter, the editor of the *Pine Cone*." She made this announcement without extending her hand in greeting. Perhaps it was petty of her, but after having read his letters, she just couldn't force herself to shake his hand.

He glowered down at her. "I want to know why you're not printing any of my letters in your paper. I got an A in my college writing class. I use correct grammar and punctuation, and my spelling is pretty decent. Maybe you people just don't believe in freedom of speech!"

"We don't print every letter we receive, Mr. Ebbert." Actually, other than his, they usually did. "And it has nothing to do with freedom of speech."

"Yeah, well, I thought the editorial page was a place where the paper allows everyone to express their opinions whether or not the editor agrees with the content. Am I not correct, *Ms.* Carpenter?" He pronounced the "Ms." as if pelting an insult her way.

"That's correct. We quite often print letters with differing opinions—the diversity adds interest to the paper. As you may recall, last summer we quite regularly published Greg Snider's letters even though he was quite critical of the views of the newspaper and of me personally."

"Right!" He growled as he reached into his parka. Maggie took a sudden step back, fearing that this man could actually be armed and dangerous. Back at the *Times*, they had security guards and metal detectors for moments like this. But he simply removed a wrinkled sheet of paper and stepped forward to wave it in her face. "Well, here's another letter that I'm certain is contrary to your views. Is there any reason you can't print it in this week's paper?"

"There may be. But I'll need to look at the letter—"

"I'm sure you will!" His voice grew loud and he snatched it back from her. Just then Scott opened his office door and leaned his head out to see who was making all the noise. Mr. Ebbert continued, "I'm sure you'd look at it *real carefully*—right as you chuck it into your trash can!"

Now she was mad. "I'll have you know, Mr. Ebbert, that I do read your letters. And for your information, the reason I don't print them in our paper is because they are filled with hatred, bigotry, and racism. And while those may be your opinions, they are hurtful and mean-spirited and bring absolutely no good to this community. So unless you can think of something else to write about, you will never see a single word of yours printed in *this* paper!"

"Fine!" He turned on his heel. "I've come up with another way to get the word out before this whole town is crawling with a bunch of *undesirables!* If we don't protect the motherland, who will? Certainly not bleeding heart liberals like yourself! You think you're going to change this town, Ms. Carpenter—well, you're in for a big surprise. There are more of us than you think. We were here long before you came, and we'll still be here after you leave!"

"For your information, Mr. Ebbert, Pine Mountain *is* my home, and I have no intention of leaving, thank you very much! And as this is my home, and I am an American, I will continue to stand up for the rights of all Americans—for no matter what our religion or skin color is, we are all Americans—and that's what this country is all about. If you don't believe me, maybe you'd better leave. Go take a look around your 'motherland,' as you put it, and you'll quickly discover that our country is made up of many people from all kinds of ethnic backgrounds."

After this little speech, Abigail, Scott, and even Clyde, who had just slipped into the reception area, burst into hearty applause and cheers.

"Speaking of leaving," said Clyde as he stepped up to Mr. Ebbert and opened the front door, "don't let us keep you.

And don't bother sending any more of your hate mail here again. It's just a waste of good paper and ink."

"A lot like your liberal rag of a newspaper!" he growled as he stomped out the door. "I wouldn't even use it to line the bottom of a birdcage!"

Clyde slammed the door behind him, then said, "I'd say that's good riddance to bad rubbish!"

"Man," said Scott, turning to Maggie. "You're like a magnet for trouble, aren't you?"

She held her hands up helplessly. "I guess so. Honestly, I don't know why I keep attracting these troublemakers."

"It's because you stand up for what's right," said Abigail, "and there's nothing wrong with that either."

"Thanks for stepping in, Clyde," said Maggie. "And thanks to you guys for standing behind me like that. It meant a lot."

"That guy's a total jerk." Scott started to head back to his office and then paused. "And I don't believe a word of his little act about how there's so many out there who think like him. I bet even the likes of Greg Snider and Rick Tanner wouldn't go in for all that hate garbage."

"You're probably right, but you know it might be interesting to do an article on Mr. Ebbert's little hate group," suggested Maggie.

Scott snapped his fingers. "Good idea! Man, I'd love to do a story about them. Do you think I could do it, Maggie? Please?"

She considered his request for a moment—it was just the sort of story she would love to break herself. It might even be something that the Associated Press might pick up if done right. But then again, she knew it was a great opportunity for Scott as well. And right now his pleading face reminded her of Spencer and she softened. "Yeah, Scott, I suppose it's about time for you to get your feet wet with something beyond the local human interest story. Besides, I'm swamped with this TS Development business and now researching for all these environmental issues. But I want to work with you on it, okay? I want you to do your best work. Remember, this is investigative reporting—be thorough and don't rush it. Get all the facts you can and take lots of photos too. Maybe even do some research about hate groups in the Northwest as a whole while you're at it."

"All right!" His face lit up. "I can't wait to start in. You know, this could be really big! Thanks, Maggie."

"Sure, and who knows, maybe in time, you'll turn into a bit of a trouble-magnet yourself."

"Cool!"

∽

Back in her office, Maggie called her mom and got the phone number for Steven Harris' parents. She wanted to finish up this little piece today, and it made sense to include a bit about Steven because he, in essence, had started this whole Michael Abundi thing in the first place.

"Hello?" said Maggie when a woman answered. "Is this Mrs. Harris?" The woman confirmed and Maggie began by introducing herself as the editor of Pine Mountain's only newspaper.

"We used to live in Pine Mountain," said the woman as if reminiscing.

"I know," said Maggie. "And you had a son named Steven?"

"Yes, but he passed away some time ago." Her voice grew sad.

"I'm terribly sorry for your loss. A dear friend of mine was quite close to your son during his school years. Do you remember Jed Whitewater?"

"Oh, yes. He was such a nice young man. Very smart and quiet as I recall. And a good friend to Stevie. Whatever became of Jed?"

Maggie filled her in on the recent details of Jed's life and how things were going in Pine Mountain in general. "The main reason I'm calling is because another good friend of your son's has shown up in town recently and I am writing an article in the paper about him."

"Oh, who's that, someone famous?"

"Not really. Your son helped him out while living in Papua New Guinea. The young man's name is Michael Abundi."

"Yes, I do remember that name from some of Stevie's letters. Didn't his parents die when he was a young boy?"

"Yes, and Steven raised him and sent him to school. But Michael was a little worried that because you and your husband had disapproved of Steven's decision to become a missionary, that you might be reluctant to discuss all this. Although, I must say, you seem very open to me, Mrs. Harris."

"Please call me Barbara. And that whole opposition thing was mostly Stevie's father's doing. He thought Steven was throwing away his life, and then when he got sick and died, my husband blamed his death on his choice to go live in some 'God-forsaken foreign country.' My husband died last winter. Ironically, he also died of cancer."

"Oh, I'm sorry, Mrs.—Barbara. Have you other children?"

"No, Stevie was our only one. He was such a dear boy. And I'm proud that he lived his life doing what he thought was important. Oh, maybe I don't completely understand it, but I respect him for it. His father spent his whole life just making a lot of money, but it sure didn't seem very worthwhile to him when we lost our only son, or even when he himself died last year. What good does it do him now, I wonder? You know, I'd trade all that money just to have both of them back—and speaking to each other again." She paused as if to catch her breath. "Goodness, I'm sorry to have gone on like that. It's as if something in me just came uncorked. I guess I still have my own issues to deal with after all."

"Well, you sound like a very wise woman to me, Barbara. And I'm guessing your son was a lot like you."

"Thank you, that's very kind of you to say. Now did I hear you right? Did you say that this young man, Michael, is actually staying in Pine Mountain right now?"

"Yes. Strange as it sounds, he came here because of Steven."

"How very odd."

"Yes, it is rather unusual. Michael said that Steven's dying wish was to return to Pine Mountain and share his faith with his friends there. Michael promised Steven to go himself, and although it took him all these years just to save up enough money to get here, he has finally come."

"Oh my..."

"But he's a very sweet and sincere young man. And he's already having quite an effect on our community. I'm sure your Steven would be proud."

"How fascinating."

"Anyway, I wondered if I could ask a few questions about your son to include in my story."

Barbara readily agreed, and in just a few minutes they were done. "Thanks so much for your time," said Maggie as she closed her notebook. "It's been a real pleasure talking with you."

"You know, I was just thinking..." she began slowly. "Would there be any accommodations in town...if I decided to come for a little visit?"

"Why, yes, as a matter of fact, the Pine Mountain Hotel has been completely refurbished—and beautifully done, I might add. I know for certain they're not full up right now, but we've just gotten snow so that could change soon. Are you seriously considering coming for a visit?"

"I think so. I've always loved that little town. It was my husband's decision to leave. There were so many memories there, he just couldn't get over losing Steven. In the end, it was simply easier to move away."

"I can understand that. I lost my husband a few years ago, and it wasn't until I left Los Angeles and came up here that I actually began to get over losing him."

They chatted a while longer, then Maggie gave Barbara the number of the hotel, encouraging her to make reservations right away. She told her to call if she could be of any more help and then hung up. How utterly amazing! Steven Harris' mother might actually be coming back to visit Pine Mountain. Who knew, she might even get here in time to meet Michael Abundi. What a curious meeting that could be. She wondered what they might think of each other.

She picked up the phone again. She couldn't wait to tell Jed this news! But halfway through dialing, her hand stopped and she hung up the receiver. She suddenly remembered last night's agreement to put their relationship on hold. She bit her lip and thought for a moment. Did this mean she must weigh every action, consider every word that was directed toward him? What was acceptable in a "normal" friendship-type relationship between two people of the opposite sex? And how could this ever be a "normal" friendship anyway? Wasn't that just a lie? Would a mere phone call about this good news suggest that she was trying to get things back to where they were? Or was this whole thing just suddenly making her extremely paranoid? She wanted to be patient and understanding, but why did life have to become so complicated?

Nine

Only two days after the first snow had fallen, and before the ski resort ever received enough to open, an unseasonably warm wind began to blow from the south and within twenty-four hours the streets were rapidly running with melted snow. The warm spell continued to the end of the week, and Pine Mountain grew soggy and damp, with shopkeepers and businesspeople growing more worried and dismal than ever.

"Guess we better get that island man to do some more praying," said Dolly as she arranged two large bowls of vegetarian chili in front of Maggie and Scott, taking a moment to refill their water glasses.

"Well, you know Michael's from the tropics," said Maggie as she stuck her spoon into the chili. "I guess when he prayed for snow, he just forgot to specify that temperatures should remain cold."

Dolly laughed and headed back to the kitchen.

Scott glanced around. "You better not tell my mom I ate in here."

Maggie laughed. "Rosa knows I come in here about once a week, and she thinks it's great. She likes Dolly and Jinx—and it's not like these guys are in any serious competition with your mom's deli. The menu and atmosphere differ greatly."

"Yeah, I suppose you're right. Mom doesn't usually get truckers in the deli. Also, I know for a fact Buckie won't step foot in here."

"Okay, let's not get distracted. Remember, this is supposed to be a business lunch." She broke some crackers into her chili.

"By the way, Mag, good story about the wetland issues. I can't believe you haven't heard anything from our development boys yet. I thought for sure Greg Snider would send in one of his nasty letters of protest."

"Well, I did hear from Cherise just yesterday that he and Rick are pretty furious about the whole thing."

"And she's still speaking to you?"

"Cherise and I are friends, and it's no secret around town that she and Greg are having some problems right now anyway. I think she's enjoying watching him squirm a little."

"Do you think they'll stay together?"

"I think Greg's a fool to treat her the way he does. I doubt he'd ever do any better than Cherise and, despite everything, I think she might still love him. For both their sakes I really hope they can work things out."

He nodded and took another bite of chili. "It's nice to see you don't bear a grudge against Greg personally. I don't know if I'd be that gracious."

"Sometimes it can be hard to separate your personal feelings when covering a story, but I got lots of practice at the *Times*. The funny thing is, I've found it's even more challenging here in Pine Mountain. I think it's because it's a small town, and I find myself so involved with all the people, but I'm still trying to keep a balance."

"That's good. Especially since people around here tend to talk, if you know what I mean. Best to keep a level head. Hey, speaking of that wetlands article, did you send a copy to the Environmental Protection Agency or anyone else that might be interested?"

She winked at him. "I'm not supposed to know, but dear Abigail took care of all those little details—and anonymously too." She broke off a piece of bread. "Now, tell me, Scott, where exactly are you at on that Ebbert story—is next week too early to expect anything?"

He frowned. "There's really not much to tell. I went out to his place, and it didn't look like much more than a small working ranch. Oh sure, he has a couple of compounds built and a big flagpole next to the driveway, but I didn't see anything unusual besides the rebel flag bumper sticker on the back of his pickup. No marching fanatics, no burning crosses..."

"Hmm. What about that flyer his son has been posting around town this week? What do you think that's all about?"

"Well, now that's something, isn't it? I mean, you can tell what he's getting at beneath all his rhetoric about patriotism and whatnot, but his verbiage is a little toned down from his usual hate mail, don't you think?"

"Yes, definitely. I wonder if he's not trying to recruit others by trying to sound a little less controversial—all that talk about preserving our country's moral integrity mixed in with his usual antigovernment spiel might appeal to some of our more conservative folks, especially if they're not aware of any hidden agenda."

"That's what I thought too, kind of like the old proverbial wolf in sheep's clothes. But just the same, I doubt anyone will take him seriously. I mean, my dad's pretty conservative, but he'd never be taken in by someone like Randy Ebbert."

"I know Sam wouldn't..." She glanced around the diner, filled mostly with men she recognized but didn't actually know by name. To the casual observer, they were the types who wore plaid, flannel shirts with frayed cuffs, some with suspenders, some with down vests—most of them probably drove four-wheel-drive pickup trucks. Not all that much different than Clyde Barnes, just younger. And probably more open-minded than many outsiders would suspect. Although, how could anyone know for sure? "I guess I just hope that no one else reading those flyers falls for Ebbert's propaganda. It almost makes me wish I'd printed his original letters in the paper—just so everyone would be aware of his true colors. But at least I had Abigail file them in case he ever did anything questionable. That way we could pull them for a story, or maybe, although I hope it never comes to this, even submit them as evidence."

"Good thinking. Maybe I'll study them and try to see if I can figure him out a little better. One thing I've learned about this guy—he's not stupid. I mean, other than believing in a very ignorant philosophy."

"Did you talk to him much when you went out there?"

"I tried to. At first he seemed somewhat suspicious, but I tried to act pretty nonchalant. I told him I felt bad we couldn't print his letters and wanted to learn more about him and his political views and such. Then he warmed up a little and started to talk—but kind of guarded, you know. I was surprised that he let me take some photos, but he stayed right with me the whole time. I don't think he wanted me snooping around too much."

"Hmm. I know he has a couple sons—is there a wife?"

"Actually, he has three sons—one high school age, and the other two just a little older. They all work on the ranch. And he has a wife and a younger daughter, but I didn't see them. Ebbert told me, quite proudly I might add, that none of his kids have ever gone to public school, that his wife homeschools them all because, as he put it, 'they don't want the government filling their kids' heads with a bunch of liberal garbage.'"

Maggie sighed. "I wonder what *he* fills their heads with?"

"Yeah," agreed Scott. "Shouldn't that be considered some sort of child abuse or something? I can't believe it's actually legal to keep American kids from going to a real school and being around other kids."

"Well, the issue isn't really about homeschooling. I happen to know people who teach their children at home and do a fantastic job of it. But this thing with Ebbert is something completely different."

"He did say one thing that got my attention." Scott lowered his voice. "He's pretty ticked off that Michael Abundi is still here. That might even be what set him off on this new crusade of his. He said it's just a matter of time until the minorities (well, he didn't say it quite like that) would be taking over this whole area—just like down in California. Then he looked at me as if I were a case in point." Scott laughed uneasily. "At first I didn't know exactly what he meant. I know it sounds strange, but I sometimes forget that my mom has Mexican roots. She seems so American to me."

Maggie shook her head. "She *is* American, Scott. The fact is, we Americans are all just one big melting pot of many different cultures. I just don't understand why people can't see that. Anyone with half a brain can see that all this purebred white Aryan business is nothing but a bunch of nonsense conjured up by some narrow-minded bigots with too much time on their hands."

"Can I quote you directly on that?" He teased, and then grew more serious. "Sorry, I haven't been able to shape this into much of a story yet. So what do I do now? Any ideas?"

Maggie could think of several ideas offhand; for instance, investigating into Ebbert's past connections, checking out any groups he belonged to, and so on, but she didn't offer any suggestions. It was important that Scott figure this out for himself. "What do *you* think?"

He dropped his spoon into his now-empty bowl. "I think this chili is surprisingly tasty." He grinned, and then absently scratched his head. "I suppose I should continue with my research. I found a number of hate groups on the Internet that I can quote from. I just wish there was some way to infiltrate into Ebbert's little world so I could get some real juicy tidbits. But I don't have a chance at being taken seriously by him, being a 'half-breed wetback' as he so kindly put it."

Maggie studied Scott's appearance. Of all of Rosa's children, he had the most of the Latino features. He was dark and strikingly handsome. Why were people like Ebbert so threatened by such small and superficial differences? "I'm sure it'd be an eye-opener to get an inside look," she said, "but I don't know that it would be wise."

"Hey, I used to take drama," said Scott. "Maybe I should get a blond wig and dress up like a freckle-faced redneck."

She laughed. "Now that'd be funny. But even so, I don't recommend it, Scotty. You never know about people like Randy Ebbert." She remembered how frightened she'd felt when he'd abruptly reached into his jacket the other day in the office. "You never know—it could get dangerous. And I'm certain that Chloe wouldn't like the idea of you putting yourself in that situation either."

"Well, I'm not giving up yet," he declared. "I'll keep on with the research and figure out some way to get what I need—just you wait and see."

"I'm sure you'll come up with something, Scott." She placed money and a tip on the bill and stood. "By the way, I think you had an object lesson today."

"Huh? What's that?"

She waited until they were outside to answer him. "I think you were just slightly prejudiced against Dolly's Diner before you went in and tried it out for yourself."

He nodded sheepishly. "Point well taken."

᧍

When she got back into her office there was a message from Barbara Harris explaining that she planned to arrive in Pine Mountain on Wednesday of next week, and would Maggie please convey this information to Mr. Abundi and perhaps arrange a dinner meeting for the following night. Maggie had already told Michael about her conversation with Steven's mother but, not wanting to raise his hopes unnecessarily, she had chosen not to mention the possible visit. Now she was eager to do so. Instead of calling Jed to convey this new information, she decided to leave a message through Leah. As much as she wanted to hear Jed's voice on the phone, she knew it would be easier, and probably better in the long run, to allow Leah to pass the happy news along. But first she called and made reservations for a table at the hotel for the following Thursday.

"I'm not sure how many," she told Cindy. "Why don't we say four just to be safe."

Cindy laughed. "It's not like it matters, Maggie. Most of the tables are empty every night anyway. If the snow doesn't come back, and soon mind you, we may cut down to serving dinner only two or three nights a week."

"I'm sorry, Cindy. I know this is hard on everyone. How's your chef taking all this? Hopefully, he doesn't think it's any sort of personal reflection on his culinary skills."

"Fortunately he's still in the honeymoon stage with us and Pine Mountain in general. He says the slow pace is just what he needs to recover from the years of stressed-out city living. Only I'm worried he'll get all better and want to zip back to Seattle before we ever have a chance to really take off here."

Suddenly Maggie felt guilty for not having frequented the hotel restaurant yet. In truth, she'd been hoping that Jed would ask her out and her first dinner there would be with him. But now because they were "putting their relationship on hold" who knew when that dinner date might actually happen—or if ever. "Well, if it's any comfort, I think we'll be coming for dinner on Saturday night. I know Mom and Leah have eaten there before, but Spencer and I have missed out on the pleasure."

"Great. Shall I put you down for four then?" She laughed again. "Not that you need a reservation, but it just makes me feel better to see the actual names written into my book."

Maggie smiled. "Yes, there will be four of us—and let's say about six-thirty."

"Thanks, Maggie. Wow, that's two sets of reservations with one phone call. I think that must be a record for me so far."

"Don't worry, it'll get better, Cindy. Someday people will be complaining that they can't even get a table at the Pine Mountain Hotel."

"Wouldn't that be something!"

After Maggie hung up, she called Leah and told her all about Barbara Harris' upcoming visit as well as the dinner reservations. "I thought Jed might like to see her again too, and as Michael doesn't drive..."

"Great," said Leah. "I'll tell them both this afternoon. But you said the reservation is for four. Who is the fourth?"

Maggie felt her face grow warm. Actually, she'd wanted to join them herself. After all, she was the one who'd connected with Barbara in the first place, and she'd sort of assumed that Barbara's message about dinner reservations was meant to include her as well. But somehow she just couldn't say this to Leah. "Well, maybe you'd like to join them too, Leah?"

"Yeah. It sounds like it would be interesting, Maggie. Thanks for letting me know. I better go since there's a real, live customer coming in here right now—that is, unless she's just lost and looking for directions. That happened yesterday. Needless to say, it's been pretty slow..."

Maggie hung up the phone and swiveled her chair around to look out the window. She tried to ignore the disappointment growing inside of her. She told herself she would not stoop so low as to be jealous of Leah. "Just grow up, Margaret LeAnn," she whispered sharply to herself. Just then a big black pickup pulled up and parked right in front of the newspaper office. A shiny magnetic sign proclaimed "TS Development" in bold white letters. As if anyone in town could mistake those two imposing four-wheel-drive vehicles. She mentally braced herself as she watched Greg Snider walk briskly up the walk and into their building; then, just as she expected to hear Abigail's voice announcing his presence on the intercom, her door burst wide open and Greg stormed into her office waving this week's newspaper right in her face.

"What the heck do you think you're trying to do here?" he demanded hotly.

She leaned back in her chair and studied him before answering. "Basically, I'm trying to run a newspaper, Mr. Snider. And in the future I'd prefer that you check at the front desk before blasting into my office like this." She spied Abigail's sturdy brown shoes from behind the still partially open door. "It's okay, Abigail," she called out with reassurance. "I'll let you know whether I need you to call security or not." Then she forced a laugh at her own joke and looked directly at Greg.

His eyes narrowed, but he glanced over his shoulder as if to see whether or not she was serious.

"Would you care to sit down, Mr. Snider? Or have you said everything that you came to say?"

He gave the paper another loud shake. "I want to know where you get off writing this kind of stuff? Just who do you think you are anyway?"

"Who do you think *you* are, Greg Snider?" She stood now, her desk safely between them. "First you act like you're some flaming environmentalist who's totally against all forms of growth and development, then you and Rick practically steal Arnold Westerly's farm, and now you want to turn it into some sort of shoddy development for whatever rich fools you can lure in here who'd be crazy enough to buy into such a thing—"

"And now I suppose you think you're going to stop us with all of your overblown environmental concerns!" He laughed cynically. "Well, let me set you straight. Nobody in Byron County gives a flying fig about your ridiculous wetland issues— I already talked to the boys down at the county and they think what we're doing is just great, thank you very much!"

"So, what exactly is your problem then?"

"My problem is a certain Miss-Know-It-All editor who can't keep her nose out of other people's business. And I've had more than enough of your biased press coverage on TS Development."

She forced a saccharine smile to her lips as she spoke to him in what she knew was a patronizing tone. "But, unfortunately for you, *we* haven't had enough yet, Greg. And our readers still find this whole thing very fascinating. It's just *so interesting* how someone so opposed to development less than six months ago is now in the process of trying to develop the biggest chunk of property in Pine Mountain. And it's *so interesting* the way you guys swindled an old man—"

"Yeah!" he snapped. "And look where *that* story got you! The old guy dropped deader than a doornail just as soon as he read your stupid article. Doesn't that tell you anything, Maggie Carpenter? How many other writers can boast that their reporting actually *kills* people? Maybe you should have a warning label on the front of your paper. 'Reading the *Pine Cone* could be hazardous to your health!' Or maybe I should get the sheriff in here and see if he can't charge you for murder—or at the minimum, manslaughter."

A wave of sadness washed over her as she remembered the vivid image of poor Mr. Westerly slumped over his newspaper. She was instantly at a loss for any witty comeback or sharp retaliation. Why had she even lowered herself to Greg's level in the first place? To engage verbally with Greg Snider was almost always a lose-lose situation. She held her chin up and looked him squarely in the eye, determined to deny him the pleasure of witnessing the deep hurt he'd just inflicted upon her.

He tossed the newspaper to the floor, then leaned forward, planting both palms on the edge of her desk. "Why don't you just do everyone in Pine Mountain a great big favor and move on now. I think we've all had enough of your kind of help." He spat out that word. "Putting up your silly little lampposts and park benches isn't going to save this town from financial ruin. We're ready for some *real* development, and it looks to me as if you and this one-sided newspaper are the only obstacles standing in our way at the moment."

"You're right about one thing, Greg, this town does want and need development. And for your information, so do I. But I believe the majority of people want *good* development, and not at the expense—"

"You don't know this town as well as you think you do. You haven't been here long enough to understand our ways or our history—you're the newcomer here and I, for one, am pretty certain you've worn out your welcome! And not that you're even invited, but I happen to be having an important meeting this weekend for those local businessmen who are ready for growth and development in Pine Mountain—folks who will stand behind me for the sake of *our* town. But maybe you should send out a reporter—not that you guys will ever get your stories straight—but because the people of Pine Mountain have a right to know the truth!"

She sank back into her chair as he stormed out of her office. Lambasted by his words, she felt unsure of anything at the moment other than the fact that he might have missed his calling! The way he could confuse the issues and turn the tables on his opponents, he really should've become a lawyer or maybe even a politician. Not that all lawyers and politicians were like him, but Greg could've made some of the worst of them look pretty decent.

"Are you okay, honey?" asked Abigail after the front door slammed loudly.

"Just peachy." Maggie forced a smirkish smile to her face.

"Don't you worry about a single word he said," soothed Abigail.

"That's right," agreed Scott, also poking his head in the doorway. "I couldn't help but overhear his blustering, and most of what he said was nothing but blatant lies."

"And what wasn't an out-and-out lie was completely twisted anyway," added Abigail.

Maggie closed her eyes and exhaled slowly.

"Want me to cover that meeting for you?" offered Scott.

She briefly considered this tempting offer, and then sadly shook her head. "No, but thanks anyway. You've got the Ebbert story to work on, Scott. Unfortunately, TS Development is my baby."

"And what a spoiled rotten baby it is!" exclaimed Abigail. "I think all it needs is a good paddling!"

This made them all laugh.

Later that afternoon, Clyde stopped by her office. "I heard you had an irate visitor today. How're you holding up, old girl?"

"Okay, I guess. Got a minute, Clyde?"

"Sure, I was about to ask you the same." He sat down across from her and leaned back in the chair. "Now, don't you go letting that Snider boy get to you none. It's all just a lot of hot air and bluster, you know."

"I *don't* know that, Clyde. I've been wondering... remember Buckie's pro-development comments at my house on Thanksgiving?"

"Sure, but you've been doing the research about this developer, right? And writing what you know to be the truth?"

"That's right. Although, I must admit I do find pleasure in exposing the very worst of the things I've heard about him—not that I've heard anything good."

"Do you think you're being unfair in any way?"

She thought for a moment, wanting to be completely honest with herself and Clyde both. "No. I think I'm just telling it like it is."

He smiled. "Well, that's all anyone expects." He reached into his pocket and pulled out a piece of neatly folded paper. "Just got this from Gavin."

"Oh, really? How is he? Did he receive my letter apologizing about my accusation over his paternity identity with Leah?"

Clyde chuckled. "Yes, and I think I was as much to blame as you for that little misunderstanding. But with Gavin's history, it was an easy mistake to make. Anyway, he said to tell you thanks for the letter, and that he'll tell you in person that there are no hard feelings."

"In person?"

He nodded grimly. "Yep. Gavin wants to come back to Pine Mountain."

"And how do you feel about that?" She studied his face.

He shrugged. "Don't rightly know yet. Guess it depends mostly on him. I'll tell you this though, Maggie, I'm sure not getting my hopes up for that boy."

"But you'll give him a chance?"

"A chance? For what?"

"To show you that he's changed."

"What makes you so sure he has? I've known him his whole life. He's never changed before."

Suddenly she felt unsure about a lot of things. She'd always considered herself a fairly intuitive person, but lately she was questioning her own intuitions on many levels. It was possible to make mistakes. "I don't really know, Clyde, and I suppose I could be wrong about him. I guess I just want to hope for the best."

He frowned. "Well, I agree that hope's a good thing— *most* of the time. I'm just not too sure about it when it comes to Gavin."

She smiled. "But at least you're willing to talk to him, right?"

"He's my only flesh and blood, Maggie." His voice grew raspy. "I guess I can't very well turn him away, now can I?"

She shook her head. "Especially if he's trying to make amends with you."

"So, I suppose I can at least give him the time of day."

"Good for you, Clyde. I don't think you'll be sorry."

He grunted. "I wouldn't be too sure of that."

Ten

*M*aggie wished she could go incognito to Greg and Rick's development meeting in the grade school library on Saturday. But because that would be fairly childish, not to mention slightly paranoid, she decided instead to simply slip in just as the meeting was scheduled to begin and then to sit inconspicuously in the back by the door. She felt a little concerned about who might be in attendance and why they'd come; she certainly didn't want to give the impression, by her presence there, that she supported TS Development in any way, shape, or form. And on top of everything else, she knew it was imperative that she keep her mouth shut—no futile debates with Greg Snider today! So she prayed for grace and wisdom as she walked across the parking lot. A surprising number of cars were parked there—the majority she recognized as locals—and disappointingly a number of them belonged to the same folks who belonged to the Pine Mountain Business Association. But then, why shouldn't they be here? It was probably an excellent opportunity for them to hear firsthand what was going on with TS Development.

She glanced up at the sky as she walked toward the front door of the school. Still perfectly clear—not a single cloud in sight! And the temperature had to be close to sixty, which was downright balmy for early December in this part of the country. Yet only days ago their hopes had been so elevated by the snowfall. The late opening of the ski season would probably make worried businesspeople very open to Greg and Rick's ideas of growth and development. And who could blame them? The livelihoods of many hung in the balance right now. Perhaps opposing TS Development was becoming a fool's errand. As she walked down the quiet hallway toward the library she wondered if this was how David might have felt when going to face the mighty Goliath. No, she reminded herself calmly, this was not a battle. She was confronting no one. Her only purpose today was to cover this story, to collect the facts and then get out of there—and quick!

She sat next to the door, shielded from the front by others who were already seated. She had no desire to be observed by either Greg or Rick, and she had no intention of creating a scene of any sort. She opened her little notebook and hunched slightly over, her eyes focused on her notes as she listened intently to Greg rambling on and on about what a good thing this project would be for the entire community. He could actually be quite compelling and charismatic when he put his mind to it, and obviously this development was important to him. He had much to gain by its success. She wondered if Cherise was here today. She'd barely seen her this morning during her workout at the fitness center, but on her way out she'd noticed that Cherise's eyes were red and puffy. Not a good sign.

"And now," continued Greg as if finally coming to the main point, "I'd like to introduce you all to Mr. Colin Byers, our idea man and the visionary for designing this community. Meet the man who will partner with us as we continue to develop Pine Mountain Estates." The crowd applauded politely but, to Maggie's pleasure, without much enthusiasm.

That was the first time she'd heard mention of a name for the development. She jotted it down and glanced up to see if she could get a good look at this Colin Byers person. She'd already researched and read enough about him and his shoddy developments to feel as if she knew him personally. She imagined him to be a fast-talking, sixtyish, potbellied, slightly balding man, probably wearing a light-colored suit with shiny white shoes and a gold chain or two around his thick neck. But to her surprise, a rather attractive gentleman, tall, tan, and blond, and probably only in his late forties, stepped up to the podium and shook Greg's hand.

"Greetings," he began in a friendly tone. "What a beautiful region you folks all live in. I can see now why they call this God's country." He paused to look around the room at all the faces, as if trying to recognize each one individually, then he continued. "However, I've heard that you've come upon some hard times with your local economy and some of you are struggling right now just to keep your businesses afloat. And for that very reason you should all be extremely thankful for Greg and Rick here. These guys have the kind of foresight and vision to realize an opportunity that will bring this town back on its feet. They are presenting your community with a fantastic opportunity to stabilize and escalate your economy throughout the new millennium." He paused, like a showman, as if waiting for approval or applause, but only a few people responded. The majority seemed reserved, or perhaps simply unsure, and a number of them still appeared fairly skeptical. Somehow their reaction relieved Maggie considerably, and she leaned back into her chair and relaxed a little, waiting to see how this smooth-talking developer from California planned to convince them otherwise. She hoped folks would remain dubious, remembering Greg and Rick's questionable methods for attaining their land. The townspeople were smart. Surely they couldn't be persuaded by a charlatan, no matter how good-looking he was!

Colin continued. "Now, I understand that I've gotten some bad press up here." He laughed lightly. "Well, that's not surprising because I've gotten some bad press down in

California too. But I'd like the chance to explain a few things. I'm sure you all believe that a man should be allowed to defend himself—after all, isn't a man still innocent until proven guilty? Anyway, it just so happens that land development is a highly competitive business, especially where I come from. It's a real dog-eat-dog world down there. And there are those who will resort to anything to discredit a man's reputation. But I'm not a spiteful person, and most of the time I don't fight back. I allow the success of my developments to speak for itself. Now, if you'll allow me—Rick you will want to get that video going now—and Greg, maybe you'd like to dim the lights. We'll let the good folks of Pine Mountain judge me for themselves."

Maggie sat up straighter to see the big-screen TV set up in the front. The room grew quiet as they all watched a very slick video, complete with soft classical music and some well-written narrative, that proudly displayed all the so-called amenities of a few of Colin Byers' developments. There were long, lingering shots of crystal-clear pools, lush green golf courses, lovely-looking homes with perfect landscaping, and interiors that were decorated to the hilt, and throughout the video were lots of smiling, attractive people (probably actors). It was all quite convincing, and for a moment Maggie wondered if she might not have been all wrong about him. But then she wondered what it was that he wasn't showing. Having been a reporter, she knew that what you read or saw was only part of the whole picture and could sometimes be very misleading. It was what *wasn't* said that could make all the difference, and she wasn't convinced.

The lights came back on and people quietly commented among themselves. It was obvious that many had been impressed by Colin Byers' tricks. Next he invited their questions. To her delight, many asked the very questions that she had posed in her previous articles. Queries were made about the longevity of management plans, use of quality construction materials, legal labor practices, and whether local workers might bid for contracts themselves. Colin Byers smoothly and graciously fielded each and every question without batting an eyelash, and in the end the crowd seemed satisfied. Either he had rehearsed all this before or he really was on the up-and-up. She doubted the latter, and for a moment considered challenging him herself, but stuck to her earlier resolve to keep her mouth closed. This was neither the time nor the place. Just as Greg began to finish up, she quietly closed her notebook and slipped out the backdoor, then hurried to her car without talking to anyone. The whole thing was rather unsettling. This guy was incredibly smooth. Once again she questioned herself—what if her research had been flawed? But then again, even if she was wrong about this out-of-state developer, she knew that what Greg and Rick had done to Mr. Westerly was terribly unfair. But then, perhaps that was her main problem. Perhaps she needed to step back and make sure she wasn't just reacting emotionally to this whole thing based on her feelings for Arnold Westerly. She remembered the balance she had just recently described to Scott...how a good reporter must guard against letting her opinions take over. Just get the facts, she reminded herself. Just report the truth. Then let the people decide for themselves. She must always remember to limit her opinions to the editorial page, otherwise she would compromise the entire paper. And, as with all news stories, it was never purely black and white—good versus evil. No, most stories were layer upon layer of varying shades of gray. Only once in a blue moon did you uncover the truly wonderful tale of the valiant hero who rescued someone out of pure chivalry. And even then, you often learned later that there was more to the story...

∽

Maggie decided to take full advantage of the mild weather by taking both dogs out for a walk in the woods. Bart dashed energetically ahead, and then quickly returned to nose Lizzie as if to say, "Come on, old girl!" He'd really taken to the older dog, and she seemed surprisingly comfortable with his companionship, although Maggie was sure Bart's limitless energy tried Lizzie's patience from time to time. Especially lately, for between Spencer's broken foot and Leah's long hours at the shop, the dogs hadn't had as much walking as Bart had been used to in the past. Maggie enjoyed having an excuse for a walk today. The ground was still slightly moist from last week's melted snowfall, and the trail was coated with a thick blanket of rusty-colored pine needles, so that it was like walking on a soft, thick carpet. The sky was a dusky periwinkle blue, and the smell of clean pine permeated the air with its freshness. She breathed deeply and wondered once again how she had ever managed to live most of her life away from all this beauty. But now that she had found it, she felt certain Pine Mountain would always remain home.

When she returned to the house, Spencer was all dressed and ready to go to dinner at the hotel. He was waiting downstairs wearing a clean shirt and pants, and she hated to inform him that their reservations weren't until six-thirty. But she was glad he was excited about going out. That broken foot had slowed him down some, and as a result he'd seemed to lack some of his normal youthful enthusiasm. But just yesterday, Audrey had taken him in to get a walking cast put on his foot and now he was getting around quite well compared to when he'd needed crutches. This alone had greatly improved his disposition. Maggie hurried upstairs to clean up, and before too long they were all on their way to dinner.

"Cindy said it's been pretty slow here," she told the others as they walked down the sidewalk toward the hotel's entrance, "but I made a reservation for us anyway."

"Yeah," said Leah. "Last week when Jed and I came here, there were only a couple of other tables filled. I felt sorry for Cindy. I mean, she has fresh flower arrangements on every table. It seems such a waste."

"That's too bad," said Audrey as they stepped inside the lovely foyer. "But, hey, it looks like they're busy tonight."

Maggie glanced around in surprise. Sure enough, the restaurant was nearly full, and it looked as though even Brian was helping to wait tables.

"What's up?" she asked Cindy after a short wait.

"Isn't this great? I think it's all due to that nice Colin Byers—he gave us some great free promotion at the end of the meeting today. He mentioned what a fine hotel this was and how the food here was really first-rate." Then she lowered her voice. "He even said we're comparable to some of the five-star restaurants he's eaten at."

Maggie blinked. "Wow. That's high praise. Well, good for you guys."

"Thanks. Now, right this way to your table."

As chance, or Cindy, would have it, their table was just opposite where Colin, Rick, Greg, and a couple of other men were already seated. Maggie pasted a smile on her face and nodded politely in their direction. Thankfully, Greg and Rick said nothing, but she did notice Colin smile and nod in return.

"Don't look now," she spoke quietly after they were all seated. "But that's the developer I told you about. He's sitting right next to Greg just across the way."

"I overheard what Cindy said about the little promotion he gave them," said Audrey. "For a skunk of a developer, he seems like a rather nice man."

"Unfortunately, he does come across extremely well. I even found myself questioning whether I'd researched him correctly or not. He is *so* smooth." Maggie glanced quickly at their table and uncomfortably realized they were looking her way at just the same moment. It felt as if they were telling Colin Byers who she was—unless she was just becoming overly paranoid. "Why don't we change the subject," she said with a stiff smile.

"I think I may have found a spot for the library," said Audrey. "I finally heard back on one of the vacant buildings that had been confiscated by the county for back taxes several years ago. And after they heard the proposed use, they were very interested. We just might be able to strike a deal that will make everyone happy."

"That's great, Mom. Where is it?"

"It's that old building right behind Galloway's Deli, next to City Hall."

"Oh, yeah," said Spencer. "The place with those ratty-looking awnings. Didn't it used to be a store or something?"

"Yes, the lady at the county said it used to be a clothing store. But despite those horrible awnings it seems to be fairly well built, and it's just the right size to house our little library."

Though the talk swirled around her, much of the fun of the evening—the excellent food and the company of those she loved—was lost on Maggie as she continued to be aware of the men just adjacent from them. Each time she glanced at them, which she did only rarely and inconspicuously, it seemed to her that Colin was looking directly her way, smiling even. Finally, just as they began to eat their desserts, Maggie noticed the men walking over to their table, with Greg in the lead. Surely he wouldn't dare to make a scene in here!

"Excuse me," he said in a distinctly cool but formal voice, "I don't like to interrupt your meal, but my friend here was very determined to make the acquaintance of the *Pine Cone's* editor. Maggie Carpenter, I'd like you to meet Colin Byers."

Colin extended a hand and Maggie stood and took it. "I heard you speak this afternoon, Mr. Byers."

"Ah, spying on the enemy?" But his words were warm and he looked directly into her eyes. "And so, may I ask, what did you think?"

"I think it was very impressive. But I'm confused because it's all quite contrary to what I've discovered in my research."

"And do you believe everything that you read, Ms. Carpenter?"

She blushed. "You make a good point, Mr. Byers. And yet, when all your sources seem to say the same things, you do begin to take them at their word."

"They also say that seeing is believing. Have you ever considered visiting one of my developments in person?"

"Unfortunately, your developments aren't handy to Pine Mountain. And our little newspaper just doesn't have the budget for researching. I tend to rely on the Internet and a few other sources I consider to be reliable."

He smiled. "Then why don't you allow me to fly you down to see one of my places for yourself?"

She was somewhat taken aback by his friendliness and personal manner. Suddenly she grew very self-conscious, for it seemed that the entire restaurant had grown quiet and it felt as if every head had now turned their way. "Well, I just might consider that, Mr. Byers." She quickly fumbled in her purse and managed to produce a business card. "If you're really serious about your offer, why don't you give me a call and we'll see what we can do?"

He took her card. "I'll do just that. And forgive me for interrupting your dinner. It's a pleasure to meet you, Ms. Carpenter," then he bent toward her and lowered his voice. "And by the way, you're nothing like the *dragon lady* these fellows described to me." Then he winked at her.

She couldn't help but chuckle. "Well, thank you very much—I think."

She sat back down and watched as the men exited the dining room. "Well, go figure," she said to the three sets of eyes now focused tightly on her.

"Wow, Maggie," said Leah, "you handled that really well."

"That Mr. Byers is one smooth number," commented Audrey as she turned her attention to her berry cobbler.

"I didn't like the look in his eyes," observed Spencer dryly. "This guy seems sort of slippery if you ask me."

Eleven

By Monday, the weather hadn't changed a single bit, and the forecast was for a continuance of this unwelcome warm spell. Only yesterday at church, a few people had suggested they should get Michael Abundi to pray for snow again. Maggie felt relieved for Michael's sake that Jed, wanting to make the most of this mild spell of weather, had closed his shop for the whole day and driven Michael and Leah over to see the Oregon coast. Leah had arrived home late last night with wonderful tales of all they'd seen and done, even touring a completely renovated clipper ship that had been docked near a seaport town for a few days. Maggie had listened with what she hoped appeared to be delighted interest, but at the same time had silently chided herself for the small ripples of envy that floated through her. How she wished she could experience a trip to the coast with Jed too. Maybe someday. In the meantime, if the warm weather continued, perhaps she should plan a similar trip with Spencer and her mother.

In the morning's mail she discovered an envelope, addressed to her, from Gavin Barnes. She opened it to find a short but well-written letter of apology to the whole town, with a small note attached asking her if she would please print this in the newspaper. His letter to the town seemed sincere and remorseful and she saw no reason not to print it, but decided to run it past Clyde first. She found him puttering around in the printing room. "Hey there," she called. "Got a moment?"

He set his push broom aside and dusted his hands on the sides of his faded black work pants. "Always got time for you, Maggie girl. What is it?"

"I got a letter from Gavin today. Actually, it's for the town. It's an open letter of apology for all that drug-trafficking business. As you can see, he doesn't take personal blame for the actual drugs, only for opening the door—and for that he seems truly sorry, don't you think?" She handed him Gavin's letter and waited for him to adjust his glasses and read.

Finally he folded it and handed it back. "It's up to you—you're the editor." He sniffed. "Don't know as I'd believe every word myself. Don't know that a snake can change his stripes that easily."

She frowned. "But you said you were going to give him a chance."

"It's one thing, me giving my own nephew a chance. He's my own flesh and blood, what else can I do? But it's something else altogether in encouraging the whole town to take the same kind of chance."

"Well, like you said, I'm the editor. And I happen to be willing to take this chance with Gavin. If he somehow blows it, well, then printing his letter will be on my head—right?"

Clyde grinned. "Seems to me you've got a lot riding on your head these days."

She lifted her brows. "Meaning?"

"Meaning, I heard some good ol' boys yacking away at the hardware store yesterday. Seems everybody's real taken with this California developer man. And seems that some folks think a certain newspaper editor's all wet in reporting on him the way she did."

She exhaled in loud exasperation, and then threw up her hands. "Well, what am I supposed to do, Clyde? Just believe everything this guy says and forget about everything else I've heard and read that's contrary to that?"

"Not as long as I'm around! I want you to stick to his trail like a hound on a coon. Don't you be taken in with all his fine, smooth talk."

"He invited me to go down and see some of his developments."

"You going to take him up on it?"

"I don't know…I'm certain I'd get a very carefully guided tour, only showing me exactly what they want me to see, and I'm sure everything will be impeccably perfect—just like that slick video he showed on Saturday."

Clyde smiled slyly. "But now, you're smarter than them, Maggie. You could easily do a little snooping around on your own, ask some questions, take some photos. Isn't that what they call investigative reporting?"

"I suppose so…" The idea of sleuthing around one of Colin Byers' developments did sound intriguing in a Nancy Drew sort of way. "Who knows, maybe I'd find out I'd been all wrong about him all along—but then at least I'd know for sure myself."

Clyde shoved his hands in his pockets and scowled. "Well, for Arnold Westerly's sake there's nothing I'd rather see than that whole darn TS Development business shut down once and for all!"

"But what if this guy's legit? What if we can't stop the development? What then?"

He made a growling sound. "It just gets my goat to see the likes of Snider and Tanner profiting by taking advantage of old Arnold."

"I know," she said soothingly. "But we might have to consider the bigger picture here. What if this developer can really bring growth and progress to Pine Mountain? That wouldn't be so bad, now would it?"

He eyed her with suspicion. "It sounds almost as if you're consorting with the enemy."

She shook her head. "Not at all. I'm just trying to be open-minded and fair. The honest truth is I'd love to see that whole development fall flat on its face too. But a lot of that is based on my own personal feelings, not what would be best for this town. And I do care about this town, Clyde. I don't want to see one single business lost."

"I know, I know...but we aren't doing so bad, are we? Why, just look at all the great progress that has taken place in the last year—and most of it was due to you—"

She shook her finger under his nose. "Don't you forget, Clyde Barnes, it took the *whole* town to accomplish those things. And unfortunately, despite the improvements, this town is still painfully dependent on something as undependable as the weather. You know as well as anyone that these aren't the old timber days where weather had little effect on the local economy. Right now, we need tourism to survive—and lack of snow for just one winter could shut this place down completely."

"Maybe we should get your Michael friend to pray again." Clyde looked at her from the corner of his eye and then grinned.

"Or maybe we should try to be a little more open-minded to this new development. "

Clyde groaned. "I can't believe you're giving up, Maggie. I thought you were such a fighter."

"I'm not giving up. I'll keep investigating the whole thing. I just need to find out if this Byers fellow is really who he says he is or not. And if it turns out that he's really on the up-and-up, we'll be open to this whole thing, right?"

"And if he's not, will we slap his sorry story all across the front page?"

She couldn't help laughing. "You bet we will!"

~

Barbara Harris arrived in Pine Mountain a day earlier than she had planned, and Maggie met her at the hotel for tea the following afternoon. Barbara was a fragile and refined-looking woman, and though probably only a little older than Audrey, in some ways she seemed to come from a generation long past. With her perfectly coifed snow-white hair, soft powdery face, and pastel blue woolen dress complete with a single strand of pearls, she reminded Maggie of someone from the Victorian era, especially by the way she held her teacup so daintily with her little finger gracefully pointing down.

"I'm still so amazed to be back here in Pine Mountain," she said as she set the fine porcelain teacup carefully back into its saucer. "Everything looks so wonderful. Much nicer than when we left. In fact, much better than I ever remember it being. This hotel has never been this lovely before."

"How long did you live here?"

"I came as a young bride just after the war. My husband's family ran several businesses in the area. I was originally from the East—I met Steven Sr. while volunteering at a dance for servicemen soon to be shipped off to fight in Europe. I was only seventeen at the time, but totally smitten by this handsome young man in uniform. I gave him my address and we wrote regularly throughout the war. I guess we fell in love long distance. And during that time I promised that if he survived the war I'd marry him." Her eyes grew misty.

"And so you did." Maggie smiled. "Then you came here?"

"Not at first. We stayed with my parents for a while. But Steven missed his home and family—he'd been through so much during the war—I thought the least I could do was to come out here. I didn't realize at the time that we'd settle here permanently. I must admit that I hated it at first, but over time I grew to love the mountains and the fresh smell of pine trees. After many years of waiting, our little Stevie was born here; then life was complete for me. Oh, it was a quiet sort of life, to be sure, but I had a few good friends and belonged to a bridge club. A couple of my old friends still live here, and I plan to try to see them during my stay."

They visited for about an hour, but Maggie could see that Barbara was still worn out from her trip. "I think I'll let you get some rest," she said. "I know you're probably still on East Coast time, and the traveling must've been exhausting."

"Yes, it's funny I do feel very tired, but I also feel rather invigorated at the same time. I must admit I was a little worried about adjusting to the higher elevation. They say it can be more difficult as we grow older, but I'm already feeling adapted to it." She smiled warmly. "I'm just so very glad that I came."

Maggie gave Barbara her home phone number and told her to call if she needed anything at all, and then she told her about tomorrow night's arrangements to have dinner with Jed, Michael, and Leah, taking a moment to explain about Jed's daughter. Barbara inquired about whether Maggie might also join them, but Maggie gracefully declined, saying that she had previous plans. For some reason, she wished she could better explain to this thoughtful woman who had known and liked Jed since his boyhood days that she and Jed did indeed share a deep and promising relationship, which for the time being was put on hold. Sometimes it all seemed so unfair!

"I'm so looking forward to meeting Michael, and I can't wait to see dear Jed again. I do thank you for all your help, Maggie. I certainly hope I'll get to see more of you too while I'm here in Pine Mountain."

"Well, if you have the time I'd love to have you out to my house—it's the old Barnes place. I'd like you to meet my mother and son."

"It would be my pleasure. I used to be fairly good friends with Betty Barnes—well, at least we played bridge together. But she and her son moved away some time before we did."

"Then you remember Gavin?"

"Ah, yes, Gavin. A handsome boy, but full of the devil. I think his mother spoiled him a bit too much. It was a good reminder to me though—when you only have one son it's easy to spoil him."

Maggie thought of her own son and laughed. "I know exactly what you mean. Anyway, I'll have to fill you in on Gavin later. For now you need to get some rest. I know you'll be comfortable here. Cindy and Brian are great hosts."

⤙

In Wednesday's paper, Maggie had run the story covering the Pine Mountain Estates meeting on the front page. Nothing sensational, nothing inflammatory, just what had transpired in Saturday's meeting. But in her own column on the editorial page she raised questions about whether their town was willing to wear blinders regarding the dubious way TS Development had acquired its property in order to "ensure growth and development for the entire town." She didn't want to incite anyone, but rather hoped to raise their consciousness level. She further expressed her concern about the spirit of Pine Mountain—how she didn't want to see it compromised or watch it in essence sell its soul just to attain what it assumed would bring financial security. Obviously, she knew Greg and Rick wouldn't appreciate her views. When had they ever? But it was the editorial page, and as editor she was entitled to strong, well-founded opinions. If anyone cared to respond, honestly and in writing, she'd be more than pleased to express their views as well. She also ran Gavin's letter of apology with a footnote of her own saying she felt everyone deserved a second chance from time to time. Risky, she knew, but she also felt she owed him one for accusing him of fathering and then abandoning Leah. Maybe they were even now.

Just as she was getting ready to go home, Abigail told her that a Mr. Byers was holding on the line for her.

"You're probably just about to head for home," he said apologetically, "but I thought I'd try to catch you first—that is, if you can spare a moment out of your busy schedule."

She laughed. "The *Pine Cone* isn't exactly what you'd call busy. It's steady, but nothing like the hectic demands of working for a big-city paper. What can I do for you, Mr. Byers?"

"Well, I was wondering if you'd had a chance to think over my offer to see some of my developments for yourself."

"Actually, I'd been thinking that if you were still interested, I just might take you up on it."

"Great. And in that case, I wonder if you'd be willing to meet with me to discuss this further, maybe nail down a date and some other details." The phone connection grew scratchy. "As you probably guessed, I'm on my cell phone right now, and I'm afraid it's almost out of juice."

"Oh, I didn't realize you were still in town."

"Yes, I've been doing a little planning and research out here at the property site. But I plan to fly home tomorrow morning. Do you think it would be possible to meet with me before then?"

"Sure. Would you like to come by the office right now?"

"No, I'm a muddy mess from traipsing around these fields, but it sure is beautiful out here. How about if we meet for dinner at the hotel, say around seven. Would that work for you?"

She considered this for a moment and could see no reason to decline. "Sure, that sounds just fine. I'll see you then."

⌒

Maggie dressed with care before dinner. Not for Colin Byers, although she did want to look professional, but for Jed because she knew he'd be at the hotel for his dinner with Barbara Harris. Maybe it was silly or even somewhat immature on her part, but she wanted Jed to see her and perhaps think about what he was missing out on by setting their relationship aside. Not that she had any intention of pushing Leah out of the picture. Not at all. But all this being put on the back burner was taking its toll on her self-image. Besides, it wasn't very often she had the opportunity to dress up in their rural mountain town. She finally decided on a black wool designer suit that she hadn't worn since last winter in L.A. It was a fine wool, the heaviest weight you could get away with in a warmer climate, but cut to perfection. Beneath this she donned a cranberry-red silk blouse with a strand of black pearls that had been her grandmother's. She started to pull her hair back in the usual barrette, and then changed her mind and let it fall loose upon her shoulders. She added matching pearl earrings and a touch of cranberry-red lipstick. She had to admit that the overall effect was very classy.

"Wow, don't you look great," commented Audrey as Maggie stopped by the kitchen to tell her and Spencer goodbye.

Spencer's eyes grew wide. "*Mom,*" he said as only a teenager can. "I thought this was just a business dinner with that slimeball developer. Why'd you get all fixed up for him?"

Maggie laughed. "It *is* a business dinner, Spence. And sometimes it's worthwhile to look just as sharp as you can—it builds up your confidence level and gives you the upper hand." She winked at her son.

He nodded wisely. "Okay, I think I get it. Well then, give him what for!"

She squeezed his arm. "You sound just like Clyde!"

"And don't you be out too late, young lady," chided Audrey with a twinkle in her eye. "It is a school night, after all!"

Twelve

$\mathcal{T}$he hotel restaurant wasn't as busy as it had been last Saturday night, but at least there appeared to be several tables filled. Maggie glanced around to see if Colin Byers was already seated while at the same time carefully searching for Jed's party.

"Good evening," came a male voice from behind. She turned to see Colin approaching, wearing a brown tweed sports jacket over a fine-gauge sweater, probably cashmere. He smiled and shook her hand. "Thank you for meeting me on such short notice, Ms. Carpenter. Cindy reserved a spot for us right over there." He gently took her elbow and guided her to a table next to the big fireplace. "Will this be too warm for you?" he asked as he politely pulled out a chair for her.

"Not at all. It's perfect." She sat down and looked up, and just a couple tables away she spotted Barbara Harris with Jed seated to her right. He was staring directly at Maggie with what seemed to be a confused expression. She smiled pleasantly and waved his way to signal that all was well and not to worry. Barbara waved back then turned to make a comment to Jed, smiling and nodding at Maggie as she did so. Maggie suspected the older woman was speaking of her, but felt no concern as she turned her attention back to Colin Byers.

"This is such a small town," she said apologetically. "It's impossible to go anywhere without seeing people you know, so you just learn to expect it. But I do think that's part of its charm too."

"Pine Mountain is certainly charming," he agreed. "I'm surprised it's gone so long without much development—until now that is."

Cindy approached their table, and Maggie could tell by her eyes that she was full of questions, but she simply smiled and asked if they'd like to order drinks and then recited the specials of the day to them. Maggie knew she'd have to tell Cindy the details about this later. She didn't want to give anyone in town the wrong impression. Hopefully, they wouldn't see this as an endorsement of the development, but as a sincere effort on her part to be truly nonpartisan.

Colin was excellent at making small talk and, without really saying much, managed to keep the conversation flowing smoothly until the waitress came to take their orders. Then he moved on to business matters. "I figured you might like to come down to see a development as soon as possible," he began. "There's a community in Nevada called Desert Winds that has its own airstrip, and it isn't a very long flight from here. That might be a good place for you to start."

"That sounds fine. But first, Mr. Byers—"

"Please, call me Colin." He smiled. "That Mr. Byers stuff always makes me feel old. I think it could send me straight into a midlife crisis."

She glanced quickly at his left hand. No ring. But that didn't always mean anything. When she looked up she knew that he'd caught her peeking and hoped he didn't assume it was because she was interested in something beyond a business relationship, which she certainly was not! So with a journalist's curiosity she asked, "You must travel a lot. Do you have a family?"

"I'm divorced, going on ten years now. Both kids are grown. One in college, he graduates this year. And one who's about to make me a grandfather." He laughed. "I think it's Heather's way of getting revenge at me for me leaving her mother. Although I've never heard her mother complain much, because California law stipulated that I leave her with half of all my assets. Not such a bad deal for her." Surprisingly, he said all this without the slightest perceivable trace of bitterness. "And what's your story, Ms. Carpenter?"

"Well, if I'm to call you by your first name, you had better do the same. My husband died several years ago. I have a fifteen-year-old son. Then my mother lives with me, and another young woman we've sort of adopted." She glanced over at Leah, who looked very grown up as she visited with the other three adults. "And we have two dogs, also adopted."

"Sounds like a nice little extended family. Lucky for you. It's not that much fun being alone." He took a sip of water.

"What I was about to say, Mr.—I mean, Colin, is that before we get this trip all settled I'd like to lay my cards on the table for you. I want you to understand fully where I'm coming from—"

"You mean, like how you plan to really scrutinize the quality of my developments? That you intend on uncovering and exposing anything that looks even slightly suspicious or questionable? That you'll grill my employees and look under the rugs? Things like that?"

She nodded, suppressing a grin. "Yes, as a matter of fact, that pretty well sums it up."

"Good. That's exactly what I hoped you'd do. And when it's all said and done, I also hope that you'll write an honest appraisal of my work, and perhaps I'll get some good press for a pleasant change."

She was baffled. Either this guy was good—or he was *really* good. He almost had her believing him, and nearly to the point where she might consider simply saying, "Oh, let's just forget about this whole trip, you've got me convinced."

Bethel Baptist Church
P.O. BOX 167
AUMSVILLE, OR 97325

But then she remembered Clyde's warnings. She couldn't be *that* gullible. "Great," she said. "Then it looks like we understand each other."

"Fantastic—"

"Excuse me," said Cindy. "Mr. Byers, you have a phone call. The man sounded like it was urgent. Do you want to take it at the front desk?"

"Sure." He turned to Maggie as he casually stood. "I'm sorry about this. You know how it is when you're out of town for a few days; everyone suddenly thinks they need to talk to you. I'll try to keep it short."

With Colin gone, Maggie glanced over again to Jed's table. This time when he looked her way their eyes locked for a long moment. She felt her heart begin to beat faster as she looked straight into his dark eyes. They seemed laced with what she feared might be sadness, and she longed to run over and explain to him that this was absolutely nothing more than a business meeting, and that she had only dressed up to catch his eye! She couldn't bear to hurt him, not even slightly. And yet, at the same time, it seemed silly to make too much of this. Perhaps she was only imagining she saw any hurt in his eyes in the first place. Uncomfortable with her confusing feelings, she smiled once more at him and then forced herself to look away, focusing her eyes instead upon the fireplace. To distract herself, she watched the graceful motion of flames. Unlike her childhood memories of the big log fires that were lit in here on a cool summer night, this river rock fireplace was now fueled by natural gas. Still, the cement logs and orange flames looked amazingly realistic, and although it wasn't quite the same as the snapping of pitchy wood, it was warm and friendly. She glanced furtively back at Jed, who was now immersed in conversation with the other three. She sighed and hoped they were all enjoying their time together. She wished she could see Michael's face, but his back was toward her. She knew she'd soon hear what Michael thought of Barbara Harris. Judging by Barbara's face, she was impressed with Michael. That was a huge relief.

"Sorry about that," said Colin as he slipped back into his chair just in time for the waitress to serve their entrees.

"Business?"

"Yes. A problem that couldn't wait until I got back." He looked down at the plate before him and picked up his fork. "Once again, this looks absolutely delicious. The chef here is really first-rate, you know. I sneaked into the kitchen and tried to entice him into going home with me and working in one of my restaurants, but he wouldn't hear of it, and then Cindy very nicely but firmly escorted me out of the kitchen."

They chatted as they ate. Dinner was very pleasant, very congenial. Maggie had to remind herself from time to time that Colin, according to Clyde, was still the enemy. But to her surprise she almost found herself hoping that she'd been completely wrong about him. Really, wouldn't life be much simpler if she could just step away from this battle with TS Development? After all, wasn't this exactly what the town wanted and needed? Maybe it was time to let bygones be bygones, after all. Besides, they had other, more serious, issues to pursue anyway. Things like Randy Ebbert and his hateful, racist views. Even today he'd circulated a new flyer suggesting that the town needed a conservative newspaper to balance the liberal views of the *Pine Cone!* That had made her laugh out loud. As if she'd ever been considered a "liberal" in any other circle! Why, her old editor at the *Times* had often laid into her for what he called her overly "conservative" views. Politics were funny.

Just after Maggie and Colin were served their dessert, Jed and his party began rising to leave. Barbara walked directly over to Maggie's table and laid a gentle hand on her shoulder. "So nice to see you again, my dear."

Maggie introduced Colin to her friends, briefly explaining to him that it was an unusual reunion of sorts. Colin politely rose and acknowledged the two women with a friendly greeting, then took a moment to shake hands with both men.

"I understand now why you couldn't join us tonight," said Barbara in a knowing voice as she gave Maggie a nod that suggested she suspected the two of them to be here on something of a romantic date. "But we've had such a lovely time. And dear Leah has invited us all to dinner at your house this weekend. I do hope that's all right with you."

"Of course it is." She smiled at Leah. "Good thinking, Leah."

"Now, we won't keep you two from enjoying your wonderful desserts," said Barbara with a twinkle in her eye. "The food here is simply outstanding."

Maggie glanced up at Jed uneasily. But he only nodded and said a brisk goodnight. Suddenly she wished she hadn't gone to such trouble to dress up. This wasn't at all how she'd wanted this to go. But hopefully, she could explain everything to Jed this weekend—and bless Leah for inviting them all for dinner!

By the end of their meal, it was decided that Maggie would visit one of Colin's developments the first of next week. He would send out his private plane to pick her up. His goal was that she might gather her information in time to reveal her findings in next week's edition of the *Pine Cone*. He didn't try to conceal the fact that he wanted to change his tarnished image in town, but he wasn't pushy or offensive about it either. No doubt about it, Colin Byers was a charmer of the first degree. Despite herself, she liked him.

∾

Maggie arrived home shortly after Leah, and Audrey already had a pot of fresh tea waiting in the library. "Come sit with us, Maggie," she called. "Leah was just about to tell me about her dinner."

"Mrs. Harris is really nice," began Leah. "She and Michael hit it off just great. He told her lots of things she didn't know about her son, and that seemed to mean a lot to her. And

Michael was totally relieved to find out that she'd never been angry about Steven's choice to become a missionary. I think she was just sad to have him go away so far from home."

"Not to mention that he never came back," said Maggie. "I can understand her feelings. I know how much I'd hate to see Spence go off to the ends of the earth like that. But just the same, I'd have to support him in whatever his choices might be. By the way, where is he?"

"I think he's doing his homework," said Audrey. "And now, tell us about your dinner, Maggie."

"It was all right. Colin is actually quite nice."

"I'll say," said Leah. "You should have seen the way he was looking at Maggie all gaw-gaw eyed—"

"It wasn't like that at all," she countered quickly. "He's just one of those really smooth guys who knows how to treat a lady. And, of course, he's trying to get on my good side for the sake of good publicity at the paper."

"Well, Mrs. Harris was certain that he was your 'beau'— I that's how she put it." Leah giggled.

"Oh, good grief!" exclaimed Maggie in horror. "Well, I hope you set her straight, Leah."

"Well, I didn't know for sure what was going on myself," said Leah defensively. "It wasn't until I got home just now and asked Audrey what was up that I even knew what was going on. And to tell you the truth, I thought maybe you two *were* on a date. I mean, stranger things have been known to happen." Was it just her imagination, or did Leah appear to be somewhat smug?

Maggie groaned again. "And I suppose that's what Jed thought too?"

Leah shrugged. "I don't know what he thought. He didn't really seem to care. At least he didn't say anything about it. But Barbara kept making comments about what a handsome-looking couple you two make, and how she understood now why you weren't able to join us for dinner tonight. By the way, Barbara thinks you're just the greatest, Maggie." Leah smiled brightly.

"That's nice," said Maggie, her voice void of expression. "She seems like a sweet person." Then she turned to her mother. "Leah invited them all for dinner this weekend, so you'll get to meet her. I think she's a little older than you, but I'm sure you're going to like her."

❧

Before going to bed, Maggie considered calling Jed just to make sure he understood that her dinner with Colin Byers was nothing more than strictly business. It made her sad to think that he might be feeling hurt about any of this. And yet, she felt uncomfortable calling him—probably stemming from an old-fashioned notion that women shouldn't call men. Just the same, she couldn't make herself pick up the phone. She stared at the phone by her bed for a long moment, willing him to call her but, of course, it never rang. In frustration, she decided to write a much-overdo email to her friend Rebecca.

Dear Rebecca:

Sorry it's been so long. Fortunately, I know we both lead very busy lives, so I doubt you've been pining away waiting to hear from me. So much is going on here, I hardly know where to begin. When you come for Christmas we'll have time to really sit down and catch up. I can't wait to see you! By the way, little brother Barry is coming too. Still single and more handsome than ever. I was telling Mom that the age difference between you and him no longer seems like much of an issue to me—not that I'm playing matchmaker. Actually, if I was playing matchmaker, I might introduce you to the man I had dinner with tonight (strictly business, mind you—my heart still belongs to Jed!). But anyway, this guy, who is supposed to be my "enemy" (long story…), turns out to be incredibly decent—only my first impressions, of course. He is a little older than us, I think, and divorced, and there may be good reasons for that…but I found him surprisingly good company—pleasant, thoughtful, and polite. He's the "money man" behind a controversial development going in up here (part of that long story). Anyway, I'm going to go check out some of his developments to see if he's really for real or not. You may have heard his name before—Colin Byers. Know anything about him? The fly in the ointment is that Jed saw me with him tonight, and I'm sure he didn't understand. It doesn't help that we've "put our relationship on hold" for Leah's sake. (Jed's decision.) By the way, do you ever call men? Just wondering.

Love you.
mc

Just as she hit the "send" button, an idea occurred to her. Jed had an email address. She had seen it on his business card. She wondered how regularly he checked it. Somehow the idea of communicating via email wasn't as intimidating as calling him on the phone. And who knew, perhaps this was a way they could remain in contact without drawing Leah's attention to themselves. Anyway, she figured it was worth a try. She only hoped that Leah didn't access his email at work. Perhaps she could keep the content somewhat generic in this message and simply see what happened.

Hi Jed,

I was just online and remembered that you get email, and I thought perhaps you might enjoy getting a message. Although, I'm not sure how regularly you check your in-box...As you saw, I had dinner with "the enemy" tonight. My purpose was to attain more information about the development and to try to maintain an objective viewpoint about this whole controversy. But when I saw you, I wished we could talk. I miss our talks, Jed. I thought maybe we could "talk" through email. Or would that be taking our relationship "off hold" so to speak? I just figured this might be a private way to sort of hold things together during the interim. Let me know what you think.

Maggie

Thirteen

On Friday afternoon, Colin Byers' personal assistant called Abigail and then followed up with a fax of Maggie's proposed flight schedule and itinerary. "Are you sure you want to do this?" asked Abigail as she handed the paper to Maggie. "Seems to me you'll be hopping right out of the frying pan and into the fire—or maybe it's the dragon's lair. I'm not too sure about my metaphors, but just the same, I don't think it's a good idea for you to go down there."

Maggie laughed. "You haven't met him, have you, Abigail? He actually seems like quite a nice person, and he has almost everyone in town convinced that he's okay. And who knows, maybe he is telling the truth about how his competitors have slandered his name in order to get a leg up in the development business."

Abigail frowned. "Well, if he's anything like the company he keeps—like Snider and Tanner, I mean—then I wouldn't trust him no matter how nice he seemed. And I don't think you should either."

"Believe me, I understand your sentiments. But this is a good opportunity to find out if this guy's on the level or not. I plan to really snoop around and ask lots of questions. If there's anything disturbing, I'll be the first one to blow the whistle on him. But Pine Mountain Estates may be coming whether we like it or not. I feel I owe it to our readers to find out the truth about Colin Byers and the quality of his developments, and to do that I need to see his work with my own eyes."

Abigail nodded solemnly. "I suppose you're right. Just you be careful. Are you all packed up and ready to go?"

"Well, there's plenty of time for that." Maggie glanced at the itinerary. "Wait—it says here that I'm to fly out tomorrow morning and return on Monday!"

Abigail nodded. "His secretary called and said that early next week doesn't work for him. She was very apologetic, but she explained that he thinks it's so important for you to come that he cleared his weekend in order to tour you around himself. She said they hoped you wouldn't mind giving up a weekend and that they promised to show you a good time."

Maggie groaned. "Well, I guess I don't have much of a choice, do I? Maybe it's best just to get this over with anyway. I think I'll head home early and try to get some things in order before I have to leave."

As she drove home, she realized that by leaving tomorrow she'd miss the dinner with Barbara, Michael, and Jed. Perhaps she could get Leah and Audrey to postpone it until she returned on Monday. She knew Barbara planned to stay at least another week.

Spencer and Leah went to the high school basketball game after dinner. Leah had kindly offered to chauffeur "the two handicapped kids" as she teasingly called Spencer and Daniel. But at the same time, she seemed to be aware of how badly Spence had wanted to play basketball on the freshman team this year, and because of that Maggie suspected Leah was being more helpful and empathetic to him of late. Fortunately it was only a week or so until his cast came off, while Daniel would probably wear one until after Christmas. Maggie would never admit it to anyone, but she was just slightly relieved that their injuries had slowed these boys down some. Spencer, although only fifteen, seemed to be too independent and was growing up too fast these days.

After cleaning up the dinner dishes, Audrey and Maggie settled in front of the fireplace in the library, Audrey with her knitting and Maggie with her most recent edition of the *L.A. Times.*

"I must admit I'm a bit concerned about you going down there," said Audrey as she set down her knitting. "I know you're a grown woman and able to take care of yourself. But that smooth-talking Colin Byers worries me a little."

"You don't need to worry, Mom. Everything will be just fine. And if it makes you feel any better, I'm taking my cell phone with me. If Colin decides to tie me up and leave me out on the railroad tracks, I'll be sure to give you a call, okay?"

"And just how will you push the buttons with your hands all tied up?" asked Audrey wryly.

"I guess I'll just have to use my nose." They both chuckled over this image, then Maggie added, "Really, Mom, I did stories that are much more threatening than this when I was down in L.A. Remember that piece about the Russian mob? This will be a piece of cake compared to that. Who knows, it might even be fun. And honestly, despite what we may have thought before, Colin Byers appears to be a perfect gentleman."

"Yes, but looks can be deceiving, and Spencer didn't seem to like the way he was looking at you that night we had dinner."

Maggie laughed. "Spence is very protective, which I happen to think is quite normal and rather sweet. But think about it, Colin Byers wouldn't dare do anything to offend me. After all, he knows I'm a big-mouthed reporter. Why would he risk his reputation in such a silly way?"

"Yes, I suppose you're right. Besides if anything happened to you he'd have half of Pine Mountain, not to mention a very angry Jed Whitewater, down there giving him what for!"

Maggie smiled. "Yes, so don't worry. And speaking of Jed, I was hoping that you and Leah might be able to postpone that dinner engagement with Barbara Harris until I get back—if it works for everyone."

"That shouldn't be a problem. I'll mention it to Leah. By the way, how are things with you and Jed lately?" Her tone seemed to implicate concern. "I don't mean to interfere, but it seems to me that something's not quite the same between you two. Anything I should be aware of?"

Maggie hadn't told her mother about their decision to slow down their relationship for the time being, and she wasn't sure she wanted to discuss it now. Besides, she was still hoping Jed might answer her email and decide to continue their relationship electronically. But she had to say something. "No, we're doing okay. We just thought for Leah's sake that we should cool things down a bit—give her more time to adjust to everything, you know."

Audrey's brows arched. "Do you think that's such a good idea?"

Maggie studied her mother's face. Was this the counselor or the mother speaking? "I don't really know, Mom. I mean, the truth is, I'm not too thrilled with the whole arrangement, but then Leah has so much to adjust to...I guess it just seems more fair to her. She's had such a hard life..."

Audrey nodded. "Yes, I understand about her life. But do you realize that it's not up to you and Jed to make all that up for her?"

"What do you mean?"

"I mean, Leah is bound to have a lot of needs—it's to be expected after all she's been through with that irresponsible mother of hers. And I'm absolutely certain that Jed is being a wonderful father to her now, but he needs to realize that there's no way he will ever replace or make up all the years that have gone by. And if he tries to do it all now, he may be setting a precedent that will be very hard to maintain in the years to come. Do you know what I mean?"

"I think so...maybe..."

"For Leah's sake, she shouldn't expect that Jed is always going to be her superdad, the guy with all the time in the world for her. He needs to be able to have a life of his own. Anything else is just not normal—not to mention humanly impossible. Having such elevated expectations will only hurt her in the long run...when she discovers that, like her mom, he's only human."

"But he's certainly doing a lot better than her mom did," defended Maggie.

"Yes. But Leah needs to keep standing on her own two feet. Of course, Jed's her father and he'll always love her. But she's a young adult who needs to continue getting on with her life. She needs to accept that Jed can't be her all in all."

"Won't that take time?"

"I don't know for sure. But I do worry that she might get too caught up in *his* world. I mean, she's working so hard in the shop these days to the exclusion of other things, like continuing her schooling or spending time with friends her own age. The more time that lapses, the more she will depend on him. And what if Jed wanted to have more time for something else?" Audrey eyed Maggie sharply.

"Like another relationship..."

"Exactly."

"But what can I do about it?"

"You could talk to Jed."

Maggie moaned and ran a hand through her hair. "I just don't see how I can bring this up without sounding rather selfish. I mean, between you and me, I'm already a little jealous of the amount of time he spends with Leah. I'm afraid if I tell him what you just said it'll sound like I'm trying to push her right out of his life. And I'm not, because I really do love Leah, Mom. I don't want to hurt her in any way."

Audrey considered this for a moment. "Maybe I could talk to him about it."

Maggie brightened. "Oh, would you?"

"Sure, if the right opportunity comes along. Maybe I can drop some hints with Leah too while I'm at it. She seems to listen to me."

Although they'd never been a demonstrative family, Maggie threw her arms around her mother. "Thanks so much, Mom!"

~

Audrey drove Maggie to the airport the next morning, waiting to see the small twin-engine plane take off with only Maggie and Colin Byers' company pilot inside. Maggie was glad the pilot didn't seem to want to talk, and instead she looked out the window and enjoyed the scenery below. Pine-covered mountains with clear blue lakes spotted here and there, and then on to the browns and tans of the barren desert. After just a few hours they were landing on an airstrip.

The pilot helped her to climb from the little plane, and then they crossed the tarmac toward a small metal building that said "Desert Winds" over the door.

"Does this airstrip belong to the development?" asked Maggie as they walked in the door.

"Yes. Some of our homeowners have their own planes." He set her bag inside the door and glanced around. "Mr. Byers is supposed to pick you up here, but I don't see him just yet. Why don't you wait over there?" He pointed to some chairs by a window. "I have to fly over to Vegas to get someone else right now, and I'm already running late. Will you be okay?"

"Sure. Thanks for the nice flight." She picked up her overnight bag and walked over to sit down and wait. After several minutes, a woman walked in and sat down at a desk in the corner. Maggie thought perhaps she should check with her about Colin and make sure he was actually picking her up.

"Hi," she said in friendly voice, observing that this woman was about her age, dressed quite stylishly, and was very pretty with long, curly auburn hair.

"Hello," said the woman in a tone that suggested she'd rather not be bothered.

"I was supposed to be picked up—"

"Are you waiting for a salesman?" asked the woman sharply. "Because if you are, you're in for a long wait—"

"No, actually I'm waiting for Colin Byers. He was supposed to pick me up."

The woman's left brow arched with suspicion. "You're here to see *Colin?*" Something about the way she said his name implied a familiarity beyond just business and Maggie wondered if this might be a girlfriend.

She hurried to explain. "Yes, I'm a reporter from Oregon, and I'm here to see Desert Winds in order to find out more about Mr. Byers' developments. I am covering a story in our paper." For some reason she felt the need to make it clear to this woman that her visit was strictly business.

"Sorry, I must've sounded rude," said the woman. "I'm June Emerson." She stood and extended a hand. "I thought you were a prospective buyer or something. And well—to tell the truth—I've just quit and I came in here to clear out some things from my daughter's desk. She also just quit. She used to work part-time out here."

"Oh, I'm sorry to bother you." Maggie glanced at her watch. "It's just that I thought Mr. Byers was supposed to meet the plane."

"Well, why don't I give you a lift over to the clubhouse?" She eyed Maggie with open curiosity. "You say you're a reporter?"

"Yes. And to tell the truth, I was really hoping to look around a little without an escort. Do you think that's possible?"

June laughed. "Boy, did you run into the right person. The stories I could tell you—"

Just then a door opened and June glanced quickly over Maggie's shoulder. "Oh, hi, Colin," she called out. "This woman was just telling me that she was supposed to get picked up by you." Before Colin reached them, June slipped a card into Maggie's hand and winked. "I was just about to give you a call."

"Thanks, June," he replied without even looking at her. "Welcome to Desert Winds," he said to Maggie, offering her a warm handshake. "Sorry there was no one out here. We're a little short-staffed today." He looked over to the waiting area. "That your bag?"

"Yes." She glanced at June in time to see her mouth the words "call me," then with a nod she slipped June's card into her pocket and turned to join Colin.

"Sorry about the wait. And my apologies for the terminal. It's not the greatest, but it's just temporary. We have plans for a much nicer one to be built out here by the end of next summer."

Maggie briefly glanced around the drafty metal building. "I suppose it's better than nothing." She waited for him to open the door and then lead the way to a luxury SUV that looked as if it had just rolled off the car lot.

"I thought we'd have lunch at the clubhouse first, then give you some time to relax a little this afternoon. You can hang around and enjoy the clubhouse facilities, golf if you like, or visit the spa. Unfortunately, something urgent has come up and I have some pressing business I need to attend to today. Then, if you don't mind, I'll meet you for breakfast tomorrow morning, and afterward give you a complete tour with me as your personal guide. How does that sound?"

"Great," she replied, eager to have a free and unsupervised day to explore the development on her own.

"We have a wonderful spa facility, an Olympic-sized pool, and a state-of-the-art workout area. I even reserved a masseuse for you at three o'clock." He glanced over at her. "I thought you might enjoy some R and R while you're here. You know what they say about all work and no play."

She smiled. "No problem. I think it sounds just perfect."

The clubhouse was fairly impressive upon first glance, with its large pond and fountain situated just outside the entrance and tall, open-beamed ceilings inside. But upon closer inspection, in the ladies' restroom, for instance, she noticed numerous things that suggested less than the best workmanship and materials, not to mention poor mainte- nance. She spotted several cracked tiles, a loose soap dis- penser, and even some places where the wallpaper was starting to peel off the walls. Certainly not the sort of things most people might notice, and maybe no big deal, but she was trying to be watchful. She snapped a few photos and then quickly jotted these observations down in her note- book.

Soon they were seated at a window table that overlooked the golf course. "It must take a lot of water to keep those greens up," she commented as she scanned over the menu.

"Yes, but we have an excellent well system. We had to go through about a thousand feet of solid rock, but it was worth it. We have some of the best water in the world here."

"How old is Desert Winds?"

"It's been about two years since we first opened the club- house and Phase One of the housing." He pointed to a sec- tion of impressive-looking homes off in the distance, circling the southern perimeter of the golf course.

"So it's fairly new compared to your other communi- ties?"

"Yes, it's our most recent project. That's exactly why I thought you should see it as it's probably very similar to what we have planned for TS Development in Pine Moun- tain Estates."

She glanced around the restaurant. It was about half- filled, mostly with people who looked to be of retirement age. She also noticed that most of the waiters appeared to be of Hispanic background. Not that she had anything against that, but she remembered the stories she'd heard of illegal workers. However, the girl waiting their table was a perky blue-eyed blonde, probably not much older than Spencer. She greeted Colin by name as she took their orders.

"Does everyone know you here?" asked Maggie as she started on her salad.

He laughed. "Not everyone. But this is my special table, and Christy's dad is an associate of mine."

"I noticed that a lot of the waiters are Hispanic..." She studied his eyes for any clues as he answered.

"So we're an equal opportunity employer." He shrugged without any real show of concern.

But she wasn't about to be cowed by his confidence. "Do you know for sure that all your employees are legal U.S. citizens?"

He shrugged. "Does anyone?" Then he smiled warmly. "Actually, my personnel director handles these things. You can take it up with him if you like. I'll give you his number."

"Thanks." She smiled apologetically. "I hate to seem like such a pest, but you know it's the reason why I came."

He pretended to frown. "It wasn't just for my good company after all?"

Playing his game, she frowned back. "Well, then I'd have been terribly disappointed about being abandoned for the day, wouldn't I?"

His eyes lit. "You mean you are? I could try to wind things up in time for dinner tonight..."

She waved her hand in dismissal. "Oh, no, no. Don't worry about me. I'll be perfectly fine, really. I'm looking forward to relaxing. I even brought a good novel along."

He seemed unsure. "Are you certain, Maggie?"

She nodded, feeling a bit like a hypocrite as she fingered June's business card resting in her pocket. "I'm certain, Colin. Like I said, some R and R sounds just wonderful to me." But perhaps, she told herself, the "R and R" might actually stand for *reconnaissance* and *research*...

Fourteen

*A*s soon as Maggie was settled into her luxurious suite across from the clubhouse, she called the woman she'd met at the airstrip.

"This is June," came a crisp reply.

"Hello, this is Maggie Carpenter," she began tentatively. "I met you today at the little airport." Suddenly she wondered if this woman's offer had been in earnest or not. And furthermore, whether or not she could trust her. Still, what did she have to lose?

"Oh, I was just telling my daughter about you, Maggie. What can I do for you?"

She explained a little more about the nature of her mission, how she was now stuck at the clubhouse for the remainder of the day without a car, and how she really wanted to see more of the community without being under the watchful surveillance of Colin Byers.

June laughed. "Yes, you can be certain, Colin will only show you what he wants you to see. And without a doubt, he's brought you to one of his best-developed communities, hoping to impress you, I'm sure."

"Does that mean there's nothing here that's really out of line?"

June laughed even louder now. "Oh, don't kid yourself. Desert Winds may be better than the other developments, but believe me, it has its share of problems. That's exactly why I can't stand to stick around for one more day. It's really ironic that I ran into you out at the airport today, but somehow I think there's a reason for it. Anyway, my daughter and I are sick of the greed and deception that goes on here. I tried to convince myself when I first came out that this place was different, and in some ways it is. But to be honest, I know it was only the lure of big money that made me look the other way all this time."

"So there's quite a bit to be made in these developments?" Maggie was already taking vigorous notes.

"Oh, yeah, if you're into easy money, it's here for the making. They say there's a new sucker born every minute," she made a groaning sound, "but I've had enough—I'm fed up with the whole biz. I mean, once I realized how it was affecting my daughter, I decided it was time to split. I'm sorry to go on and on about this—I guess it's because I've kept it all bottled up inside for so long. Anyway, we're all packed up over here, and I can spare you an hour or two. Would you like me to pick you up right now?"

"Do you mind? I mean, I know you're in the middle of moving and everything. I hate to take your time—"

"No. All that's left to do is a little cleaning, and, as usual, my Annie's got everything under control. I'm thinking that if I can help you to get this story out, it might just be my personal way of apologizing for my involvement here—sort of like paying restitution, I guess."

"You make it sound pretty bad." Maggie wondered what she was getting into.

"Well, I guess it all depends on how you look at it. Colin is certainly able to justify everything and he manages to do *most* things within the legal limits of the law—why, he's even had me believing he was totally legit. But then one morning you wake up and realize how many innocent people have been hurt...and well, I'll explain everything when I get there.

Watch for a white Jaguar out in the circle drive in front of the condos. I don't dare come inside—you don't want to be seen with me. I'll be there in about twenty minutes."

Maggie called to cancel her three o'clock massage, then headed out to the lobby to wait for June. While she was waiting, discreetly wearing her dark glasses and already assuming her new role in undercover espionage, she overheard tidbits of a heated conversation from the front desk.

"Look!" said an older man, probably in his sixties. "My wife and I drove all the way over here from the bay area, and now there isn't a drop of water at our house, and according to maintenance there won't be. This is unacceptable, and I demand that you find us a room with running water immediately."

"I'm sorry, sir," said the woman in a strained voice. "As I told you before, all the rooms are full." Just then Maggie noticed a white car pull up outside. She hurried out to see June waving from behind the wheel of a sleek Jaguar, then climbed in. Obviously, working for Colin had paid off financially for the woman.

"You have no idea how much I appreciate this," said Maggie as she closed the door and buckled herself into the cool leather seat.

June nodded and quickly took off. "I'm just glad to get the chance to help someone else for a change. Only last week I heard Colin talking about this new Oregon development, bragging about how it would be the first one in that state, and I thought to myself then that this man will never be stopped. Maybe he won't, but it won't be for lack of trying."

Maggie grimaced. "Colin is *so* convincing. I had almost expected—in fact, I'd even hoped for the sake of our town— that I'd come here and find everything to be just as he had described."

"Believe me, you would have."

"That's what I was afraid of."

"Colin would kill me if he knew what I was doing..." June glanced nervously out her rearview mirror.

"Not seriously!" Suddenly Maggie imagined June's car being followed by a hit man in a dark sedan.

June laughed. "No, I've never heard of Colin committing any murders. Although one old guy became so frustrated over a home he'd purchased last year that I think it gave him a stroke, and for that I blame Colin."

"There was a man in the lobby who sounded pretty upset. He was complaining that he had no water at his house."

"He must have purchased a home in Phase Three. Their well ran dry last week. Some people are having huge stainless steel storage tanks installed, but they run about $20,000 each and there's already a long waiting list. Once they're installed the homeowners will have to pay to get them refilled all the time, and of course their landscaping, which is supposedly required for each house, has all died. Nothing can survive out here without water. That's how Colin was able to get the land so cheap to start with. On top of all that, they raise the homeowners' fees every time you turn around. A lot of these people are forced to sell for below market value just to get out without losing everything. It's really quite sad."

"I never considered how all this could impact the consumers," said Maggie. "I was actually more concerned with the quality of the development from the outside community's standpoint. I hadn't given much thought as to what a headache it might be for the unsuspecting people who buy into these places."

"I was in sales." June pulled up to a parking area on a small ridge that overlooked the golf course and clubhouse. "And all we ever did was think about the folks who buy into these places, always coming up with another new method to lure them in and then get them hooked."

Maggie gazed over the lush green golf course and well-planned clubhouse buildings. "This really looks quite nice from up here."

"It's supposed to. We always stop here on our sales tour. We brag about the golf course and clubhouse facilities, and while they really are very nice, they have problems too which will only get worse over time. You'll probably notice a few things before your stay is over, although I've no doubt that Colin put you in one of the best suites with instructions for everyone to treat you like royalty. Let me guess—you're in suite 305?"

"That's right!"

"Anyway, after the tour of the clubhouse, we take you to see Phase One. We have a beautiful model home that we walk you through. Naturally, it's the only one of its kind, well-constructed, immaculate, and decorated to the nines in Ralph Lauren's classiest southwest decor. Of course, it's right on the golf course, and we usually invite you to sit on the deck for plenty of drinks and appetizers—the royal treatment. Then we show you maps of the property, and a schmaltzy video showing the other phases—rather *parts* of the other phases. We usually know exactly which lot we want to sell, and we tell you that we have this really special lot—the only one of its kind—and only available because someone died or something dramatic like that."

"And do people buy it?"

June nodded sadly. "Many of them have had a few too many drinks by then, and they're caught up in all the glamour. We help them to imagine themselves suddenly living out their fantasies of the lifestyle of the rich and famous. In other words, they buy in haste and repent in leisure."

"Is *anyone* happy here?"

"Oh, some might actually be happy, but they're the ones who have money to burn. And, of course, they all live in Phase One. We'll drive through that first. We can stop at the model home if you like."

"Let's do that. It might be effective for me to get the whole 'royal treatment' as you put it."

June laughed. "Maybe I should sell you a lot while I'm at it too."

"Actually, I'd probably make a likely victim. I bought a house sight unseen last year—not the smartest thing I've done in my life. It could've turned into a real nightmare but, fortunately, it's been more like a dream come true." Maggie told her about Clyde selling his house to her as they drove through Phase One. "This looks quite nice in here," she observed. The houses were large and impressive with well-watered and immaculate lawns.

"Yes. Unfortunately these are the minority of home-owners in Desert Winds. But they have paid dearly for these showplaces. Everything done out here on the desert is highly inflated—nothing comes cheap, except for the quality of workmanship and materials, that is. Of course, some things will only show up over time. These homes are only a year, or two at the most, old. But my guess is that in five years they will be having some major problems."

"Are you saying that even the best homes aren't well built?"

"They cut lots of corners, have very low building standards, and often use inferior materials."

Maggie jotted all this down. Then they toured the model home, and she was honestly impressed by its open, flowing design and expensive decor. With classical music piped into every room, computerized heating and cooling systems, remote-controlled window coverings, and many other of the very latest innovations, she almost became convinced that she'd rather have a house like this than her own dear house back in Pine Mountain. "Are all the homes in Phase One like this?"

"Some come close, but nothing is quite this nice. It would cost a fortune. But, after a few drinks and some persuasion, most people assume that *this*," she waved her arm around dramatically, "is what they'll be getting when they sign on the bottom line. Of course, if they'd only read the fine print they might suspect otherwise. But don't kid yourself, Colin is very careful to obey the letter of the law. For the most part people are incredibly trusting and gullible—especially some of the older ones. I want to show you a couple of the vacant houses so you can get a better look at some of the construction problems—one in this phase, and the other in the latest phase. Then you can decide for yourself."

Maggie couldn't believe the difference between the vacant houses and the model home. She took photos of uneven sheet-rock on the walls where nail heads had popped out, wobbly toilets, cheap lighting fixtures, thin vinyl flooring with bubbles, and one bathroom where the plumbing wasn't even connected to the sink. On top of this, June explained how many people were having problems with improperly installed, but very expensive, septic tank systems that sat aboveground and were becoming environmental and health hazards.

"You can see why I want to get out of here," said June after they finished touring the last house.

"Do you know much firsthand about the other developments?"

"I've seen enough of them to know that this is truly their best one."

"I guess then what I've read about the other places might be true as well."

June nodded soberly. "It's all because of greed. Colin and his associates have made millions, maybe billions—at the expense of others. And this may be only a rumor, but I've heard that Colin has some lawsuits pending. I'm sure it's all a matter of public record. It shouldn't be too difficult to get the details."

"Have you ever heard of any actual settlements?"

June shook her head. "Colin keeps all that kind of stuff under pretty tight wraps. The only reason I heard about the pending lawsuits was because I was dating him at the time. And *that* is something I don't want to talk about."

Maggie surveyed the golf course again. It was really quite an attractive contrast with the surrounding desert. "It's too bad they had to take all those shortcuts and do such a shoddy job of developing everything. I don't understand—"

"That's because you're basically a good person. You don't understand that a lot of folks in this world only care about the bottom line."

"But surely they still would've made plenty of money if they'd done things right from the start. Then at least they'd be able to sleep at night."

"Greed does strange things to people, Maggie. It can really mess up your perspective. Believe me, I know first-hand. I allowed myself to be pulled into this. But like I said, the day comes when you have to look at yourself in the mirror—" her voice broke, "or into your daughter's eyes."

"Your daughter sounds like a very sensible girl. I think you're doing the right thing to get out of this."

"Yeah, I'm so thankful for Annie. She's really got her head on straight. I could learn a lot from her." June pulled up in front of the condo complex and stopped. "I'm sorry I can't spend more time with you, but we're trying to get out of here today. I'm driving the U-Haul and Annie's driving the car. We have a ways to go before we reach my folks' place by nightfall."

"Thanks so much for all your help, June." Maggie handed her a business card from the newspaper. "If you're ever in the neighborhood, stop in. And God bless you and your daughter as you travel."

Maggie went immediately to work on her article for next week's paper, calling room service to order a small dinner to be sent to her room. She knew she couldn't enjoy using any of the luxurious amenities in the clubhouse now, knowing how these little niceties were created at the expense of the unfortunate homeowners, not to mention being used as bait to lure in even more unsuspecting buyers. To her dismay, she realized she hadn't packed her computer modem for her laptop and was consequently unable to access any informa-tion online or check her email. She didn't expect to hear from Jed, but she was still hoping.

As she finally prepared for bed, she dreaded the idea of spending the entire day with Colin tomorrow, but could think of no real escape short of hiring a taxi to drive her over a hundred miles to Las Vegas, which was the nearest city to Desert Winds. Though she would never mention June's informative tour to Colin, she wanted him to know that she was well aware of Desert Winds' unpleasant secrets—at least some of them. June had intimated that there were more, but seemed reluctant to say too much. Not that Maggie blamed her. People like Colin Byers' usually had a number of slick corporate attorneys in their back pocket. June was smart to get out while she could. Maggie knew that June had had more than just a business relationship with Colin, and her reluctance to speak of it was understandable. But surely she hadn't told her all this just to spite him. No, it had seemed more of a confession of sorts, an attempt to clean the slate before she moved on. Maggie prayed for June and Annie as they traveled across the desert to a new life. She remembered distinctly how that had felt—the excitement, the apprehension. Hopefully it would go as well for them as it had for her.

✦

Colin's tour on Sunday held no surprises, beginning with an elegant and leisurely breakfast served out on a terrace right next to the golf course. Then they played nine holes of golf, and somehow Maggie managed not to embarrass herself too badly. Phil had taught her how to play golf in their early married days, but she had been young and impatient with the slow-moving game back then, promising him that one day, when they both grew older, she would play with him on a regular basis. This thought made her incredibly sad now.

Colin was polite and considerate, showing off every amenity of the clubhouse facility with an air of grace mingled with pride. It was clear he thought Desert Winds to be his best effort so far, although he made no apologies for any of his other developments, implying that their standards were always of the very highest. He took more time than June had in showing her the beautiful model home, careful to point out and demonstrate each and every luxurious detail. When Maggie asked him how this house compared with the others, he diplomatically answered that no two homes were the same, and that this fact was what made his developments so special. She had to look the other way to hide her disgust as she remembered how there'd been only three different sets of blueprints used in the houses in the Phase Three section, each one only slightly different. She questioned him about things such as water, electricity, and waste disposal. But each of his flawless answers flowed smoothly, implying that other than the occasional problem, all went very well at Desert Winds. He even stopped to show her his own home, which not surprisingly, was equal in every way to the model home.

Shortly after lunch, Maggie began to feel unwell. She wasn't sure if it was a result of the stress from playing a double agent or from the restaurant's overly rich food, but her head was throbbing and she honestly felt ill. She thanked Colin for everything and quickly excused herself to her room, collapsing onto the bed to rest. Mostly, she was relieved to get away from him. His smooth charm had begun to work on her again, and she had almost believed him when he'd rambled on and on about his vision for his future developments. He promised her that Pine Mountain Estates would be far superior to Desert Winds. He even invited her to become involved on the ground floor, offering her a special "early investor" deal and guaranteeing her that property values would only increase as the community continued to be developed.

Surely, that was enough to make anyone sick!

Fifteen

ortunately Maggie didn't have to see Colin again before she flew out of Desert Winds on Monday morning. He had called the evening before to check on her, but while she'd reassured him that she was somewhat better, she had declined his dinner invitation. He had a basket of goodies sent to her room, which she gave to the maid. The young woman, who didn't speak a single word of English, and was most likely in the country illegally, seemed truly grateful.

Maggie restrained herself from falling to her knees and kissing the ground after the twin-engine airplane finally landed. Instead she thanked the pilot, gathered her things, and jogged over to meet her mother, who was waiting at the gate.

"It feels like I've been gone for a month," she exclaimed as she hugged Audrey.

"So how did your little investigation go?"

Maggie told her mother the whole story as they drove back to Pine Mountain.

"I must admit I felt slightly deceitful, but I told Colin from the beginning why I was there," she said as they pulled into town. "But I just couldn't tell him about June's tour. I didn't want to get her into trouble."

"Or yourself," agreed Audrey. "Don't worry, he'll hear about your findings soon enough."

Maggie sighed. "I honestly wish it had gone differently. I really wanted to be pleasantly surprised. For the sake of everyone in town, I wish I could write a good report on Desert Winds."

"Just write the truth—that's good enough."

Maggie treated her mother to lunch at the hotel. As they ate Audrey told her about the conversation she'd had with Jed when she called him to change the dinner date with Barbara Harris. "He seemed very concerned about you going down to Nevada with Colin Byers on such short notice."

Maggie made a face. "What? Did he think I was eloping or something?"

Audrey laughed. "Maybe. Although I assured him it was strictly business. Just the same, I'm not sure he was convinced."

"Did you talk to him about Leah?"

"I tried to. But he seemed pretty defensive. I think he's carrying a lot of guilt over abandoning her as a baby, and I have a feeling he's willing to do whatever it takes to make up for her earlier life."

"Did you tell him why you don't think that's very healthy?"

"I tried." Audrey shook her head. "But I don't think he heard me."

"Poor Jed. He's such a decent person. I know he only wants to do what's right. It has to be hard on him trying to understand all these things."

"And all these women in his life..." Audrey chuckled.

"Plus he's spending so much time with Michael these days. I suppose I just need to be patient and cut him some slack until he gets things figured out." Yet at the same time, Maggie couldn't wait to get home and see if he'd answered her email.

"You might be right to just play it cool," agreed Audrey. "Anyway, I invited them all for dinner on Wednesday night. Will that work for you?"

"Sounds great."

⁓

Maggie decided to go to work for the rest of the afternoon, but Scott stopped her in the lobby before she could even get into her own office. Like a kid with a new toy, he was eager to have her read his story about Randy Ebbert's white supremacist group.

"Apparently he has some real card-carrying members," exclaimed Scott. "I found his website on the Internet and he was boasting of increased numbers."

"Well, that could just mean his wife's having another baby."

Scott laughed. "Man, you won't believe the kind of stuff these guys write about online for the whole world to see. I even called the FBI to make sure they're keeping track of all these little fringe groups. Apparently they are. A woman told me they even have a special division for it."

"I'm sure they'd have to watch them. You never know what one of these fanatics might do." She scanned his story. "This looks really good, Scott, but do you think it's complete yet?"

He frowned. "Well, I thought I could run this piece now, and then continue following it up, you know—sort of an ongoing report about what's going on in Randy Ebbert's hate camp."

She nodded. "I suppose so. But we want to be careful not to give him too much attention. Sometimes these guys eat this kind of thing up."

"But everything I've said is so negative. I didn't pull any punches, Maggie. I can't imagine that Ebbert's going to be pleased."

"Probably not." She handed the story back. "I'm sure when he reads this, he'll be more likely than ever to start printing his own newspaper."

Scott laughed. "Great. Competition is healthy."

The front door opened and they both turned to see Gavin Barnes. At least it looked like Gavin, but something about him seemed very different. Maybe that old swagger was gone, or perhaps he'd lost that hard glint in his eye, but somehow he reminded Maggie of an errant boy who'd just been sent down to the principal's office. She extended her hand in a friendly greeting. "It's really good to see you again, Gavin. I didn't even know you were in town."

"Good to see you too, Maggie. I just got here and thought I'd stop by to see my uncle first." The way he said *first* suggested he didn't know what he'd do after that—or perhaps whether he'd even be welcome at all.

"Hey, Gavin," said Scott. "I liked your letter."

Gavin glanced uneasily at Maggie. "Did you print it?"

"Last week. And I've already heard some nice feedback."

He seemed relieved. "Is Clyde here?"

"He's out back," said Scott, "having a problem with one of his cranky old machines, and the words are flying."

"Maybe I can give him a hand," said Gavin. As he walked toward the back he stopped by Abigail's desk. "How's it going, Abigail?"

Her brows shot up. "Just fine—thanks." After he was out of earshot, she shook her head. "Now, if that don't beat all. Gavin's never given *me* the time of day before."

"People can change," said Maggie as she headed to her office. To tell the truth, she was almost as surprised as Abigail, but she hoped, especially for Clyde's sake, that Gavin had truly changed.

She quickly went online with her computer, going directly to her email. She found a note from Rebecca and a couple of other things, but not a word from Jed. She told herself it didn't matter and went into a search for any record of lawsuits pending against Colin Byers. A couple of phone calls and faxes later, she had just what she needed in her hand. And although the court date for an impressive-looking class-action lawsuit wasn't set until next August, the insinuation of wrongdoing was as plain as day. She knew just where she would work this little bombshell of information into her story. Just as she finished her last rewrite on the Desert Winds article, she heard a quiet knock on her door. "Come in," she called as she hit the "save" button and exited from her document.

"Got a minute?" asked Gavin tentatively.

"Sure, come on in."

He sank into the chair across from her desk and exhaled loudly. "I just talked to Clyde."

"How'd it go?" She leaned forward with interest.

"Actually, better than I had expected." He forced a smile. "He didn't tell me to leave town. But on the other hand, he didn't invite me to stay either."

"Are you staying?"

"I'd like to."

"Do you have a place? I'm sure there are lots of rooms available at the hotel. It's pretty slow over there."

He shrugged. "I guess I could stay at the hotel, but they've fixed the place up so nice I'm afraid it's gotten pretty expensive. And to tell you the truth, I'm a little low on cash right now. I haven't had much income lately."

Suddenly she wondered if the only reason Gavin had come back was to weasel some money from his uncle. But something about his demeanor made her think not. Still, she couldn't be sure. "What exactly are your plans, Gavin?"

He shrugged again. "I don't know. I just needed to come back here, Maggie. For some reason this place feels like home to me. I just don't know where else to go."

"I always thought you were more of a big-city guy, Gavin."

"I suppose I've changed."

She smiled. "I can see that. But if you stayed here, how would you make a living? Any plans?"

His eyes lit up. "You hiring?"

She thought about that for a moment. Just last week, she'd mentioned to Clyde she'd like to hire someone for the sole purpose of selling ad space. The paper's only profits came from selling advertising, and yet none of them enjoyed doing it. "Well, actually, we might have an opening, Gavin. Although it's only part time to start—and it's not very glamorous."

He straightened up in his chair. "That's okay. What is it? Delivering papers? Cleaning up? Believe me, Maggie, I'm willing to do whatever it takes."

She laughed. "Well, I suppose it could include those things. There's no doubt a lot goes undone around here, but I was thinking more about getting someone to sell advertising for the paper. We've been toying with the idea of doing two editions a week, and we're already understaffed."

"Hey, I was always good at selling ads. Just pull out some of the old papers and you'll see."

She remembered the old ad-filled papers with hardly any news stories, then grinned. "No offense Gavin, but I think you were better at selling ads than you were at running the paper."

He nodded eagerly. "I was. Want to give me another shot? Do you think Clyde will agree?"

She drummed her pencil on the desk while she considered this. "Well, I'm the one who'll decide, but I'd like to run it past him first. I want him to be supportive of the decision. And you know, Gavin, Clyde's not getting any younger, and he still insists on doing most of the presswork himself. Although Scott tries to help him out in the pressroom, it's not the best use of Scott's time when he's trying to become a serious journalist."

"I'd be glad to help out in the pressroom—that is, if Clyde will let me. Honestly, Maggie, I'm willing to do whatever it takes to prove to him that I've changed."

"I believe you, Gavin." She studied him carefully. "But can I ask you something very bluntly?"

"Yeah, sure, anything. Go for it. I had to get used to this at rehab."

"Well, I know it'll be on Clyde's mind…and mine too." She wasn't sure how to ask, other than just to cut to the chase. Besides, she wanted to closely observe Gavin's initial reaction. "Okay, the thing is, I need to know if you're just trying to get into Clyde's good graces in order to secure an inheritance."

She studied him carefully. Gavin looked down at his feet for a moment. She suspected that her question might have hurt his feelings, but then he looked back up, his gaze evenly meeting hers. "That's a fair question, Maggie, and under the circumstances it's not all that surprising." He cleared his throat and continued. "I know you'll find this hard to believe, but money has become a lot less important to me since I quit drinking. Suddenly I've become a lot more interested in getting a *real* life. You know what I mean, a life with family and friends, and hopefully finding work that I enjoy. I feel like I'm starting all over again. Only this time, I'd like to do it right."

She felt his genuineness and smiled at him. "Good. I'll talk to Clyde about the job."

Relief washed over his face. "Thanks. I appreciate it."

"Now," she glanced at her watch, "it's quitting time."

"Well, thanks again for everything." He rose to leave, and she wondered where he'd go, where he'd stay. She considered offering to help out, but then wondered if that was such a good idea. But in the same instant, she recalled something she'd heard Michael say recently about how when they helped people in need, it was like helping Jesus. Gavin certainly seemed to be in need.

"Um…as you know," she began with some uncertainty, "we have extra room at my house. I mean, the top floor hasn't been totally renovated yet, but it's not all that bad either. You could stay up there for a while, if you want…that is, until you figure things out."

"Are you serious?" He was incredulous. "You'd put me up at your house?"

"Well, we're not a bed-and-breakfast yet. And you might need to be on your own for meals—"

"I wouldn't expect you to feed me or anything. Don't worry. I can fend for myself. But it would really help to have a place to stay, at least for now. I thought I'd sell my car after I got here, you know, to have some money to tide me over at first. But of course I haven't had a chance yet."

She nodded, then glanced out the window, remembering how Audrey had dropped her off at the office. "Speaking of cars, could you give me a ride home?"

She told Gavin about her trip to Desert Winds as he drove to her house, explaining all about Greg and Rick's plans to develop the farmland, as well as how they swindled Arnold Westerly out of his property.

"I've done some pretty slimy things in my life," admitted Gavin as he pulled into the driveway, "and I know in many ways that I'm probably much worse than those two guys, but what they're doing is really wrong! For the sake of the town, I hope they can be stopped before it's too late."

"Oh, look," cried Maggie when she saw her house suddenly beginning to glow with hundreds of little white lights. "They put up Christmas lights while I was out of town this weekend. Oh, doesn't it look wonderful!" She leaped from the car and ran up to the front porch to see Spencer hobbling around on his walking cast. "This looks great, Spence!" She hugged him. "But please don't tell me you climbed up on a ladder with that cast."

He laughed. "I would've, but Grandma wouldn't let me. Leah and Jed did all of the high stuff and I did the places I could reach from the ground."

She looked at the evergreen wreath on the door and at the garlands wrapped around the porch handrails. "This is so lovely. What a beautiful homecoming."

"Yeah, that was Grandma's idea. Hey, who's that?" asked Spencer, looking over at Gavin as he carried a suitcase from his car.

"It's Gavin Barnes. He's going to stay with us a while." Then, lowering her voice, "He's really changed, Spencer. You won't believe it."

Audrey had never met Gavin before, but after Maggie discreetly took her aside and explained everything, she warmly welcomed him into their household, even inviting him to help her in the kitchen by peeling potatoes. Without complaining, he rolled up his sleeves and pitched right in.

After dinner, Audrey took Maggie aside and offered to let Gavin use the guest house while he stayed with them.

"No, Mom. I don't want to push you out of your little nest."

"But is it proper for him to stay with you in your home?" asked Audrey with a concerned brow.

Maggie considered this. "Well, how would it be any different if I were running a bed-and-breakfast?"

"I suppose you're right. After all, it's not as if you're romantically involved with him." She peered at Maggie curiously. "You're not are you? I mean, he's awfully nice, and rather good-looking too."

She rolled her eyes. "Don't be ridiculous, Mom. Why is it that everyone assumes if I spend any time with a man that I must be romantically involved with him?"

"Well, you just never know." Then taking on a teasing tone, Audrey continued, "And you must admit, you've been seen with a number of attractive men lately. I'm sure it's just a matter of time until you'll have all of Pine Mountain atwitter."

Maggie laughed. "And what would be new about that?"

～

Leah came home late. She'd been helping Jed to organize some things for his trade show next week. "Michael's going to drive up to Seattle with him," said Leah as she ate from the plate of leftovers they'd saved for her.

Maggie turned the heat up beneath the teakettle. "How's old Jed doing?" she asked, hoping to sound nonchalant, though just speaking his name seemed to make her heart pound a little faster.

"Okay, I guess. Probably working too hard to get everything just perfect for this crazy show. He's renting a big truck to take everything in. It's sure good that he has Michael to help him with all the loading and unloading. I just hope this show is worth all his effort."

"I'm sure it will be. Once people see the quality of his furniture, he can't help but line up lots of work."

Leah brightened. "Yeah, I'm sure he'll be a huge success. I wish I could go too, but I need to stay home and keep the shop open. Hey, did you hear we got some new snow up at the higher elevations last weekend? Jed says just one more good dump and the resort should be open. Then we'd be really busy in the shop."

Maggie explained to Leah about their new houseguest, then made herself a pot of chamomile tea and said goodnight. In her room she looked longingly at her laptop computer. Was it possible that Jed had answered her email? Did she want to chance looking and be disappointed? And yet, how could she not? It felt as though years had gone by since they'd last spoken. She quickly plugged in her modem and waited for the computer to connect. What if this brief span in their relationship had actually weakened things? Could it undo something important? Yet if their feelings for each other were real, wouldn't they be able to withstand a small break? At last the line connected, and with trepidation she opened her email. First was a message from Rebecca, which she skipped because the next return address was whitewaterworks.com! Quickly she opened it, almost afraid to read.

Dear Maggie:

What a surprise to go online and find that you had sent me an email! I don't check my email every day, but I sure will from now on. You have no idea how good it is to feel a connection with you again. I've missed you so much, my Maggie! When I saw you at the hotel restaurant on Thursday, it was all I could do to remain in my seat and keep my conversation focused at our table. You looked so beautiful, and I must admit I felt some furious jolts of jealousy seeing you there with Colin Byers. Yet all the time, I kept telling myself you were only there on business—what else could it be? But Barbara seemed set on thinking that you and Colin were Pine Mountain's hottest new couple. And, of course, what could I say without revealing everything? But when I got your email, I knew I'd been right to believe the best in you. I suppose the heart can be a fickle thing when it comes to hurt and love. And I must admit to my weakness in that area when Barbara carried on about you two. I felt the bitter taste of some serious hurt. And I didn't like it, not at all! But I realize that's the risk of loving someone—a person could get hurt. And, as you may already suspect, I was hurt once before. It was a long time ago, and I'll tell you all about it someday. But since that time, I suppose I've kept my heart locked up safe and sound. That is, until you arrived in town. Well, it's very late, my dear one. But I hope to continue this conversation with you later. And hopefully, it won't be long until we can be more open with our relationship. I do think Leah is growing more confident all the time, but I must admit, I sense troubles with her whenever I bring up your name. I think it has something to do with her mother, but I can't be sure. In the meantime, know that my feelings for you are as strong (no, stronger!) than ever.

Love,

Jed

Maggie felt tears of happiness in her eyes, and immediately began her answer.

Dear Jed,

Thank you for your wonderful email letter. It means so much to me. I have missed you desperately. Even tonight I worried that this little "break" might mess up something between us permanently. But now I feel certain that it won't. I wish this thing with Leah could be over, but I do understand, and I know she needs more time. Honestly, I'm willing to wait as long as it takes. I think if we can just keep in touch (even if it's only through email) I'll do much better. I guess I must be pretty insecure at heart, for it's easy for me to think the worst sometimes. I'm sorry, but it's true. Maybe you can relate, because what you said about loving and being hurt makes a lot of sense. I feel like I'm laying my heart right out on the line and giving someone (you) the power to really make me feel bad (not that I think you will), but just because I feel vulnerable. I really want to hear more about what happened to you, Jed, what it was that made you lock up your heart. And forgive me for this, but I guess I 'm glad you did because that meant that I got to be the one to see it being unlocked. Oh, I could go on and on, but I'm just totally exhausted—a long and tiring weekend. So until we "chat" again.

Love,

Maggie

Next she opened Rebecca's message and quickly read, her eyes almost refusing to stay open until she reached the end.

Hey MC:

No, I gave up calling men back in junior high school. And, no, it has nothing to do with not being liberated. I just enjoy being pursued, and if other women wish to call their men, it's fine by me. Now, tell me, how did it go with this Colin Byers? Yes, I do know the name. He's quite rich, but according to my sources, somewhat unstable. (And between you and me, he may have some pending lawsuits…) I strongly suggest you stay away from this one! And what's the deal about Jed "putting your relationship with him on hold"? I don't get that. If your mystery man is serious about this relationship, then what's the problem? Maybe he's one of those guys who are deathly afraid of certain "C" word—commitment. I've known a few of them in my time. Watch out, Mag, you could be wasting your time on him. I laughed out loud when I read your matchmaking thoughts about me and little brother Barry. Although, I must admit I've always thought he was very sweet and cute. Can't believe some smart girl hasn't grabbed that one up yet, but I can't imagine that he and I would find much in common either—and we live a lifetime apart. Just the same, I'm really looking forward to sharing some good times and laughs with you guys at Christmas. Can't wait to catch up. Hey, you got any snow there yet? I better not be packing my skis for nothing! See you in a couple weeks.

RB

Sixteen

Maggie asked Gavin not to come into the office until she had had a chance to inform Clyde of her plan to hire his nephew. Then she'd call Gavin when the coast was clear. But to her dismay, even after several minutes of persuasive pleading, Clyde remained stubborn and resistant to the idea.

"It's one thing for Gavin to come out here and apologize," he declared. "But I don't know why he thinks we should give him a job."

"As I said, it was *my* idea, Clyde. And you know as well as anyone that we really need someone to sell ad space, not to mention help with a dozen other little odd jobs that have gone undone around here on a regular basis." She glanced at an overflowing trash can sitting right next to the door.

"I'll get to that," he growled. "Do you seriously think Gavin would lower himself to take out the trash around here?"

"I think he should have a chance to try."

"He's had chances!"

She folded her arms and glared at him. "Clyde, you told me when you first hired me that running this newspaper is

177

my responsibility. Does that or does that not mean I may hire whomever I please?"

Clyde looked at the floor, then grumbled without answering. That's when she knew she had him.

"I say we give him a chance." Then she grinned slyly. "Besides, it's not like we have to pay him in advance, you know. If he doesn't work out, the least we'll get is a little free labor—that should make you happy. And if we're not satisfied with his work, we'll just send him packing, okay?"

"You ever hear that story about the camel who sticks his nose in the tent to get warm? Before you know it, the whole durned animal is inside the tent and there's not room for you!"

She waved her hand at him. "Don't you worry, I'll take full responsibility for Gavin. If it doesn't work out, you can blame it all on me."

He made a noise that sounded like "hrumph," and then shook his head. "You can be mighty stubborn when you set your mind to something, young lady."

"Isn't that why you hired me?" She playfully poked him in the chest and saw a faint twinkle in his eye.

"Yeah, and I suppose it's a good thing too because I heard we've got us a big battle coming up with those development boys. I never did hear the whole story of how your little visit went with Mr. Big Bucks."

She told him all about Desert Winds and her disappointing findings there. "I've got my story and photos all ready for this week's paper, but I honestly wish I could've come back with better news."

He rubbed his hands together. "Well, let's give 'em what for, Maggie. I'm ready for a good fight."

She sighed. "I'm sure we'll get one after this week's paper comes out."

He chuckled. "Yep, that's what this business is all about."

"You know, with your love of controversy, you should've run a big-city newspaper, Clyde."

He considered this, then he shook his head. "Nope, then I would've missed out on a whole lot of good fishing and hunting. The way I see it, I got me the very best of both worlds."

Back in her office, Maggie called Gavin and told him to report for work. They agreed that office space might be unnecessary to start with as selling ads could be done by phone or by visiting the businesses. For now he would use the mobile phone and keep track of his mileage, and perhaps if things went well, they'd eventually set up an office for him. Besides, Maggie figured this arrangement would keep Gavin out of Clyde's hair for the time being. Gavin told her that he'd already called a car dealership in Byron that was interested in helping him to trade down in vehicles. He hoped to get a fair amount of cash for his big sports utility vehicle and still afford a small economy car. "I'm willing to do whatever it takes to make it here," he assured her. "I want you to know I'll begin looking for a place to rent in town as soon as possible."

"It sounds as though you're off to a good start. Come in sometime this afternoon, and Abigail will get you set up with everything you'll need."

∽

Just as Maggie was winding down for the day, Jed stopped by her office. She tried to conceal her pleasure as she closed the door behind him. Inviting him to sit, she admired his squared shoulders and straight posture. He wore a soft suede vest, and she tried to remember if it was the same one he'd had on the first time she'd seen him last spring. She studied his even features as she sat back down behind her desk. Perhaps after her last email message he had decided to end their little "break." Then she noticed that his expression seemed different today. Something seemed to be troubling him. Whatever it was, she felt ready to face it. She smiled hopefully and leaned across her desk in anticipation.

"How are you doing?" she asked finally.

"I'm okay, I guess." He pressed his lips together as if considering how to begin his next sentence. "How are *you* doing?" The way he spoke the words seemed to imply he was inquiring about more than just her health and well-being, but she wasn't sure how best to answer.

"Oh, I don't know..." She looked to him for some sort of clue. "Did you get my email last night?" She smiled again.

He shook his head. "No, I haven't even turned on my computer today. Look, something's really bugging me right now. I guess I need to ask you what you are doing."

Now she felt thoroughly confused. "What do you mean?"

He stood now, and began to pace in front of her desk. "I'm getting kind of confused here, Maggie. I mean, I'm trying to believe the best in you. And even when I saw you having dinner with Colin Byers, I kept telling myself to take it easy, that it was nothing more than business. And then I got that email from you and felt like everything was okay." He stopped pacing and looked at her. "Did you get *my* email?"

"Yes! And it was so—"

"I don't really want to talk about that right now." He sighed deeply and then went on. "Anyway, the next thing I know, Leah is telling me how you've flown off with Colin Byers, in his private jet for a weekend down in Vegas—"

"Now, wait a minute—" She rose from her chair.

"Please, Maggie, let me finish. This isn't easy for me to say. First all this stuff with Colin Byers, and now I hear that Gavin Barnes has come to live with you. Will you please tell me what is going on?"

She blinked in surprise. "Hold on a minute, Jed. You had better get your facts straight before you come in here and start making accusations."

"That's why I came. I want to hear the facts."

She felt flustered, not even sure where to begin. "Did Leah tell you all this?"

"Not everything. I saw you with my own eyes at the hotel, remember?"

"Yes. But you knew it was only business—"

"That's what I told myself, and it wasn't easy with Barbara carrying on about how great you two looked together—"

"But Jed, you know—"

He held up his hands as if to stop her words. "Look, I really didn't come in here to tell you how to live. And maybe I'm butting in right now, but I really thought...we had something..." She heard the break in his voice, but before she could say a word, he continued, this time with a stony expression and steel in his words. "But I have to say, as Leah's father, that I think it's completely unacceptable for you to invite a strange man to come live in your home while she's there. I'm sure you know that all this has been very upsetting to her."

Maggie felt as if she'd been slapped, and all of her defenses sprang into action. "But I talked to Leah about it just last night, and she said it was fine. Besides, Gavin has really changed, Jed, you should talk to him. And not only that, but my mother's there most of the time, and Spencer too. I don't see how it would be much different if we were running a bed-and-breakfast..." Her voice faltered and she knew by his flat expression that her reasoning was lost on him. Was this jealousy? Or hurt? Or simply an overly protective father trying to shield his daughter? Whatever it was, it felt narrow-minded and unfair.

"It's just not right, Maggie." His features softened a little now. "Can't you see that? Leah feels really uncomfortable there now."

She was too irritated to answer rationally. "Well, what do you suggest, Jed? Should I just throw Gavin out onto the street?"

"If Michael wasn't staying out at my place, I'd suggest that Leah come and live out there, but you know how small it is. I only have two bedrooms."

"Well, maybe you'd like to trade," she said sarcastically, his words of accusation still stinging. "Why not have Michael come stay at my house? Then Leah could go live with you."

"You know, that's not such a bad idea. I think it might work."

Maggie sank into her chair and stared at him with unbelieving eyes. Who *was* this man? And how had she ever supposed that he loved her? Or she him? "Fine," she said in a subdued voice, looking down at her desk. "Whatever makes Leah happy."

"I'm not trying to placate her, Maggie. I'm just trying to be a good dad."

She felt tears burning in her eyes, and she was determined not to let him see how much his words had wounded her. His choice seemed clear; Leah was more important. It's understandable, she thought hopelessly. After all, if she had to choose between Spencer and Jed, there would be no contest. But why did they have to choose at all?

For a few moments neither one of them spoke. She couldn't bring herself to look into his eyes. "If that's all settled, I have work to do," she said in gruff voice, sticking out her chin and pretending to focus on the papers before her. She waited until she heard the door close quietly behind him before she allowed the tears to flow freely.

She called home to tell them she'd be working late tonight. As usual, her mother was understanding, glad to start dinner and generally hold down the fort. By the time Maggie got home, Michael was already there, situated in Leah's old room. She learned that Jed had brought him over after work, and then he'd helped Leah pack up her things and had taken her home with him.

"It all happened so quickly," explained Audrey. "But Leah seemed determined to leave tonight. I suppose she's just eager to live with her dad—maybe it will feel more like her own home."

Maggie shrugged. "I thought she felt at home here."

"Well, there's nothing quite like your own kin," said Audrey, giving her daughter a warm squeeze. "I wouldn't give it a second thought, honey."

"Yeah, it's not like we still don't have a pretty full house."

"I'm wondering if you're starting to run a boardinghouse after all," said Audrey wryly as she led Maggie into the kitchen. "Look, I saved some of my special vegetable beef soup for you. I'll bet you're hungry."

"I guess so." She dumped her briefcase onto the kitchen table and sighed loudly.

"Is there something else going on here that I should be aware of? I couldn't help but notice that Jed seemed a little grim when he was making the switch tonight. And he said the two of them probably wouldn't be able to make it to dinner tomorrow. He said he's got a lot to do to get ready for that furniture show."

She suddenly felt very weary. "Well, I suppose we can still have Barbara over anyway, if you'd like."

"Sure, why not? You know, I met her at church on Sunday while you were in Nevada. She seems quite nice."

Maggie took her soup and bread to the library and sat down in front of what was left of the fire. "Did Gavin and Michael eat dinner with you and Spencer?"

Audrey nodded. "Yes, me and the boys. It was actually kind of fun. You know, I think I might enjoy running a boardinghouse, or bed-and-breakfast, or whatever you want to call it."

Maggie smiled. Maybe it was the soup, but she was feeling a little better. "You know you'd be great at it, Mom. By the way, this soup is really good. I'm so glad you're around to help out. I really appreciate it."

Audrey beamed in surprise. "Well, I must admit, it's nice to be needed."

"Where's everybody else?"

"Spence and Daniel hobbled out to the barn to make music. They weren't too happy to see Leah leave. Looks like they're back to being a duet again." She glanced up at the clock. "Actually, Daniel's grandpa should be picking him up any minute now. I'm not sure what Michael's up to. Maybe unpacking, although he only had one bag."

"I hope he doesn't feel like Jed threw him out."

"No, not at all. He seemed happy to be here. And he seemed to hit it off with Gavin too."

"What's Gavin up to?"

"He said he had some work to do upstairs, but that was after he helped me in the kitchen. You know, after all I'd heard about Gavin Barnes, I never expected that he'd be such a nice person."

"He really seems to have changed."

"Excuse me." Michael poked his head in the doorway. "Oh, I am sorry. I did not know you were eating."

"No. It's okay. I'm just finishing up. Come in and sit down, Michael. I haven't had a chance to talk to you for a while, and I've been wondering how you are doing. Are you staying warm enough these days?"

He smiled. "I am finally getting adjusted." Then his dark eyes registered concern. "But I am worried that I may have mixed things up for you, Maggie. Is everything all right? Jed said that Leah must come stay with him and that I must stay here. Is that what you want too?"

Maggie nodded. "Sure, I'm happy to have you come stay with us, Michael." She wondered how to explain this complicated scenario, and finally decided just to tell it like it was. "You see, Jed was worried about Leah's welfare because I invited Gavin to stay here at my house. I guess I never considered that it could present a problem. I felt sorry that Gavin had no place to stay and...and I think you'll understand this, Michael, because it's what you said about how when we do things for people who are in need, we're doing them for Jesus. Well, it just seemed right to offer Gavin a place to stay until he's able to get a place of his own. Does that make any sense?" She knew she was probably telling him way too much, but he was such a good listener, so easy to talk to, and before she finished his eyes lit with understanding.

"I think you have done exactly the right thing, Maggie. Already Gavin has told me about how much of his life has been wasted. And he told me about how he is changing. You have helped him. That is a very good thing."

She smiled weakly. "Really? You think so?"

He nodded with enthusiasm. "Yes! The Bible says that when we give someone help, or food, or a place to sleep, or any other kindness, it is like we are giving it to Jesus. That is a very good thing."

She sighed. "Yes. That's what I thought too. I'm just sorry that the whole thing upset Leah. But I'm glad you get to stay with us, Michael. I hope you'll make yourself at home."

Michael's words were a real comfort, and yet she still felt sadly deflated as she prepared for bed. She checked her email, only to confirm her certainty that Jed hadn't answered her latest heartfelt message—oh, how she wished she could retrieve it back from cyberspace! She couldn't even remember exactly what she'd written, she'd been so tired at the time. Perhaps after what happened today, he wouldn't be checking his email so regularly anymore.

That whole episode with him in her office had shaken her badly. She knew her reactions had been strong and probably as harmful as his, but then what could he expect? She wondered again if perhaps he simply wasn't the man she'd thought he was. Rebecca had insinuated as much in her last email message. Or perhaps Jed didn't actually love her, not the way she loved him. Maybe it was all for the best to find these things out now before their relationship progressed, or digressed, any further. On the other hand, perhaps this was all just a great, big misunderstanding; a problem that could be resolved with some serious effort from both of them. Maybe she should just give the whole thing some time to cool down and sort itself out. She tried to take comfort in Shakespeare's words, "The course of true love never did run smooth." Besides, she chided herself, didn't she have enough on her plate right now? Here she was running the paper *and* what suddenly appeared to be a boarding house for homeless men. Not to mention she had guests coming for Christmas. She looked at the days of December left on her calendar and actually gasped. Why, she hadn't even taken the time to do her Christmas shopping yet!

❧

Barbara Harris came to dinner the following night, and while Leah and Jed were missed, the others still enjoyed a pleasant evening. It was plain to see that Barbara was growing quite fond of young Michael. She even mentioned how she saw a lot of her Steven in him, jokingly saying that she just might adopt him as her own son.

"I was so impressed with Michael's sermon on Sunday," she continued as they ate their dessert. "I think he has a rare gift; I, for one, have never been quite so touched by a church service before."

Michael smiled, then spoke with sincere humility. "If you were touched, Mrs. Harris, it was by the hand of God, not my feeble words."

"Well, while I've never considered myself to be much of a God-fearing person, I do think that God must be speaking through you somehow," she said with conviction. "Tell me, what *are* your long-term plans, Michael? How long do you think you'll stay in Pine Mountain?"

"Until God tells me to go somewhere else. Or," he laughed, "until there are no more unbelievers left to preach the good news to."

Gavin had been very quiet during all this talk of religion, but finally he spoke up. "I've never been one to think much about God, one way or another," he admitted. "That is, until I decided to quit drinking. In my rehab program, they told us to look to a higher being for help. I thought it was just a big gimmick at first, but then I wasn't having any real success on my own either. So I finally asked God to help me, and

I can't even explain what happened, but it was amazing, and *that's* when things really began to change for me."

"So do you believe in God now?" asked Michael, his eyes glowing with excitement.

"I think so." Gavin seemed a little uneasy. "But I don't really know what to do about it. I mean, is that all I need to do? Just believe in God and then go about my business trying to live right and be good and everything?"

Michael smiled. "That is just the beginning, my brother. If you want to talk to me about the next steps, I would be most happy to share what I know with you."

"I might just take you up on that."

"Good," said Michael.

"Did you know that Michael prayed for snow," said Spencer suddenly, "and the next day it snowed six inches!"

"Really?" exclaimed Barbara.

Gavin laughed. "Maybe he'd better pray again. From what I'm hearing already, the business community could really use it."

"Maggie," said Barbara as if suddenly remembering something, "I read your newspaper from cover to cover today. It was very nicely done, I might add. There's quite a lot going on in Pine Mountain these days." Then she glanced uncomfortably at Michael. "But that story about the Ebbert family was rather frightening, don't you think? Do you suppose they're very dangerous?"

"I don't know. It's hard to understand those kind of people."

"I read the story about Randy Ebbert too," said Michael gently. "And I have made him number one on my prayer list. But you must know that there are people like him everywhere. There will always be those who hate others because they are different. It will never stop until they learn to think differently themselves." His voice grew dramatic. "For instance, in my village, there was a group of men who hated us because we were Christian. Certainly our skin was the same color as theirs, but their hate became like a big wall between us. But in time, we learned how to break down that wall."

"How?" asked Maggie.

"With love." He smiled. "Instead of getting angry or demanding retribution for the mean things they would do, we did what Jesus said to do. We chose to love our enemies. We prayed for those men who tried to destroy us. And, in time, every single one of them became believers. All, except for one. Bilami—he was a very angry man. He finally gave up and moved from the island to live in another village, but we sadly learned that he died within that very same year."

"That's a cool story," said Spencer. "I don't know why you couldn't be the preacher at church every Sunday."

Michael laughed. "Thank you, but I do not wish to take the pulpit away from any of your leaders. I am content to simply do whatever God has for me to do. I know I have come here for God's purpose, and that is enough for me."

"But what if part of that purpose is to lead a church?" suggested Barbara.

Michael folded his hands in his lap. "Then God will have to show that to me."

Seventeen

Audrey tried to talk Maggie into taking Thursday morning off to do some Christmas shopping in Byron with her. "Look, honey, you gave up your whole weekend last week for work, and you work half your evenings. You know what they say about all work and no play. Christmas shopping is the least you can do for yourself." Audrey was determined to win this argument. "Come on, Maggie, you need to get out and relax a little. Have some fun. I'll even take you to lunch at that new restaurant Elizabeth Rodgers has been raving about."

"Okay," said Maggie finally, throwing her hands up in surrender. "You win, Mom. Actually, it does sound wonderful. Besides, I'm expecting to be lambasted by TS Development about my article today, and I'm sure not looking forward to that."

"So, why not put off the inevitable and have a good time?"

And that's just what they did. Audrey was familiar with Byron, and in just a few hours they managed to hit all the best shopping spots. At their last stop, a Northwest gift shop, Maggie discovered a beautiful collection of inlaid wood pocketknives she felt certain Jed would appreciate. She selected her favorite and bought it.

"Who's that for?" asked Audrey as the woman wrapped it up.

Maggie shrugged, unwilling to admit that it was for Jed in light of their recent disagreement. "Oh, I don't know. We'll see…"

Her mother nodded knowingly. "It's always good to have a few spare gifts on hand. Did you see the handmade sweater I got for Barry?"

They compared their purchases at lunch. Elizabeth had been right on target about the restaurant. Situated in a beautifully restored Craftsman house, it was set up like an old-fashioned tearoom with antique tables and chairs on hardwood floors. And fresh flowers, white linen, and delicate china graced each table. The restaurant was renowned for its delectable deserts, but its menu also included light lunches—perfect for shoppers.

"Have you talked to Jed lately?" asked Audrey as they studied the carefully handwritten menus.

Maggie knew it was time to tell her mother exactly what the status of their relationship was. To her surprise, it was almost a relief to relate the whole miserable story of how he'd recently confronted her about Gavin staying at her house.

"It sounds as if he's jealous," commented Audrey as she sipped her tea.

Maggie shook her head sadly. "Maybe. But I think he's mostly just concerned about Leah's welfare."

"I don't know. It seems to me he may have been hurt more deeply than that." Audrey looked intently at Maggie. "Now, honey, don't take this wrong, but sometimes I'm not sure that you understand where Jed is coming from."

"And you do?"

Her mother smiled. "Let's just say I see him from a different angle. For instance, do you consider Jed to be insecure?"

"Not really."

"See, there." Audrey sounded as if she'd made her point. "I happen to think that he is. In fact, I suspect that somewhere along the line, that man has had his heart broken—and maybe badly."

Maggie remembered his words in the email. "Actually, you're probably right about that. How did you know?"

"It was just a guess, but I'd be willing to lay odds on it."

Maggie studied her mother curiously. "I only learned of this recently, and I still don't have any details. Are you telling me that you suspected this all along?"

She nodded smugly.

"But what makes you think so?"

"Well, think about it, Maggie. He's extremely attractive, very intelligent, and basically a really good person. Why do you suppose he's never married?"

"Because the right woman never came along?" suggested Maggie weakly.

"What makes you so sure? Have you ever asked him?"

"Well, no...I guess I just assumed that if anyone did the heartbreaking, it would've been Jed. I mean, take Kate, for instance. I think *he* broke her heart."

Audrey waved her hand in dismissal. "I think Kate was only slightly wounded, and Buckie's done a good job of fixing her up."

"I suppose you could be right. But what does that have to do with anything?"

"Well, it stands to reason that if Jed had his heart broken once, he could be somewhat insecure when it comes to a relationship where his heart is deeply involved again. Like with you."

Maggie nodded hopefully. "He almost said as much."

"And he may need some extra encouragement and bolstering to take some risks in this area. And you need to remember that your independence might send a wrong message. He could be assuming that you aren't as interested as he is. And then add to that how there seem to be a lot of other men around you, and the whole thing might make him feel like he can't trust you. And that might be why he comes across the way he does."

"I...I hadn't really looked at it like that."

"Well, try to put yourself in his shoes. How would you feel if he'd flown off for a weekend with an attractive female client? And then taken in another attractive female boarder?"

Maggie's eyes opened wide. "Wow, I see what you mean!"

"So, you just might want to cut the poor man a little slack."

"I suppose so. But what about this whole thing about putting our relationship on hold?"

"You must know that Jed only did that out of concern for Leah, not because he loved you any less."

"But how can you be so sure, Mom?"

"I don't know. Just a gut feeling, I guess."

"Well, you've certainly given me some things to think about." Maggie smiled hopefully.

For the remainder of lunch, they made lists and plans for Christmas and ways to entertain their guests. Thankfully, Audrey was more than happy to carry much of the load of the preparations. "You know I love this sort of thing, Maggie."

"Well, I don't know what I'd do without you, Mom."

"Until I get that library off the ground, it's nice to have things to keep me busy. Oh, by the way, do you want me to take Spencer in to get his cast off tomorrow?"

"Is it time for that already? Yes, I'd appreciate that. Poor Spence has been complaining about his foot itching like crazy lately. I'll bet he's already waxing his snowboard. Now, if only we could get another good dump of snow! I've promised both Barry and Rebecca that we'll spend a day or two on the slopes."

"And I'd love to see a white Christmas."

"Well, there's still plenty of time." She glanced at her watch. "Speaking of which, I had better get back to the old grindstone."

"But aren't you glad you decided to take some time off and come shopping with me?" asked Audrey as they finished their desserts of creme caramel custard.

"Yes, it was really fun. We should do this more often, Mom."

"Now you can go back to face the inevitable."

Maggie rolled her eyes. "Oh, boy, I can hardly wait."

～

She had barely stepped into the reception area when the onslaught began. "Greg Snider's been by twice already," reported Abigail with exasperation, "and he's acting like he owns the world too!"

"Randy Ebbert stopped in as well," added Scott as he held up a flyer. "He delivered an official notice announcing the birth of his new newspaper, the *Conservative Code.* Don't know what the code stands for. Maybe it's a secret handshake for members only or a special swastika ring."

"And Colin Byers asked that you return his call as soon as you step in," said Abigail with a deep sigh. "He's called several times already, and for the *gentleman* that you described, he sounded slightly rude—if you ask me."

Maggie ran a hand through her hair. "I'll bet he's already read the *Pine Cone* from our website. Oh man, I can hardly wait for *that* conversation. My guess is he'll bring in one of his high-powered attorneys to scare us a little."

"Oh, I almost forgot," called Scott just as she was trying to slip into her office.

"Now what?"

"Actually, this has nothing to do with business," he began somewhat apologetically. "And it's probably the very worst timing on my part, but I promised. You see, Chloe wants to know if we can get married in your house."

Maggie stared at him speechlessly.

He laughed self-consciously. "I told her I thought you had your hands full right now, but she was so upset last night that I promised her I'd ask you the moment I saw you today. Feel free to say no, Maggie. I know it's a lot to ask anyone. I mean it's crazy, really."

"But why? I thought you were going to get the hotel or the church. And it's such late notice—don't you have your invitations printed already?"

"We thought we could get the hotel, but we hadn't nailed it. Then we found out last night that Brian and Cindy had already invited a bunch of their Seattle friends for a big New Year's Eve bash. It's their way to drum up some business, I guess, especially since this year's ski season is looking so gloomy right now. And then, of course, Jed's shutting down the church—"

"*Shutting down the church?*" She was incredulous. "I hadn't heard that."

"Yeah, it kind of surprised me too. But that's what he told my dad yesterday. It's always been pretty inconvenient for folks to get up there, especially during the winter months, and as a result they end up missing a lot of Sundays because of the snow and ice and bad weather. Anyway, he told Dad he thinks it's time to turn the building back into a house like he'd always planned to. I guess now that his daughter's living there he needs more room. Can't say that I blame him either. Man, what I'd give to have a place like that for Chloe and me."

She didn't know what to say. "Well, let me talk to my mom about the wedding idea, Scott. I would really need her cooperation to do something like this."

"Really?" His dark eyes grew wide. "You mean you'd consider doing this?"

"Of course I would." She couldn't help smiling at him. Maybe a wedding would brighten up some of the gloom that seemed to be descending upon her. "My mom's going all out to make things really special for the Christmas holidays—and by New Year's Eve, well, our guests will all be gone anyway, so we might as well make the most of all her cleaning and sprucing up, right? That is, if she's not totally exhausted by then."

"Mom and Sierra and Chloe will take care of all the food and decorations. Audrey won't have to lift a finger, I promise. And you know how Mom is such an organizer and all. And we'll only invite a small group of friends and family; Chloe and I want a very casual and intimate wedding. We're not even sure if her folks are coming yet—they're so put off about the whole thing. Chloe says they think if they don't cooperate with us on the wedding that they can keep us from getting married, but when they see how serious we are, they'll probably come."

"For Chloe's sake, I hope she's right. Okay, I'll talk with my mom tonight and get back to you as soon as I know something for sure."

"Thanks, Maggie. It means a lot that you're even considering this. We've thought about going to Reno—you know, one of those cheesy little chapels where you get married by an Elvis look-alike or something."

"Don't do that yet! And honestly, I feel honored that you asked, Scott. It sounds like it would be a whole lot of fun, but I'd like to get my mom fully on board first."

The phone rang, and Abigail nodded to Maggie as she spoke into the receiver. "Oh, hello again, Mr. Byers. I'm not sure if she's in yet. Hold on and I'll check."

"I'll take it in my office," Maggie answered firmly. "Just give me a few seconds to brace myself."

"Don't let him get to you," encouraged Scott. "All you did was print the truth. If he can't handle it, that's his problem."

She sat down, took a deep breath, and then picked up the receiver. "This is Maggie."

"So this is the way you repay me for all my cooperation?"

"I told you from the beginning, Colin, I wanted to report truthfully. And that's exactly what I did—"

"What I want to know is, where did you get all your so-called information from? Though I think I have a pretty good idea."

"My sources, as always, remain confidential. And if you read the article carefully, I'm sure you'll find that I didn't print a single word that was untrue."

"I wouldn't be so sure. Our lawyers are already looking into it very carefully."

"I was sure they would. Did you notice how I praised your club facilities and your lovely golf course—"

"If you think saying that, and I quote, 'the lush greens of the golf course are a sharp contrast to the thirsty residents with no running water due to a dried-up well' is praise, you're out of your mind. And who told you our well had run dry?"

"I happened to overhear a chagrined homeowner trying to get a room in the hotel so his wife could take a shower. And they were refused a room, although I later learned there were plenty available. I didn't even print that in my article. Admit it, Colin, all is not well in Desert Winds."

"You are a mean and spiteful woman, Ms. Carpenter. Believe me, you haven't heard the end of this yet."

She sighed. "I didn't figure I had. Take care, Mr. Byers." Then she hung up. That mean and spiteful part stung just a little. Was printing the truth about how a poorly done development could adversely affect an entire community mean and spiteful? She didn't think so.

"Excuse me," said Abigail as she cracked open the door. "I saw you were off the line with Mr. Byers, and while you were still fuming over him, I thought you might as well take a look at these." She held out several letters.

"Let's get it over with," said Maggie. "Are they pretty bad?"

Abigail frowned deeply. "It appears that some business owners think that bad development is better than no development at all—especially when the weather isn't cooperating." She glanced out the window at the clear blue sky. "Anyway, here's a real cranky one from Cal—no big surprise there. That man has absolutely no taste anyway. And then here's one from the hardware store owner. Of course, he'd support something like this—he stands to profit from all those irate homeowners beating a regular path to his door for all their household repair items."

Maggie chuckled over this as she fingered through the small stack. "Good point. It looks like we've got all the contractors ganging up on us about this too. I'm sure they think with all the potential construction going on that they'll get a piece of the pie. But the way Colin Byers goes in for cheap and sometimes illegal labor, I'm afraid they're barking up the wrong tree." She made a note. "The next article should probably address the whole labor issue more directly. That might make the contractors think twice about supporting a venture like this."

"Good thinking," agreed Abigail. "A lot of these guys are union too. I'm surprised they haven't considered these things already."

"Well, who knows what kind of promises Greg and Rick are making right now."

"Did you hear Greg has officially quit his postmaster job?"

"No. I hope he's not sorry about that later."

"I also heard he's already flattened and removed all the old buildings from his folks' property. Everything's in the process of being surveyed for the streets and utilities. And I heard if the weather holds out, they might start working on it right away."

Maggie groaned. "There seems to be no real way of stopping them, but at least we can put up a good fight. Say, Abigail, would you give Mr. Westerly's niece, Jeanette, a call?" She wrote down the number and handed it to her. "Find out if she's learned anything from their lawyer yet, even though I assume that because we haven't heard from her they haven't uncovered anything to make a difference."

Suddenly Abigail sat up straight in her chair. "You know, a letter came today. It looked like some sort of government thing, but not that interesting compared to all this local riffraff. I figured it could wait until later, but now I'm wondering..."

Maggie followed her out to the reception area, and then waited while Abigail slit it open. She smiled as she handed it over. "It's from the EPA, and I'm guessing they read your wetland issues article that I sent."

Maggie quickly skimmed the letter and then let out a whoop. "They're sending an investigative team as soon as they can mobilize!"

"Wonderful!"

"What is it?" asked Scott.

Just as Maggie was about to read the letter out loud, Gavin stepped in. "You better listen to this too, Gavin." Then she read about how much their organization appreciated thoughtful journalism like hers that brought these issues to light, and how it took everyone working together to preserve important lands that were becoming more and more rare and endangered.

"Way to go, Maggie," exclaimed Gavin. "You'll be pleased to hear that some of the local businesses are behind you a hundred percent in your stand against TS Development now that they read your latest investigative report. Not all of them, of course, but some. I actually sold some ad space today."

"Good for you!" Maggie patted him on the back.

"Thanks. By the way, I have an idea I'd like to discuss with you and my uncle. Do you think we could all meet for dinner tomorrow night at the hotel? My treat."

"Sure, if you think Clyde is free..."

"Or do you mean willing?" asked Gavin.

"Well, you know how he's been lately. Anyway, he's already left for the day, but if you like I can invite him first thing in the morning."

"It might help to get him there."

"Can I tell him what this pertains to?" She was wondering herself.

"Just tell him it's an idea that could help all of Pine Mountain."

She brightened. "Okay, he just might be interested in that."

Eighteen

*I*n the morning Maggie called Scott into her office. "I asked my mother what she thought about hosting your wedding on New Year's Eve," she began in a serious tone, her face somber as if to convey unfortunate news.

He nodded with understanding. "So, I suppose it was a little overwhelming for her?"

"Well, it's pretty last minute, you know."

"Yeah, I figured it was too much to expect of anybody. It was Chloe's idea, really. But I appreciate your thinking about it. I can understand Audrey's reservations—"

"Are you kidding? She's totally jazzed about the whole thing. My mother absolutely loves weddings—they're her favorite event on the entire earth. It's her Italian roots, I think. Anyway, she's slightly furious that you've put this whole thing off until the last minute, and she even suggested you wait until next New Year's Eve so we could go all out with a really big bash of a wedding. Then I told her about your Reno suggestion, and she threw a complete fit and demanded that we host the wedding at my house or else!"

Relief washed over his face. "I really hated the idea of trying to get hitched in Reno on New Year's Eve. I know Chloe's not that into her family or social functions right now, but I really do enjoy mine. And my little brother, Max, is coming home from the Air Force for the first time since he enlisted, and I was hoping this could be a really special time for everyone."

"It will be. Go ahead and let your mom and Chloe know, and tell them my mom will call them sometime today. She wants to have a wedding planning meeting tomorrow morning—and won't take no for an answer. And she also wanted to know if Chloe has a wedding gown yet."

By now, Abigail had stuck her head into Maggie's office and Maggie waved for her to come in. "Actually, I was wondering the very same thing too," said Abigail with a maternal sort of concern.

Scott nodded. "She's going to wear an old turn-of-the-century gown that was her great-grandmother's. I haven't seen it yet, but Chloe says it's absolutely gorgeous." He frowned doubtfully. "I just hope it doesn't fall to pieces before the night is over."

"Chloe's smart about these things," said Maggie. "I'm sure she knows exactly what she's doing."

"I was talking to a friend of mine with a greenhouse," said Abigail. "She has some lovely white tea roses that are budding right now, and should just be starting to open by then. They're very old-fashioned and sweet, and they would make a beautiful bouquet."

"Maybe you should call Chloe," suggested Maggie. "Or better yet, why don't you come to the meeting at my house tomorrow?"

Abigail grinned happily. "I know exactly how Audrey feels. I love weddings too!"

"I think Chloe's in good hands, Scott." Maggie turned on her computer. "And somehow you guys just might be able to pull this thing off."

During her noon hour, Maggie walked over to the fitness center with plans to work out and hopefully relieve some stress. Already this morning she'd been personally presented with a petition signed by many, though not all, of the local contractors demanding that the newspaper back down from its opposition to Pine Mountain Estates or lose their ads to another paper. Maggie wondered, were they thinking of the *Conservative Code?* If so, that would make Randy Ebbert awfully happy. Maybe he'd call up and thank her.

It was the first time she'd been in all week, and she was curious about Cherise's reaction to Greg quitting his postmaster job. Their marriage already seemed fairly unstable; adding more financial stress wouldn't help it any. But Cherise seemed happier and perkier than ever as she flitted around helping her customers. And the fitness center was busier than usual with nearly a dozen people all working out at the same time. Maggie actually had to wait several times for the various machines before she could complete her own workout.

Just after she finished a quick shower and was about to leave, Cherise came over to greet her. "Gosh, I've missed you, Maggie! Sorry I didn't get over to say hi to you sooner, but can you believe how busy it is here? This is fantastic!"

"Yes, I'm so glad for you. That special coupon you had in the paper last month must really be working."

"It is! The timing couldn't be better."

Maggie nodded as she took a sip from her water bottle. "Yes, I suppose with Greg quitting his regular job, you'll need to make a little more here."

"Oh, no, that has nothing to do with it." Cherise's blue eyes grew larger. "Didn't you hear the news?"

"What news?"

"Greg and I split up," she announced. Then lowering her voice to almost a whisper she continued, "I haven't officially told anyone just yet. Everyone thinks I'm remodeling the upstairs in order to expand the fitness center, but I've been living up there for the past week."

"Oh, Cherise. I'm so sorry. I didn't know it was that bad."

"It's okay, Maggie." She patted her arm soothingly. "I mean, sure, I cried my eyes out the first couple of days. But then I moved all my stuff upstairs and got everything all settled and it wasn't so bad. Right now I'm having a bathroom and kitchen installed and it's going to be really cool. My mom's helping me out with money for the remodeling, and in the meantime I just run down here to take a shower or whatever. Really, it's been kind of fun. To tell you the truth, I haven't been this happy in a long, long time."

"Well…" Maggie didn't know what to say. "I'm sure everything will work out."

"I know you think marriage is real important, and I do too. But Greg has always been on my case about something or other. According to him, I never do anything right, and it's not like I didn't try."

"I know you did."

"Now that I'm on my own, I just can't believe how free, and happy, I feel. I mean, I do miss him a little." She laughed. "But only a little. Hey, you want to come up and see my place?"

"Well, sure, but I can't stay too long. I need to get back to work pretty soon."

Cherise led her up a narrow stairway and into a large loftlike room where in one corner a carpenter was framing in a wall, and in another corner knelt Sam Galloway, busily working with some copper pipes.

"Hey, Sam," called out Maggie. "Looks like you're keeping busy."

"Hi, Maggie." Sam stood and smiled. "I'm trying to get Cherise all set so she doesn't have to keep running downstairs for water."

"And he's doing a great job too," said Cherise. "Sam's the best plumber."

"I know, he's had a hand in my house too." Maggie made a mental note to quiz Sam about labor union rules and how union members would feel about the way that Colin Byers developed his properties. "Don't let us keep you, Sam. Hey, by the way, we want Scott and Chloe to have their wedding at my house."

Sam let out a big sigh. "Rosa will be so relieved. I swear, it's been keeping her awake at night, even though I kept telling her everything would work out."

"Oh, that's so cool," said Cherise. "Your house would be a great spot for a wedding."

Maggie smiled. "I can just imagine a bride coming down our staircase." She didn't mention that the bride she used to imagine was none other than herself, with Jed waiting down below!

"Anyway, this is going to be the kitchen," said Cherise, returning their attention to the little tour. "I want to keep it sort of open to the rest of the room. The breakfast bar will go right here. And over there, where the carpenter's pounding, will be my bathroom."

"I love all these windows," exclaimed Maggie. "You can actually see the mountains from up here."

"I know, isn't it great?" Then she led Maggie over to where her bed was arranged, actually a futon, with a folding floor screen to separate it from the rest of the room. "That's my bedroom." She giggled. "Pretty campy, huh?" They went to another corner where a purple leather sofa was situated with a large painting of modern art hung behind it. An area carpet with splashes of very bold colors was laid diagonally across the pale wood floor, with several odd pieces of sixties-style furniture placed at various angles. Surprisingly, the overall effect was pleasant and interesting.

"Cherise, this is really fun," said Maggie. "It's very—well, it's very L.A."

Cherise made a happy squeal. "That's exactly what I was going for. Since you've actually lived in L.A., you must know what you're talking about. Greg would never in a million years let me do anything like this in our house. Everything there had to go with navy blue and look *traditional*." She said that word in a deep voice that suggested very boring. "For once in my life I just wanted to live in a space that was light and airy and just plain fun!"

"Without a doubt, you've managed to accomplish that. I really do like it."

Cherise looked intently into Maggie's face. "Do you think you'd ever come over here? Just to visit, I mean. You know, not to work out, but just for the fun of it?"

"Sure, why not? I'd like to do that."

Cherise smiled triumphantly. "See! Greg *never* really believed me, I mean, that you were my friend. Of course, I know we're really different. You're all intellectual and smart and stuff. And everyone thinks I'm this ditzy airhead. Greg always used to say they made blonde jokes up about me."

"That wasn't very nice. And it's not true. Look at you, Cherise, you run your own business, and it looks to me like you're doing a pretty good job of it too."

"Yeah. I guess I had better get back to my clients." She glanced at the workers. "These guys are supposed to be done up here sometime after Christmas. I want you to come back up then and see how it looks when it's all finished."

"You can count on it. In fact, I think we should give you a housewarming."

"Oh, that would be so fantastic."

"Just let me know when you're ready and we'll plan something."

⌒

Maggie decided to take a mid-afternoon break, as she planned to stay in town and work until the dinner hour. Somehow she'd managed to talk Clyde into joining her and Gavin at the hotel that evening. Probably it was just his curiosity getting the best of him, but she had to admit she was curious too. What sort of plan had Gavin conjured up that could help the whole town? Maybe, like Michael, he wanted to pray for snow. She smiled to herself as she walked toward the deli to meet Rosa for coffee. Michael and Gavin had spent much of the evening in her parlor last night discussing "spiritual matters" as Michael put it. She had overheard tidbits of their conversation while sitting in the library and trying to concentrate on outlining her novel—the novel she had planned to spend so much quiet time working on this winter. What quiet time? But what had amazed her most, as she listened to the two men, was Michael's ability to talk about God to just about anyone, and he did it so openly and with such ease. It was really a gift. Before turning in to bed, she had complimented him on this ability, and of course, as always, he gave the credit to God. Then she asked him what he thought about Jed's decision to discontinue the church services up in his beautiful building. "Jed told me that he has been thinking about this for some time," Michael had carefully explained. "And I agreed with him. Yes, his church building is very, very lovely, but it is too far away. A church should be located in the center of a village and be a place where people can come and go with ease. Jed's church building was too remote. And remember, it is only a building. The real church is made of people." Somehow, when put this way, she could see the sense in the decision. For such a young man, Michael was incredibly wise.

Rosa waved as she walked into the deli. "Grab a seat, Maggie, and I'll bring our coffee right over. I made you a special treat."

The deli was completely deserted. Probably not so unusual at this time of day, but dismaying just the same. Maggie knew that Rosa badly needed the business, especially with the holidays and Scott's wedding quickly approaching.

"Oh, that looks delicious," cooed Maggie as she eyed the still-steaming slice of the rich nutty dessert. "How did you know I adore pecan pie?"

"Audrey mentioned it this morning when she called to tell me about the wedding." Her brown eyes glowed with happiness. "Thank you so much, Maggie. You have no idea what this means to me."

Maggie smiled sympathetically at her friend. "Sam said you'd been pretty worried."

"Well, those kids had their hearts so set on getting married on New Year's Eve, and with Max coming home, it just seemed so perfect. But our house is so small..." She glanced around the empty room, and then lowered her voice anyway. "You see, Scott told me they're trying to keep everything in their relationship right—you know, like according to the Bible—and they decided a long engagement would be too tempting for them, if you know what I mean. But please don't repeat this to anyone. Scott only told me about this last week."

"That's so sweet. I'm glad we can help."

"Well, it's greatly appreciated. Chloe was in here at lunch, and she was so excited. She thinks you're the greatest. I'm sure they'll name their firstborn daughter for you."

Maggie laughed. "Goodness, I hope not. Margaret was a difficult name to have as a child. I wouldn't wish it on anyone."

"Are you going to meet with us tomorrow?"

"I wouldn't miss it. Have they decided who will officiate the ceremony?"

"Actually, Scott was thinking about asking Michael. He really respects that young man."

"What a wonderful idea," exclaimed Maggie. "But can Michael do it? I mean legally. Doesn't he have to be ordained or licensed?"

"Apparently, he's already taken care of that. By the way, did you know that Sunday will be our last day to gather at Jed's place for church?"

"I just heard about his decision, but I didn't know it was this Sunday."

Rosa eyed Maggie curiously. "How are things going with you two anyway? I've been trying not to be too nosy, but I haven't seen you two together for a while, and I've been a little concerned. Is everything okay?"

Maggie wondered how to explain it. "I don't know. You see, because of Leah, we decided to sort of cool things off for a while..."

"Because of Leah?"

"Jed was worried that she felt left out, you know, and he wants to be a good dad to her. Anyway, it almost seems like we may have cooled things off completely."

"Sierra told me that Leah had moved out with Jed, and I wondered what that was all about."

"Yeah, it was kind of sudden. Jed was worried about Gavin staying at my house. It seemed to be troubling Leah."

"Actually, I was pretty surprised about that too, Maggie. I thought maybe you were losing it altogether. But then Gavin stopped in here wanting to sell me some ad space, and I couldn't believe it was him. My goodness, he *has* changed! Sam said the exact same thing. Gavin seems to be working so hard for the paper. I was totally astounded."

"Yes, he's really trying. And he'll only be staying with me until he can find a place to rent in town. It's so wonderful that he and Michael have really hit it off. Though I'm sorry that Leah felt the need to leave, I'm really glad for Gavin to have this opportunity to get better acquainted with Michael."

"God really does work in mysterious ways, doesn't he?"

"I guess so, now that you mention it."

They chatted a while longer, getting caught up on all the latest news on both sides, then Maggie stood to leave. "Oh, one more thing," said Rosa suddenly. "A couple of guys were in here today—from Salem, they said. Apparently they're environmentalists here to check out the wetlands at Pine Mountain Estates." Her eyes twinkled. "I said to them, 'Oh, yes, my husband says you can see all kinds of birds and waterfowl out there, and that it's really quite special.'"

"You didn't?" Maggie grinned.

Rosa nodded smugly. "Yes, I did. And they seemed *quite* interested."

"Let me know if you hear anything else, okay?"

"You bet I will." Rosa adjusted her apron. "There's no doubt we need business in this town, and now more than ever, but we're not *that* desperate. I have no desire to see Pine Mountain selling its soul for a few pieces of silver."

"I know what you mean." She shook her head. "I'm just not sure if we can stop them."

"Well, maybe we can at least slow them down and make them think." Rosa wiped the table off. "And after the New Year, we need to schedule another business association meeting."

"Good idea. I had been meaning to get together with Kate to discuss some ideas, but everything has been so hectic lately."

Rosa rolled her eyes. "I don't know if I'd waste my breath on Kate or Buckie just now. I've heard them in here, going on about how this town needs to support TS Development. They're so worried about the Blue Moose that I'm afraid they've completely stepped over into the other camp."

Maggie frowned. "I guess I'm not surprised, although it's disappointing. If only people could be patient. Or if only it would snow!"

"I know," agreed Rosa. "I've been here since the early eighties and I've never seen a warm spell quite like this."

"And what a year for it too."

"But it could change any day," said Rosa with her ever-present optimism.

"Here's to change!"

Nineteen

*W*hile waiting to join Clyde and Gavin at the hotel, Maggie went online and began to write an email to Jed. It was just a simple note apologizing for her sharp words and suggesting they should perhaps talk things over. But when it came time to hit the "send" button, she just couldn't do it. Shouldn't Jed be the one to apologize to her? Perhaps these things were meant to be said in person. Whatever it was, she just couldn't send the message. Instead she hit the cancel button and the message immediately disappeared from her screen.

Then she immersed herself in her follow-up article about labor practices and what the town might expect in regard to hiring practices based upon Colin Byers' developments in the past. She completely lost track of time, and when she finally looked up at the clock on her desk, it was already a quarter past six. She quickly shut down her computer, locked up the office, and then began to jog the partial block to the hotel on foot. She had promised to be there at six sharp, and with some discomfort she imagined the two men sitting across from each other in stony silence. Clyde was probably glaring at his watch right now and grumbling about where on earth was she anyway. And what if Gavin grew so anxious that he actually broke down and ordered an alcoholic beverage? She increased her pace, glancing around her as she crossed the deserted street. The town looked so quaint and welcoming, all lit up with tiny white lights and Christmas decorations adorning shop windows. The old-fashioned lanterns glowed warmly. All that seemed to be missing was the snow—and visitors, of course. For the umpteenth time, she shot up a little prayer for some real winter weather and soon! Business matters aside, she thought snow would be a delight. Besides, she already had the tires to go with it!

Then just as she breathlessly reached the entrance of the hotel, she observed Leah and Jed only a couple steps ahead of her. Suddenly her heart began to pound furiously as she remembered the tone of her last conversation with him in her office the other day. Now she longed to say something—what was it she had written in that nonexistent email? There must be some way to smooth this whole silly thing over.

"Hello," she said weakly as she walked up the steps behind them, waiting as Jed opened the door for Leah.

"Maggie?" He turned in surprise, but for a moment, just a brief, split second, his eyes seemed pleased. Then it was gone, and she wondered if it had only been her imagination.

"How're you guys doing?" asked Maggie, hoping to sound cheerful.

"We're doing fine," said Leah casually. "How's it going with you?"

"Busy," she answered quickly as she walked through the door now held open by Jed. Their arms brushed and she felt certain, even through the thickness of her leather coat, that she had experienced tingles. She wondered if he possibly felt them as well. "Everything going okay out at Jed's?" she asked Leah, unwilling to look into his eyes.

"Yeah. It's so beautiful out there. Jed and Michael are leaving for the furniture show in Seattle tomorrow, so he offered to take me out for dinner tonight to thank me for holding the shop together while he's gone." She smiled up at him in undisguised admiration.

"Oh, that's right," remembered Maggie. "Michael mentioned that last night." With fresh resolve, she turned and forced herself to look directly into Jed's eyes. "I really hope you have a successful trip, Jed."

"Thanks, I appreciate it." The corners of his mouth curved ever so slightly. "Are you here by yourself?" he asked with what seemed concern.

She wondered what he'd say if she answered in the affirmative—oh, if only she were here by herself! Would he perhaps momentarily put aside all this back-burner business and invite her to join them? But she shook her head. "No, I'm here to meet with Gavin and Clyde." His eyes seemed to flash ever so slightly at the mention of Gavin's name, so she quickly added, "It's just a little business meeting. I think Gavin has some new ideas for the paper. And just getting him and Clyde together is no small thing." She forced a light laugh.

"Well, there's Gavin over there." He nodded across the room, his expression growing stony and cool. "We'll let you get to it then."

She turned to see Gavin seated at a table in the far corner of the room. But he was alone! Where in the world was Clyde? She walked quickly to the table, wondering what Jed thought of her now. Surely he didn't think she had lied and that she was meeting Gavin here alone or for anything besides business. Wouldn't he realize that if she wanted to meet Gavin alone, she could've easily done it in the privacy of her own home? "Where's Clyde?" she demanded sharply.

He looked up in surprise. "Evening to you too, Maggie. He just went to use the phone in the kitchen to call you. We were beginning to think you'd forgotten all about us."

"Oh." She sat down, slightly relieved. "Sorry I'm late. How's it going with Clyde anyway?" She glanced over to watch as Cindy now seated Jed and Leah in the opposite corner with Jed's back now facing her so he wouldn't be able to see when Clyde returned to sit down. Well, she'd just have to make a point of walking by Jed's table with Clyde at her side after they finished their meal. Why did this keep happening? She thought about what her mother had suggested about Jed's insecurity with relationships. Well, this certainly wouldn't help anything!

"There you are," said Clyde as he eased himself into the chair next to her. "Thought maybe you'd skipped out on us."

"I'm sorry, Clyde. I was working on an article and totally forgot the time."

"It's okay." A faint smile played upon his timeworn features. "Gavin and I have been having us a real interesting little chat."

Her brows raised with curiosity. Clyde sounded surprisingly congenial. "What's up?" she asked. Just then the waitress approached to take their orders, forcing Maggie to wait to hear what was going on between the two men.

"Why don't you tell her about your idea, Gavin," said Clyde as soon as the waitress got it all straight and left.

"Well, this whole darn thing with TS Development has really got me irked," began Gavin. "I've read all your articles in the back papers about it, and I've talked to various folks in town as I'm selling ad space to them. And I just kept wishing there was some way to put a stop to all their nonsense."

Clyde grinned and rubbed his hands together. "Come on, boy, now let's get to the good part."

"Anyway, as I just told Uncle Clyde," Gavin smiled across the table at his uncle, "I was out walking the dogs on your property the other day, just before dark. And as we were heading north, through the open meadow, it suddenly occurred to me that this wasn't *all* your property. I remembered how you'd mentioned one time that you only purchased twenty acres with the old homestead. Well, I figure that leaves about another three hundred acres still sitting to the north of you."

"That's a pretty close estimate," said Clyde. "I had the land divided by the county last spring in order to sell the old house as an enticement to get a certain L.A. reporter out here to run the *Pine Cone* for me."

"I didn't know you owned more acreage out there," said Maggie. "I just assumed that twenty acres was all the land that had been left. I knew that you'd sold a lot of timber land way back."

Clyde chuckled. "My parents used to own almost everything out there, clear into town. Like Arnold Westerly's folks, they came out when land was dirt cheap and they bought up all they could afford. Not a bad investment either."

"Anyway," continued Gavin in a businesslike manner. "I thought, why wouldn't *this* be a good location for a nice, well-developed community?"

"You mean to compete with Pine Mountain Estates?" said Maggie with the full realization of what this could mean slowly dawning on her. She looked to Clyde. "Is it even possible? Are you really interested in doing something like this with that property?"

He shrugged. "I'm not going to be around forever, Maggie. And while I'm still here, I'd like to do whatever I can to preserve our quality of life in Pine Mountain. I think a carefully planned development could be a real boon to our area. But not like the kind of cheap setup those development boys are proposing to do. They don't give a hoot over what happens to this town. And I wouldn't be surprised if they both don't just clear out of here as soon as they get their money in their pockets and that Byers fellow takes over."

Maggie nodded thoughtfully. "That same thought had occurred to me too."

"But there is one small concern," said Gavin. "And it involves you…"

She knew what he was hinting at. "You mean, would I mind having a few neighbors?"

"Gavin suggested this development could be designed in such a way as to keep your property somewhat protected and separate from the developed community. But there'd be no getting around things like increased traffic and that sort of thing. How do you feel about that, Maggie?"

She considered this as the waitress began setting their entrees before them. She'd certainly enjoyed her privacy out there, but sometimes it did feel slightly isolated. "You know, I've always lived in areas where I've had lots of neighbors, and sometimes I sort of miss that." She pressed her lips together. "I think if the development was done right, and the homes and everything were of high quality and not built too closely together, I'd probably like it."

Gavin sighed in relief. "I already told Uncle Clyde that I'm willing to do whatever it takes to get this ball rolling. But just so you'll know, I have no interest in profiting from this venture in any way."

"I didn't believe him at first," admitted Clyde, "but then I thought to myself, since everything's still in my name, and Gavin's not even in my will anymore, well, he's got nothing to gain anyway."

"Except maybe a little self-respect," said Gavin quietly.

"And that's worth a whole lot more than money." Clyde turned to Maggie. "I made it real clear that I'll pay Gavin a fair wage since it was his idea, but that's all I'm offering. He can take it or leave it."

"That's more than I expected," said Gavin. "I'd like to continue selling advertising for the paper too—I think I'll have time for both. It's good for me to keep busy...keeps me out of trouble." He smiled.

"But how will you do it?" asked Maggie. "Do you know anything about developing properties of this kind?"

"Well, as you may recall, I spent a couple years down in Arizona. Not that I learned so much while I was there, but my old buddy Stan Williams turned out to be one of the finest developers around. You can go down and see his places for yourself if you don't believe me. Or just do the research on the Net; this guy's been written up in some pretty prestigious magazines for his creativity and style. To tell you the truth, I used to be seriously jealous of all his success, thinking if I'd only stuck it out with him just a little longer..." Gavin shook his head. "But I probably would've just dragged him down in the long run. Anyway, I'm glad he's where he is now. And he's a really good guy—nothing like that Colin Byers you wrote about in last week's paper."

"Do you think your friend would have the time, or even the inclination, to do something like this?" asked Maggie. "We must look like pretty small potatoes to someone like him."

Gavin smiled. "I already called him to sound him out. I didn't want to get everyone's hopes up for no good reason. As soon as I mentioned that Colin Byers was involved, Stan grew very interested. Apparently, he's well aware of this creep's reputation. He said Byers is the kind of developer who gives the rest of them a bad name. Stan wants to check us out because of Byers. I've invited him to come out at his convenience." He frowned. "Now, if only we had some snow to offer. Stan mentioned he'd like to bring his wife and kids up here for a ski weekend sometime after the New Year and asked if I could work out the details for him. No problem getting rooms here in the hotel, but I don't know what to do about the lack of snow."

"Maybe we should get that Michael fellow to praying again," said Clyde with a smile.

"Maybe we should all do some praying," added Maggie quietly. Then she turned back to Gavin. "Well, this is the best news I've heard in weeks. I hope everything works out. Is there anything I can do to help?"

They talked extensively about all the possibilities and Maggie temporarily forgot about her concern over Jed's earlier presumptions about Gavin, but by the time they left, Jed and Leah's table was vacant and wiped clean. It figured, she thought, as the three of them stepped out the door. "I have more good news, Maggie," announced Gavin. "I found a small place to rent in town—a studio apartment over the health food store. I just put down a deposit this morning, and the lady said I could move in as soon as I liked. So I went ahead and moved my things over there this afternoon. Now all I need is to get some groceries before the store closes tonight."

"I'm glad for you, Gavin. But I hope you didn't think I was trying to get rid of you. There was no big hurry."

"I know, and I appreciate your hospitality. It was interesting getting better acquainted with Michael—what a character."

"So, you've met Michael?" said Clyde as they walked Maggie to her car parked by the newspaper office.

"Yeah, he's been staying at Maggie's too."

"Trying to give the hotel some competition, young lady?" asked Clyde wryly.

"I was just trying to help out," she answered stiffly, still bothered that Jed had not observed her with Clyde tonight. If only she'd been able to say something more meaningful to him before he left for his trip tomorrow. There was still email, but who knew when he'd check that? Then she remembered that Michael was going along too. Perhaps she'd get another chance to bump into Jed when he picked him up Michael at her house. "Thanks for dinner, Gavin. I'll see you two on Monday."

⌒

Once at home, her house seemed oddly empty and quiet. First, she went up to Spencer's room. His backpack was flung across his bed as though he'd been there, but he didn't seem to be around now. There was no trace of Michael either; in fact, his room was so neat she wondered if he'd actually moved out. And although Audrey's car was out in the driveway, she didn't seem to be anywhere in the main house. But then, she'd been spending more time out in her own little place lately, telling her daughter she needed to get back to being a bit more independent. Maggie had wondered if it was just to get some peace and quiet, although that should have been no problem tonight. Instead of calling her mom, she decided to walk over and see if she could find out what everyone was up to. She admired again the strings of white lights decorating the front of her house, and as she stepped from her porch she now noticed that her mother had put some lights around the window and door of the little guest house too, along with a pair of big red bows on each door post. Very cheery.

"Hello?" she called as she knocked quietly, hoping her mother hadn't already gone to bed. "Anybody home?"

"Come on in," called Audrey from inside.

Maggie stepped into the golden warmth of the little house and smiled at the familiar strains of an old Johnny Mathis Christmas album that she remembered from childhood. "Goodness, Mom, I haven't been out here for quite a while. I'd almost forgotten how nice and cozy it is."

Audrey sighed happily as she removed a tray of cookies from her small oven. "Yes, I do love it. And after everybody left today, I was sort of lonely over in your big old house, so I thought I'd better come back to own my little pad." She looked around with satisfied pleasure. "It's not half bad, is it?"

"Not at all." Maggie pulled up a pine stool and sat next to the granite-topped kitchen counter. "Where's everyone else?"

"Well, as you know, Spencer has his cast off now and I think he was feeling pretty foxy. Daniel, poor guy, is still limping around on crutches, but his grandpa took both of them to the varsity basketball game tonight. You know, that team's starting out with a pretty good winning streak. Spence says they might even go to state in their league if they can keep it up."

"So I heard. Scott's been covering them in the paper."

Audrey glanced at the clock on her kitchenette wall. "I don't expect we'll see Spence for a couple of hours."

"And you probably already know that Gavin moved into a place of his own today."

Bethel Baptist Church
P.O. BOX 167
AUMSVILLE, OR 97325

Audrey nodded. "Yes, I must admit I was sorry to see him go. He's awfully good help in the kitchen." She placed a tempting plate of fresh-from-the-oven snickerdoodle cookies on the counter in front of Maggie. "I just made a fresh pot of decaf hazelnut coffee. Want a cup to go with these?"

"I really should pass on these cookies after all I ate for dinner..." But the smell was too much for Maggie. She picked up a still-warm cookie. "These take me straight back to my childhood, Mom."

"I was going to bake Christmas cookies tonight, but I had a hankering for these instead. Don't you love the smell of cinnamon?" Audrey set a mug of coffee before her.

Maggie nodded and took a bite of her cookie. "Okay, we've accounted for Spencer and Gavin, but what about Michael?"

"Jed and Leah came by about an hour ago to pick him up. Michael and Jed are heading out quite early tomorrow, and he's going to help Jed load up the truck tonight so they'll be all set to leave first thing in the morning."

"Oh..." Maggie sighed, realizing that her opportunity to see Jed before he left had just evaporated. "I saw Jed and Leah at the hotel tonight."

"Did you get a chance to talk to him at all?"

She knew what her mother meant. "No, not really. If anything, I've probably messed things up worse than ever. I'm starting to wonder if Jed and I will ever get together. Honestly, it seems like no matter what I do, everything between us continually gets worse."

"What in the world happened tonight?" asked Audrey as she poured herself a mug of coffee and settled onto a stool on the other side of the counter.

Maggie told her the whole story of how Clyde had been on the phone and Jed had seen her meet what appeared to be only Gavin for dinner. "But you know what's really starting to make me feel bad, Mom? It's Leah. I hate to say this, but I'm really starting to resent her. And it makes me feel just horrible."

"Why is that?"

"What? Feeling horrible? Or resenting her?"

"Both, I suppose."

"Well, I feel horrible because she's just a kid who's had a pretty tough life. And I resent her because sometimes I get the impression she's actually trying to drive Jed and me apart—and then I feel guilty for thinking that."

"Well, she might be."

Maggie leaned forward. "Do you really think so?"

"Why not? Jed's probably the best thing that's ever happened to her in her whole life. I'm sure she doesn't want to lose him to anyone."

"Or even share him?"

Audrey shrugged. "Maybe not."

Maggie sipped her coffee. "Well, I've been trying not to think about this, but when Jed confronted me about Gavin staying here, he made a big point about how the whole thing made Leah really uncomfortable. But I had specifically asked her just the night before if she felt okay about the whole thing, and she had assured me she did! And then Jed said that Leah had told him that I'd flown off with Colin Byers in his private jet. Now, why would she say that? You were there; you saw for yourself that Colin wasn't anywhere around."

"I don't know why or if she said that. You need to keep in mind that you're hearing all this secondhand, Maggie. It's also possible that Jed's jealousy may have caused him to elaborate on some things that Leah had mentioned. Don't jump to any conclusions that you might later regret. Here's something I used to tell my clients, and I'm sure I've said it to you before. The safest thing in situations like this is to just assume the best in another person."

"I suppose you're right…"

"Just the same, I think you should talk to Jed directly, and as soon as possible, especially after your misunderstanding tonight. The poor guy's going to need some serious reassurance about your relationship."

"*He* needs reassurance? Good grief, what about me? I'm not even sure we still even *have* a relationship. And now he's going to be gone for the better part of a week." Maggie groaned. "And by the time he gets back, it'll be almost Christmas—and Barry and Rebecca will be here by then. Then we have the wedding to prepare for. Why, I'll be lucky if I can have a conversation with him sometime next year."

Audrey laughed. "You may be a little overdramatic about the whole thing. And by the way, don't you think we should invite Jed and Leah to join us for Christmas too? Who else do they have? And, of course, Michael is staying here..."

She brightened. "Yes. Of course, you're right, Mom. The voice of reason wins out again."

"And don't you think we should be getting a Christmas tree up soon?"

"Right. Now that Spence is out of his cast, maybe we can cut one down ourselves. I've heard that you can get a permit to cut them right out of the woods. Can you imagine? We'll be just like a real wilderness family." Suddenly Maggie recognized that the excitement of preparing for the holidays was returning to her—something she hadn't felt since Phil's death. "I just hope I can find where we put all our Christmas decorations. They may be buried beneath a pile of other boxes out in the barn, but we can dig them out."

"That's my girl," cheered Audrey. "That's the spirit."

Maggie smiled. "I guess I was kind of down, wasn't I? Well, the cookies and pep talk were good medicine, Mom."

"Sometimes, back in my counseling days, I wanted to give cookies to my patients, but I was afraid it wouldn't look very professional."

"I don't know. Just think, you could have hung out a sign that said 'counseling and cookies' and made a fortune," suggested Maggie.

"You know, you could be on to something with that idea."

Then Maggie told her all about Gavin's new idea to develop the property just north of them as a way to oppose Pine Mountain Estates.

"And how do you feel about getting a ready-made community like that?" asked her mother.

"Okay, I guess. At least I'll have the assurance that it'll be done right. And Clyde said I could sit on the board if I like, and that way I'd have a say about things. I do sort of miss having neighbors. Not that they'd be all that close—barely within walking distance really."

"My, for a sleepy little town, how quickly things change around here."

"We're all keeping quiet about this idea, at least for the time being. We don't want Greg and Rick getting wind of any of this yet."

"My lips are sealed."

Twenty

Audrey brought over a plate of cookies to share at the wedding planning meeting the next morning. Soon all the women were settled around Maggie's dining room table with Chloe as moderator, Rosa as the note-taking secretary, and Maggie as hostess.

"My mother thinks I've totally lost my marbles," said Chloe, then she dramatically imitated what must have been her mother's intonation. *"Nobody, and I mean absolutely nobody, throws a wedding like this at the very last moment. Just think what people will say! Surely they'll assume that you're pregnant, Chloe, or just terribly desperate, or that you've simply lost your mind altogether."* The women all laughed and Chloe bowed theatrically.

"Well, I have to admit I was a little surprised too," said Maggie as she refilled the plate of cookies on the table. "But I do think it's a charming idea to have a small, intimate wedding, and I'm happy to be a conspirator in the whole thing. Do you think your parents are going to come?"

"Mom keeps telling me to forget it, but I know my dad will give in and come—even if it's at the last minute. And my brother told me 'off the record' that he and his girlfriend will be here with bells on." She produced a piece of paper. "This is our guest list. Right now there are about a hundred names on it, but we figure only about half or less will show because of the holiday. We figure fifty people shouldn't be too many for your house, Maggie. I already called a motel in Byron to reserve rooms for the overnighters, although I don't expect there'll be all that many from out of town."

"And it's all worked out that Michael will officiate the ceremony," said Rosa. "He told me that he even has a suit."

"I've offered to handle all the flowers," said Abigail happily. "Chloe gave me some magazine pictures of the sort of things she likes. And Clara is going to loan me some of her antique vases and help with the arranging."

"Sierra and I will do most of the food," said Rosa, nodding to Audrey. "And Audrey has offered to coordinate everything."

"I wonder if this is how they did weddings back in the old days," said Chloe dreamily. "With family and friends all pitching in, and not all the craziness and expense—I can't believe that my friend Susan shelled out over thirty thousand dollars for her wedding last year. Actually, it was her parents who did the shelling. I think my parents should thank me."

Maggie nodded. "I know what you mean, I remember a coworker down in L.A. who became so stressed out over her elaborate wedding plans that she and her fiancé had a huge fight and ended up calling the whole thing off just three days before the wedding. She returned gifts for weeks."

"Yes," said Abigail. "My great-niece was so nervous that she broke out in hives the night before her wedding. She had to layer on so much makeup just to cover them up that I was afraid her face was going to crack when she smiled."

"But weddings are supposed to be a happy occasion for everyone," said Rosa, "including the bride and groom. I really do like the idea of a simple celebration. After all, it's not so much about the wedding but the marriage."

"You're exactly right," said Audrey. "I don't know how many times I've had to counsel unhappy newlyweds who had spent months, sometimes years, pulling off some huge, fantasy wedding but had invested literally nothing into preparing for their actual marriage."

They planned and chatted happily for a couple of hours. Scott's brother, Max, was to be best man, and Chloe had asked Sierra to be her maid of honor. The banister of the staircase would be wrapped in evergreen garlands, white lights, and white satin ribbons. All the flowers would be varying shades of white, and only white candles would be used for light. The whole thing sounded very lovely and romantic. Just the sort of wedding Maggie might have, maybe someday....When the women were finally satisfied that everything from mints to napkins had been covered, they cheerfully parted ways.

Outside on the porch, after the others had left, Rosa pulled Maggie aside. "Don't tell Scott or Chloe this, but Sam has arranged for a horse and carriage—or sleigh, if we have snow—to be used to take the couple away. Then he'll have their car parked a mile or so down the road. Do you mind if we use your barn?"

"Not at all. What a wonderful idea!"

"Oh, and I almost forgot," said Rosa. "Would you and Spencer and Audrey want to join us after church tomorrow? We're going to cut our Christmas tree—it's sort of a tradition. We traipse around in the woods for about an hour and then drink lots of hot cocoa."

"I know I'd love to tag along," said Maggie. "I'm sure Spencer and Mom would enjoy it too."

She waved from the porch as Rosa's car pulled away, and then looked over toward the mountains. A heavy bank of white clouds hung right over their tops. Perhaps not the kind that bring snow, but it was enough to give her hope as she quietly breathed another prayer for the weather to change. Only yesterday she'd received several more angry letters from agitated businessowners who felt like she was putting a damper on development to the detriment of the entire town. Although she would print some of the better written letters in the paper, she tried not to take them too seriously.

It was natural to think that some people were simply venting their frustration due to a lack of snow and the subsequent loss of business from an unopened ski season. Even this morning, Rosa had patiently explained how this hostile atmosphere would instantly disappear the very same moment when the weather began to cooperate. Maggie had heard on the news that the ski resort reported it would only take about fifteen more inches of snow to open their chairs, which, they assured with optimism, could literally happen overnight. Oh, if only...

～

On Sunday Maggie and Audrey and Spencer went to church. It made Maggie sad to think this would be their last day of meeting in this beautiful building with the fantastic mountain views (although today the mountains were completely shrouded in a thick blanket of cloud—even more so than yesterday!). She wondered if she would ever again experience another church that was so aesthetically pleasing as this. She thought of the times she had sat on the rough-hewn benches and been relaxed and refreshed as she looked out upon the mountains. And yet, she also remembered one of Jed's sermons where he said they could look to the hills for strength without finding any, for strength only came from God. Yes, that was a good message that day.

Today she glanced around the building and wondered what it would look like in here after Jed finished converted it into a home for him and Leah. She tried not to think that, not so long ago, she had actually imagined she might one day share this space with him. But now that seemed far away, if not totally removed, from reality. Besides, she had her own home and family to consider. Living out here in the woods was probably just a silly fantasy better left behind when she passed through those big wooden doors one last time.

Sam led the service today, reminiscing about the history of their little church, about how they'd pulled themselves together after their last pastor left, and what a wonderful gift it had been to meet up here for the past couple years, but that now they should rejoice for they were entering a brand new season. The school library had been secured for them to meet in until after the New Year, and at that time the board would determine how to proceed from there. "But we have also come up with a unique dilemma," continued Sam, "and last week the board decided to bring this question to the congregation to vote upon today." He glanced at the faces around the room. "Now, you've all had a chance to become somewhat acquainted with young Michael Abundi. He has preached two sermons here, and some of you have spent time with him personally. As most of you know, he was trained as a pastor in his own country, and he strongly believes that God has called him to Pine Mountain for the specific purpose of reaching out to people. Since his arrival, I know of many who have been touched by this young man's ministry. In fact, I can honestly say that I'm a better person for having spent time with him—his deeply rooted faith is a challenge to me. And I know many of you would agree. Anyway, his name was raised at our last board meeting as a potential pastoral candidate for our church. We discussed this for quite some time without reaching an agreement. Finally, we decided this was too big of an issue to decide on our own, and as both Michael and Jed are out of town this weekend, we thought today would be a good day to let the congregation discuss this possibility and make a decision. We have mentioned our interest to Michael, and he very humbly said he only wanted to do God's will. We have made no official job offer to him. What we want today is to hear from you." Sam nodded over to Jim Hanson, another board member, and Jim came up to the pulpit. "Jim has requested this opportunity to talk to you today in representation of those on the board who are opposed to this idea."

Jim cleared his throat. "It's not that I have anything personally against Michael Abundi," he began carefully. "But I am concerned about the stability of this congregation right now. We've been through a lot in the past several years, and yet we have a really good bunch of people here. I'm just worried that bringing in an outsider right now could have a negative impact on our future as a church. I'm afraid Michael might not understand our culture and our ways, and that he might alienate others in town who aren't as open-minded as some—"

"You mean because he's a black man," called Lou Henderson from nearby. He was also a member of the board.

Jim frowned. "Yes, to be honest with everyone here, the racial issue was discussed during our recent meeting. It's no secret that we already have some folks in town who are trying to make this an even bigger issue right now. We wonder, do we really need that kind of controversy for our church?"

"Jim is referring to folks like Randy Ebbert," said Lou with a scowl, "and there are those of us on the board who would rather not give *that* man the time of day, let alone let him influence our choice as to who should lead this church."

Sam stood up now and held up his hands. "Okay, guys, we've debated this enough already. I'm letting Jim present his side before we open this to discussion and take it to a vote."

"Then someone had better represent the other side," said Lou defensively, and Maggie nodded in agreement.

"I thought I already did that," said Sam.

"Not very well. I think you were trying to be too impartial." Lou looked back at Jim with impatience. "Have you said all you plan to say?"

"I just want to make it clear, I only oppose this because I'm trying to consider what will be best for our church in the long run. We want to reach out to others in town and we want to grow in numbers. And if we want to grow, we need to consider the needs of our community. Just look around this room. Do you see any other black people in here or in our town in general? It just doesn't make sense to bring in a man, not only of a different race, but also from a drastically different culture, to lead this congregation. That's all I have to say."

Sam stepped back to the pulpit. "Any comments from the congregation?"

"I have a comment." Scott stood up. "I asked Michael to officiate our wedding mostly because I like him and because I think he's got a good head on his shoulders. But before he would agree to perform the ceremony, he wanted to meet with Chloe and me a few times. I wasn't sure what for, but after our first meeting with him a week or so ago, I was really impressed. He gave us some very wise premarital counseling, and he's requiring us to read a whole list of Bible verses together." Scott looked down at Chloe. "Doing this assignment has brought us closer together. It's been really special." Chloe nodded in agreement and then Scott sat down.

"I can't believe we're even considering this," said a man who worked in the hardware store and usually remained quiet. "Oh sure, I'll agree that Michael knows how to preach a good sermon and all, but he's not one of us. I mean, he comes in here from who knows where and then thinks he can take over. Well, I'm sorry, but I think it's a crazy idea to invite him to be our leader." A couple of others chimed in agreement, and Maggie found herself standing up to speak.

"Michael is an amazing young man," she began. "His wisdom far exceeds his years and his gracious and kind spirit are the most Christian I have ever seen. I've watched him reach out and touch the lives of people of all ages, all walks, both believers and those who are still searching. I, for one, would be honored to call him my pastor. I can think of no reason to object to offering him this position. In fact, I can't believe how fortunate we are to be presented with such an opportunity."

Maggie sat down and the discussion continued. Spencer nodded to her, as if to support her stand, and Audrey patted her hand. But the group seemed clearly divided, and the deepness of the division troubled Maggie even more than the issue they discussed. When it was finally put to the vote,

Michael won, but only by a small margin. There was a fair amount of grumbling after the announcement was made.

"I know this was a tough decision," Sam said solemnly, "but I think if we're all patient and supportive, we'll see that we've made the right choice to offer this position to Michael. And we still have no guarantee that he will accept. Remember, everyone, next week we'll all meet at the library. You're dismissed."

A number of them lingered to continue discussing the controversy, but Maggie noticed that many of those who had spoken against Michael had quietly slipped out. She hoped that they would resolve themselves to the choice of the majority, but feared it might not be that simple. If only they could give him a chance, surely they would see what a gift he could be to a church like this.

"I just don't get it," said Scott. "Michael is such a great guy. He's smart, he's good, he knows the Bible. I think if his skin were a different color we never would have had this whole discussion in the first place."

"I never thought Christians would be so prejudiced," said Leah, joining their little group. "Isn't there something in the Bible that tells them not to?"

"You mean, like how we're supposed to 'love one another'?" Spencer suggested wryly.

"Yeah, aren't we supposed to love people no matter what color their skin is?" asked Leah. Until coming to Pine Mountain, Leah had never attended church before in her entire life.

"People don't always do what they're supposed to do," said Sam as he gathered a few things from the pulpit. "Just because you become a Christian doesn't mean you suddenly become perfect. We all have a long, long way before we'll ever be living the way God tells us to in the Bible. I just hope that this whole thing over Michael doesn't cause our church to split."

"I was thinking the same thing," said Maggie. "If Michael accepts the position, I hope everyone will give him a fair chance."

"Time will tell."

"Do you think it would help if I did an article about this?" suggested Maggie. "I mean, if he accepts the position?"

"It couldn't hurt for folks to be better informed," said Lou. "Prejudice is usually the by-product of ignorance."

"Exactly," agreed Scott. "That's just what I said in my story about Randy Ebbert's little hate group."

As the crowd dispersed, Maggie approached Leah. "How's it going?" she asked. "Is it lonely staying out here by yourself while Jed's gone? You know you're always welcome back at the house."

"No, I'm fine. I kind of like the solitude out here, especially after being in the shop all day."

"Has the shop been getting much business?" asked Maggie, thinking that Leah would surely have more than enough solitude there to keep her satisfied.

Leah shrugged. "Not really, but there's lots to do. I'm keeping busy enough. And if Jed gets a lot of new jobs lined up at this show, it'll be good for me to have the place all organized." Her tone had an edge of defensiveness to it, and Maggie wondered how or if she'd managed to offend her now.

"Would you like to join us in getting a Christmas tree today?" offered Maggie brightly, determined to bridge this rift that seemed to have fallen between them.

"No thanks. I have a lot to do around here." Leah glanced around the building that had until today housed the church. "Jed gave me a list of things to do to start getting this place ready for remodeling, and I can't wait to start." She smiled appreciatively as she looked around the big open room. "This is going to be such a cool place to live."

"Yes, I'm sure Jed will make it really special."

"He has plans all drawn up for where the rooms will be and everything. You won't even recognize this place by next year."

"You sure you don't want to change your mind about getting a tree with us?"

"No, but I think I'll cut one down to surprise Jed when he gets home."

"Okay, then. Be sure and call if you need anything."

Then Sam came up to get a phone number from Leah so he could reach Michael and tell him the good news. "I'd like to hear his response before we plan our next service—just in case he says no."

ᴏ̃

Audrey opted to pass on the tree-hunting expedition. She wanted to get some things done in preparation for Christmas as well as for the upcoming wedding. "I found an old recipe for appetizers I want to try out again," she had explained with enthusiasm. "And I thought I'd do some Christmas baking to start stocking the freezer." But Maggie and Spencer joined Rosa, Sam, and Sierra—all five riding in their roomy sports utility vehicle.

Sam had gotten their tree permits and driven up to a portion of the national forest where a nice variety of evergreens grew in profusion. The woods were quiet and green as they tramped along in search of perfect Christmas trees.

"Scott already helped Chloe set up a small tree in her little apartment," explained Rosa as they hiked up a small knoll with several good-looking fir trees near the top. "And they're busily working on wedding plans this afternoon."

Sierra and Spencer were dragging a little behind. "How's your ankle doing?" asked Maggie, pausing to catch her breath as she neared the top.

"It's okay," he called back. "I figure this will be good exercise to get me in shape for snowboarding."

"And judging by the sky," said Sam, "that might not be too far off."

Maggie glanced up past the treetops to see a section of low hanging clouds just about the color of pewter. "Goodness, those clouds are really rolling in fast. Do you think it's going to snow up here?"

Rosa nodded happily. "I think it might. Maybe we should get our trees picked out quickly, just in case."

Spencer selected a stately white fir to be placed in the high-ceilinged parlor of their house, and the Galloways chose a shorter tree to fit into their snug living room. Spencer and Sam took turns with the saw, and somehow between the two teens and Sam, they managed to lug down the trees without much help from Rosa and Maggie.

"Guess I just came along for the walk," said Maggie.

"And me, for the company," laughed Rosa. "But that's okay because both were worth it."

A few flakes were beginning to fall as they reached the parking lot, and Maggie couldn't help but lift her hands with delight. "Oh, isn't it beautiful!"

"Yeah," agreed Spencer as he leaned his tree against the vehicle. "I think the reason the snow waited so long was just so I could get my ankle all healed up in time for snowboarding."

"Well, it might still be a couple of weeks," said Maggie doubtfully. "You know you still have your physical therapy to—"

"I think snowboarding's a fantastic form of physical therapy!"

They all laughed and joked as they loaded and tied the trees down to the top of the SUV. The snow began to fall rapidly, coating the tops of their hats and shoulders. "Do you think it'll be snowing in town too?" asked Maggie, eager to see Pine Mountain and her house all blanketed in white again.

"You never know until you get down there," said Rosa as she offered her a cup of hot cocoa. "But at least it's snowing up here."

They sipped their cocoa and watched as the snow quickly began to accumulate. How quiet the woods suddenly seemed with the snow filling the air with its fluffy softness. Then, shaking off hats and coats, they all climbed into the SUV. "I think I might have to put on those snow tires after all," commented Sam as he switched the rig into four-wheel-drive and headed carefully down the white-covered road.

"Is Leah still staying out at Jed's, Maggie?" asked Rosa.

"Yes. I encouraged her to come stay with us, but she didn't want to."

"How does she get to work?"

"She's driving Jed's truck while he's away," Maggie glanced out at the quickly accumulating snow, "although I'm not sure she's had any experience driving on snow yet."

"You know, it can be a little treacherous getting in and out of Jed's place once the weather really turns," said Sam with concern. "I hope Leah can handle it."

"Maybe I should call and see if she's considered that," said Maggie. "As a California girl, I can relate. It still scares me a little too."

"You should just let me drive," said Spencer with fifteen-year-old confidence. "I'm not afraid."

Maggie chuckled. "Well, if it hadn't been for that broken foot, I bet you'd have your learner's permit by now."

"I have mine," chimed in Sierra, "but they hardly ever let me drive."

"I want you to take the driver's ed class first," said Rosa. "That's what I did with the boys too. It shouldn't be any different for you."

Sierra groaned. "But that's not until next spring. How will I learn to drive on snow and ice?"

Rosa relented. "I suppose you could practice a little this winter. But it will have to be with your father. My nerves can't take it."

Sam chuckled. "I guess I better go dig my old motorcycle helmet out of the attic then."

"Dad!" Sierra playfully punched his shoulder.

The snow hadn't made its way to the lower elevations yet, and it was just starting to grow dusky as they dropped Maggie and Spencer at home. Sam helped them get their big tree into the tree stand and then into the front parlor of the house.

Meanwhile, Sierra and Rosa were encouraged by Maggie to slip into the kitchen to sample Audrey's selection of appetizers.

"These are delicious," said Sierra as the others joined them. "Teach me to make these and I'll help out."

"Great," said Audrey. "I think we can freeze part of them ahead of time, and then put them together the day before the wedding."

"You shouldn't go to such trouble," said Rosa. "Remember we want to keep everything simple."

"Oh, it's no trouble," Audrey assured her. "I love doing things like this."

Rosa turned to Maggie. "You are so lucky to have her around. Do you ever lend her out?"

Maggie put an arm around her mother's shoulders. "Only to really good friends like you."

Audrey laughed. "I always wanted to have more children just so we could do lots of celebrations like weddings and the like. Between my two kids, we've only managed to have one wedding so far."

"Well, Barry's coming. We'll see if we can get him headed in that direction."

"And what about you?" asked Sierra pointing her finger at Maggie. "I thought you'd hooked old Jed good and solid."

The kitchen grew quiet as Maggie tried to think of a witty comeback to keep the conversation light, but instead she drew an embarrassing blank. Thankfully, Rosa stepped in. "All in good time—right, Maggie? One wedding just around the corner is more than enough for everyone right now."

"That's for sure," agreed Audrey. "It'll be nothing short of a miracle if we can get those two somewhat fashionably hitched." She winked at Rosa. "But I think we can!"

Twenty-One

On Sunday evening, Maggie called Leah to see how she was doing. But Leah sounded calm, confident, and just slightly cool. She asked why Maggie was even concerned in the first place.

"It's just that I wasn't sure how you felt about driving on snow," said Maggie apologetically. "I didn't think you'd had that much experience yet."

"Jed's truck has four-wheel-drive, and he showed me how to use it. We only have a couple of inches up here right now. I really don't think it should be any problem. And if it gets really bad, we also have chains and Jed showed me how to put them on if I should need them."

Maggie was impressed. "You know how to put on chains?"

"Yes. Don't you?"

"No, not really. I guess I better learn."

"I would think so. Jed said that no one should attempt to live up here in the mountains if they don't have proper respect for how quickly the weather can change. And he also said you should always be prepared for anything—like power outages or the possibility of being snowed in for a few days. Are you prepared for all those sorts of things, Maggie?"

Maggie didn't want to answer that she wasn't. "Well, thanks for all that information, Leah. You've certainly given me a few things to think about."

Leah laughed. "Isn't it funny that you called *me* because you were worried about *my* welfare. Looks like you better get it together for your own family, Maggie."

It wasn't easy being chastised by someone half your age—especially a girl you had only recently rescued from what, at one time, seemed a somewhat desperate situation. But Maggie kept these thoughts to herself. "Well, it sounds as if you've got everything under control then..."

"Yeah," said Leah with confidence. "But thanks for checking anyway."

Maggie hung up and made an irritated growl.

"So, how's our Leah doing?" asked Audrey with raised brows as she rinsed a mixing bowl in the sink.

"Just fine, thank you very much!" retorted Maggie. Then she turned to her mother. "Leah, it seems, has become some sort of survivalist mountain woman. Believe me, that girl can take care of herself." Then Maggie pulled out a piece of paper and started making a list of supplies.

"What's that for?" asked Audrey, looking curiously over Maggie's shoulder as she furiously wrote down things like batteries, candles, kerosene lamps...

"Leah's not the only one who can be a mountain woman."

Audrey laughed. "Better put a manual can opener on that list too, just in case you should ever lose your electricity. I haven't seen one around anywhere."

ᕍ

The next morning, Maggie received a surprise visit from Kate and Buckie at work. "What brings you two in here?" she asked cheerfully after getting them both a cup of coffee and settling them into her office.

"Actually, we've come to represent some of the businesses in town that are a little concerned over all the controversy surrounding the Pine Mountain Estates development," said Buckie, suddenly sounding very businesslike.

Maggie sighed with dismay. "I see. What exactly do you want?"

"We want you to lighten up, Maggie," said Kate. "I mean, we all know how you and Greg have never really seen eye to eye on—"

"Wait a minute, until recently none of the business people saw eye to eye with Greg Snider. I mean, only last summer he was Mr. Antidevelopment—"

"Oh, you know that was only a cover-up until he could get this whole thing off the ground," said Buckie quickly. "It's a tactic lots of businessmen use to hide their intentions until the timing's right to let the news out."

"Pretty extreme tactics, if you ask me," muttered Maggie.

"Anyway," continued Kate with a pretty smile. "We believe you want to see our town grow just as much as we do. All we're asking is that you simply back down a little on this attack—"

"*Attack?* All I'm doing is reporting the facts—"

"The facts as you perceive them," said Buckie, then he pulled out a sheet of paper and laid it on her desk. "This is a petition, Maggie. It's signed by a number of local businesspeople—people who regularly purchase ad space in the *Pine Cone,* if you get my drift. Everyone on this list is ready to boycott your paper if you continue this negative, antidevelopment press coverage. Can't you see that you're hurting the whole town with all this one-sided pessimism?"

Maggie pressed her lips together and closed her eyes for a moment, mentally counting to ten before she responded with something she might later regret. To think she used to consider Buckie as one of her better friends! Finally she spoke in a quiet, controlled voice. "So, are you asking me to close my eyes, put my head in a hole, and simply pretend that everything Greg and Rick are doing is just peachy keen?"

"All we're asking is for your newspaper to give a little more positive support to this development," said Kate. "Is that too much too expect? Just think how something like this could change the economy in our town. But if you keep this up, Maggie, you'll be driving a great big wedge between the local businesses—and you know what they say about a house divided, don't you?"

Buckie's expression softened. "All we want is for you to lay low just long enough for this thing to get solidly off the ground. Give Greg and Rick a chance to show you that they're going to do this thing right. Can't you just cut them a little slack?"

Maggie studied the names on the list before her. Many of them were local contractors. Even now she was working on a story about how Colin Byers' past developments rarely used local contractors and labor but instead relied heavily upon out-of-state, nonlicensed, and almost always nonunion workers, not to mention illegal aliens (although so far no charges had been pressed in this area). But to bury a story of this significance went against all that she stood for as a journalist. She sat up straight in her chair and folded her hands together on her desk as she looked at the two of them, and then she calmly spoke. "I'm sorry to have wasted your time. I'm sorry that TS Development is resorting to what I consider questionable ethics. And I'm also sorry that coverage of their activities is likely to stir up more controversy and, as you said, quite possibly divide our town even further." She paused and took a deep breath. "But I will not compromise this paper's standards and my morals to play Pollyanna just so Greg and Rick can continue to take advantage of others for their own personal gain. I've done my research in hopes that I'd uncover something more positive. Unfortunately, I did not. And I have only printed the honest results of my findings. Quite honestly, I don't know what more I can do, but you and everyone else should know that I refuse to shirk from the truth just because a few businesspeople threaten to boycott this paper. That is the oldest and cheapest trick in the book, and it doesn't worry me in the least." She picked up the letter and held it in the air. "In fact, I'm quite happy to publish this petition in this week's paper. To tell you the truth, I don't care if these people purchase their ad space from Randy Ebbert. I'm sure he'd be very happy to get their business!"

Buckie and Kate just stared at her without speaking.

Maggie set the paper aside, and said quite calmly, "Now, if you'll excuse me, I have a newspaper to run."

They stood and began to move toward the door. "Oh, one more thing," said Buckie. "I'm not saying this officially—it's just a suggestion."

Maggie looked up. "And what would that be?"

"Some of us think it's about time for you to step down from the Pine Mountain Business Association."

She blinked at him in surprise. "Are you kicking me out?"

He cleared his throat. "Well, it does seem slightly compromising to have someone who's vehemently opposed to development assisting in an association where the sole purpose is supposedly to promote commerce in our community."

She clenched her fists but remained in control. "Fine. If the association wants me to step aside, I'm more than willing. I've said from the beginning that I was only helping out initially just to get the whole thing off the ground. It was never my intention to wear out my welcome."

Kate leaned over her desk. "It's not that we don't appreciate all you've done, Maggie. I mean, you've had some really great ideas and everything..."

Maggie waved her hand. "It's okay, Kate. I understand."

"I'm sorry, Maggie," said Kate as the two of them left her office.

Somehow, Maggie believed that she was, but still the confrontation and rejection she'd just experienced stung. To think of all she'd tried to accomplish for this town, all the work she'd done to draw the business association together, and then to be thanked like this. She felt the hurt rising up in her, and she knew the immediate temptation would be to vent her frustrations by writing an angry article about the petition. But she would not allow herself to do that. She must continue communicating and exposing the truth in a sensible and controlled manner. Certainly, this petition was noteworthy news for the town, but then and there she decided to let Scott handle the story. She called him on the intercom and asked him if he could possibly get the story finished by tomorrow afternoon, which he gladly agreed to.

Then she returned to her final edit on this week's article reporting on the types of labor that had been used in other Colin Byers' developments. Pausing for just a moment, once again she considered Gavin's idea to stir up a little competition for TS Development. Suddenly, more than ever now, she longed for his plan to take off and turn into a huge success. Was that petty on her part? No, it would only be petty if her rationale was simply to punish Greg and Rick, but quite honestly, she did want growth and development for Pine Mountain—she just wanted it to be of quality and something that would profit the majority. She glanced at her desk calendar, surprised to see that the month was nearly half over, with less than two weeks until Christmas! Well, hopefully TS Development wouldn't be able to accomplish too much before the end of the year. Maybe by that time, if all went well, Gavin would get the go-ahead from his developer friend, Stan Williams, and the competition would quickly be set into motion. Gavin had mentioned just this morning that he planned to spend much of the day researching county permits and some necessary land use information that Stan had asked him about. He wanted to get everything in place just as soon as possible. The hardest thing, she thought, would be for them to keep this wonderful possibility under their hats.

"Excuse me, Maggie," called Abigail's voice on the intercom. "Barbara Harris is here hoping to see you. She said she didn't have an appointment and doesn't want to disturb you, but—"

"It's not a problem at all. I'll be right there," answered Maggie, thinking she could use a friendly face just now. She went out to the reception area and handed Abigail the petition she'd just received from Buckie and Kate. "Will you make a couple copies of this, please, and give one to Scott?" Then she greeted Barbara and led her into her office. "It's so nice to see you again, Barbara. Have a seat and tell me how you're doing."

Barbara sat down and removed her soft leather gloves. Then she rubbed her hands together and smiled as if she were keeping some delicious secret to herself. "Well, I just don't know quite where to begin, my dear."

Having no idea what she was referring to, Maggie just shrugged. "Well, why don't you just start at the beginning?"

"All right, I will. You see, I went to Galloway's Deli for one of those wonderful raisin scones that Rosa bakes fresh every morning. And I happened to mention to her that I was sorry to have missed going to church yesterday. Between you and me, because Michael wasn't preaching, I didn't much feel like going. I know that's not very good of me, but it's the truth. Anyway, Rosa told me that it was the last service they'd be having up at Jed's beautiful mountain cabin, and why, that just made me feel so very, very sad. I've never been a churchgoing person, but something about being up there, well, that, combined with Michael's eloquent sermons, just seemed very special to me somehow...so, anyway—" She stopped abruptly and looked at Maggie. "Goodness, dear, I hope I'm not keeping you from anything important."

Maggie shook her head, feeling slightly confused. "On the contrary, you've really aroused my curiosity. Please, continue your tale."

"So, I asked Rosa where the church would be meeting in the future, and she told me you'd all meet in the elementary school library—that you'd done it before, and though it was somewhat inconvenient and impersonal, it was better than nothing. Then, she told me the good news about Michael!"

Maggie nodded. "Yes, isn't that wonderful? I hope he'll accept the position."

"Why, he already has. Rosa said that Sam spoke to him for a long time on the phone last night, and Michael said that he'd been praying about this very thing for the past several days, and that he believes it is the right thing to do!"

"That's great. I'm so glad to hear it."

"I was happy for him too. You know how he promised my Stevie that he would be a missionary to Pine Mountain. Wouldn't my Stevie be proud of him now?" Barbara was beaming.

"I'm sure he'd be very proud." Maggie wondered if the news about Michael was to be the conclusion of Barbara's story. Not that it wasn't good news, and it was fun to see Barbara so happy, but she did have work to do.

Then Barbara continued. "So, I sat down to have my scone and my cup of peppermint tea, and suddenly it occurred to me that I still own a building in this town. It belonged to my husband's family, but of course, it's mine now. So, I finished my scone in a hurry—a shameful thing to do with such a delicious treat as that—and then I walked on over to take a look at that old building. And, oh my, but it certainly is a mess, at least on the outside. Well, of course, I didn't have a key. I doubt that I could ever find one, even back home, so I picked up a big rock and threw it right through the glass window in the front door, then reached in, carefully mind you, and let myself in." She chuckled. "Naturally, I had to explain all of this to the sheriff, but he was actually rather nice about the whole thing once he found out it was my own building."

Maggie was shaking her head in wonder, trying to figure out where she was going with all this. "And so, you went inside?"

Barbara nodded. "And it's not so terribly bad in there. It's clean and dry, with a wooden floor and ceilings that go up about two stories, and windows way up high letting in lots of light. I thought to myself, why couldn't *this* be a church?"

"Aha," said Maggie. "Now I see where you're going."

Barbara nodded, then raised up her index finger. "But there's one thing."

"And that is?"

"I have decided I will donate the building and the funding necessary to refurbish it into a church only on the condition that Michael is the pastor."

"But the decision's already been made, and you said yourself that he's accepted."

"I know, but Rosa also mentioned there was a little disagreement in connection to the decision."

"Yes, that's true. But perhaps this generous donation from you might help some of the dissenters to look at this whole thing differently."

"Do you think so? You know, it occurred to me that it might cause problems too. I really don't want to cause any problems, but I do so want Michael to be a preacher—he has such a gift in that area. In fact, I'm considering moving back here just so I can attend Michael's church on a regular basis. You know, I won't be around forever, and I really miss my Stevie. If there's any way I could be assured to see him again..."

"So, would you consider this to be 'Michael's church'?" asked Maggie somewhat tentatively, sensing this could present some potential problems.

"No, no, of course not. I'm sure Michael would never hear of that anyway—we've all heard him go on about how a church isn't a building but a group of people. And, certainly, I don't expect him to spend the rest of his life here in Pine Mountain. But I'd like for him to have a place where he could stand up and say all those fine things he seems to have to say for just as long as he's willing to be here."

Maggie smiled. "I think it sounds like a wonderful idea, Barbara. But, I'm curious, why are you telling me all this?"

"I guess I just wanted a sounding board, and you're the first person who came to mind. I know you're good friends with Jed and with Michael, and I thought you could help advise me on my next step."

"I think the next step would be to talk to the board." Maggie listed the names of the members of the church board, putting Sam's home phone number at the top. "Ultimately it will be their decision."

"That's what I thought too. And if they agree, do you think that they'll let Michael make the announcement in church?"

"I don't know why not."

"And would you write an article about all this in your newspaper?"

"Of course, this is an interesting news story. Maybe we should include it in our Christmas edition. In fact, it just might give us a positive way to react to all this white supremacy banter without throwing more fuel in the fire. I had already decided not to run Scott's next story on that whole business for the Christmas edition. But I'd love to do something to put a happy spin on this whole thing—and to help make some people think a little more openly. I think this is just the number!"

Barbara clapped her hands together. "Yes, that's perfect! This can be my Christmas present to the whole town. Oh, I know there are a couple of other churches in the area, but wouldn't it be wonderful if Michael's church turned out to be the sort of place where other denominations could gather too—just occasionally, you know, like for special music or something along those lines. I never did understand all these denominational divisions and differences. I mean, don't they all believe in basically the same thing?"

Maggie smiled. "I guess we'd all hope so."

Barbara rose. "Well, I don't want to take any more of your time. But I was just so excited. I felt like I was a young girl again, and I just had to talk to somebody!"

Maggie grasped her hand. "I'm glad you came to me. And I won't mention this to anyone until you give me the go-ahead, okay?"

"Thank you, dear. Oh, and one more thing. I wonder if Jed would have time to help oversee some of the renovations to the building."

"I couldn't really say. But I know if he has the time, I can guarantee that he would do a fantastic job. I can personally vouch for the quality of his work."

Barbara winked at her. "I thought you could, dear." Then she left.

Maggie couldn't for the life of her figure out what she'd meant by that last comment and wink. Certainly, Barbara didn't suspect that there'd ever been anything beyond a congenial friendship between her and Jed. And yet, just the same, it was comforting somehow to think that Barbara might have imagined more.

Twenty-Two

O n Tuesday morning the temperature dropped considerably and large snowflakes began to fall in town. Maggie called up the nearby resort for the ski report to hear that with only a few more inches of snow the lifts would be fully operational. And the cheerful person on the other end all but promised that today's snow would provide more than enough. She hung up with a shout of joy, then shared the good news with Scott and Abigail.

"Hopefully, this will lift the spirits of the local businesspeople now," said Maggie. "At the very least, it might prevent them from lynching me after they read this week's paper."

"You mean the latest news about the wetlands issue?" asked Abigail.

"Well, how could I not report on what those EPA guys told me yesterday?"

"Do you think Greg and Rick have heard about this yet?" asked Scott.

"I would think so," said Maggie as she sorted through the mail, discovering a couple of personal Christmas cards from some of her old friends down in L.A. "The EPA guys certainly didn't make any secret of it to me, and obviously, they know that my job is to print the news here. All they really said was that they'd discovered enough evidence to put a temporary halt to any more construction in the area in question until they can reach a final conclusion in their study, but at least this will slow the development boys down a little. And, as I mentioned in my article, the holidays are a good time for them to take a break anyway. No big deal, really."

Scott laughed. "Sure, no big deal, but maybe I should start packing a gun to the office just in case old Greg Snider should decide to come in here and vent a little frustration."

Maggie made a face at him. "Gee, that's a pleasant thought, Scotty. Any more Christmas cheer you'd like to spread around?"

"Just trying to be practical is all."

"Speaking of practical..." She glanced out the window as the big flakes quickly accumulated on the steps of the porch outside. "With the opening of the ski resort looking quite possible, I wonder if I shouldn't hold back on printing a couple of those especially irate letters that I selected for this week's editorial page. And maybe we should shelve that local businessowners petition story. Some of those people might be feeling a little more optimistic and positive right now."

"But then again," said Abigail thoughtfully, "It just might prove to be a good reminder to folks that moods around here can change at the drop of a snowflake. People need to remember in times like these that a little bit of patience can go a long, long way."

"That's a good point." Maggie thought specifically of Kate and Buckie's recent display. Would they still be so hard on her if they suddenly had traffic flowing through the Blue Moose as a result of this long-awaited snowfall? "I guess it's situations like this that show you who your fair-weather friends are."

By noon there was nearly two inches on the ground, and it was still coming down steadily. Maggie walked happily to the deli, eager for a hot bowl of soup. It was busier than usual with local businessowners already celebrating what looked to be a turn in the road for everyone. Maggie sat alone eating her soup, pretending to read her mail as she listened to snatches of conversation.

"Cindy at the hotel says she's already booked every single room for this upcoming weekend..."

"My brother called from Portland this morning saying he heard on the radio that our resort will be one of the first to open in this area."

"And what with Christmas vacation starting this week, we should be crawling with tourists in the next day or two...."

"Guess we had better enjoy our last day of leisure and quiet. From here on out it'll be hopping around here."

"Told you," whispered Rosa. "See how the snow comes and everyone starts singing a new song?" She set a warm cranberry scone in front of Maggie. "Compliments of the house for hanging in there with all these cantankerous businesspeople."

Maggie smiled up at her friend. "Thanks. Yeah, I guess you have to be tough to live in a small town."

Rosa patted her on the shoulder. "But it does have its rewards."

~

On her way home from work, Maggie noticed Jed's red pickup pulling out on Main Street ahead of her. Her heart gave a small tug and then she quickly remembered that Leah was using his truck while he was in Seattle with Michael. The wheels spun out a little and the back end fishtailed slightly, but then Leah seemed to regain control of the vehicle and continued on without further problems. Still, Maggie felt slightly concerned, and decided she would give Leah a call just to make sure she'd made it safely home. Leah would probably resent being checked on, but Maggie would do it for Jed.

She loved coming home to her festive-looking house, but it looked especially charming with the Christmas lights reflected in the newly fallen snow. When she opened the door, the smell of pine wafted toward her like a fragrant perfume, emanating both from the tall tree in the parlor and from the evergreen garlands she and her mother had wrapped around the banister all the way to the second floor. Tonight, mingled with this aroma, came the smell of baking and sweet vanilla, and after quickly removing her coat, Maggie headed straight to the kitchen for a sample. There she found Spencer and Daniel up to their elbows in mounds of cutout sugar cookies, and both of them immersed in the process of decorating them with frosting and other confectionery delights that Audrey must have set before them.

"Hey, you two look like a couple of overgrown elves," she said as she chose an undecorated reindeer from the pile. "Nice work, guys."

"Look at this one, Mom," said Spencer as he held up what she suspected by the shape was supposed to be a Santa, but instead of a jolly red suit, he was frosted in what appeared to be a blue tank top and shorts with a yellow number "thirty-two" piped right where his beard should be.

"What is it?" she asked.

"It's me in my basketball uniform. You know, next year, when I make the JV team." He grinned at her as he proudly set the cookie on the plate with the others.

"Very creative," she said somewhat skeptically. "Does your grandmother know about all this? Or did you guys bind and gag her before you threw her in the broom closet?"

He laughed. "Grandma had to go to the store and she said we could do whatever we wanted with them. Hey, Daniel, show Mom that cool tree you just made."

Daniel held up a tree decorated in wild, somewhat psychedelic, swirls of color. "It's kind of weird, isn't it?" He sounded apologetic.

"Actually, it looks like a piece of art you might find in some new avant-garde gallery in L.A."

"Really?" He rubbed his nose, managing to leave a streak of bright green frosting on the tip.

She nodded, trying not to laugh. "You guys are quite the talented cookie decorators. I can't wait for Barry and Rebecca to see these."

"Hello there," called Audrey as she came into the kitchen and set a bag of groceries on the counter. "Don't know what got into me to venture outside in weather like that." She took off her coat and hat and shook the snow from them on the back porch, and then stepped back inside. "But I suddenly remembered that survival list you were making the other day in case we ever get snowed in or whatever, and I thought I better go get some supplies—you know, just in case."

Maggie laughed. "I'm sorry. I forgot all about that. Do you need help bringing anything in?"

"Maybe Spence could go get the other two bags." Audrey leaned over to examine their work. "Very interesting. I see you guys mixed up some new colors." She held up a custard cup containing what looked like gray mud. "What's *this* supposed to be?"

"We were trying to make purple," explained Daniel.

Audrey shook her head. "Well, I've never seen cookies quite like these before."

Maggie smiled. "I was just telling them that Rebecca and Barry would probably appreciate them as some sort of modern art."

"Oh, that reminds me," said Audrey as she began unloading the bag, handing items to Maggie as she spoke. "Barry called today and said he'd decided to drive since there were so many flight connections just to get into Byron. He was worried that he might get laid over somewhere. Anyway, I suggested that perhaps he could coordinate his schedule with Rebecca's and pick her up at the Portland airport."

"What a brilliant idea, Mom. Was he okay with that?"

"He sounded just fine. I found her number in your book and gave it to him. He's going to work out all the details."

Maggie poked her mother in the arm. "Hey, did you suddenly decide to play matchmaker after all?"

Audrey laughed. "I've lived long enough to know that matchmaking rarely if ever pays off. In fact, I'll bet that the odds of winning the lottery are a lot better than making a successful match for someone."

"You're probably right. I'm just so excited to see them both. Did you tell Barry that Rebecca flies in on Friday, the twenty-third?"

"Yes, that's what made me think of it, since he was planning on driving down on the very same day."

"Perfect!"

ᴖ

It wasn't until after dinner that Maggie suddenly remembered her earlier resolve to check up on Leah. She finished loading the dishwasher, then, bracing herself to hear Leah's irritatingly confident voice scolding her for being overly concerned, she dialed Jed's number. It rang numerous times and finally a recorded message came on, playing Jed's voice in her ear as he announced they were unable to answer the phone right now. Just hearing his voice like that made her long to speak to him, to tell him how foolish she'd been...but suddenly the machine beeped and she was forced to leave a "brief message." "Hi, Leah. This is Maggie. Just wanted to make sure you're doing okay. So, give me a call, or I'll probably call you back again. You know me, the worrying type. Catch you later."

When Daniel's grandpa came to pick him up, Spencer talked her into letting him go over and spend the night. It seemed Daniel had been given a video-game system as an early Christmas present and the two couldn't wait to try it out. As it was Christmas vacation, Maggie agreed. Audrey seemed tired, so Maggie encouraged her to turn in early while she finished decorating the Christmas cookies. Then she turned on some Christmas CDs, lit a cinnamon candle, and proceeded to decorate (more traditionally than the boys) the rest of the cookies. Finally she finished the last one, then froze them just the way her mother had recommended, one layer at a time. She separated them with wax paper in boxes and returned them to the freezer. This way they would still be fresh for next week. Naturally, she saved a couple for her reward when she was done to be enjoyed with a cup of tea. All this time, Lizzie had been staying close to her heels in the kitchen. She had tossed the old dog a couple of broken cookie tidbits, but for some reason Lizzie seemed unusually restless. Maggie wondered if she could be missing Bart, who had taken to sleeping in the guest house with Audrey (after she had been delighted to discover that the smart dog could climb the ladder up to the loft where he still liked to sleep sometimes).

"What's wrong, old girl?" asked Maggie as she ran her hand over the smooth black head. "Are you missing Bart? Or maybe Leah. I know you were awfully close to her too." Suddenly Maggie realized she hadn't heard back from Leah all night. She glanced up at the clock and saw that it was now after ten. Although she hated to disturb Leah this late, she knew she wouldn't be able to sleep herself out of worry for the girl. She quickly dialed the number, but this time got an operator's recording saying that the call could not be connected. She hung up and looked down at Lizzie. The dog looked up with pleading eyes and whined.

"What is it, girl?" Maggie turned from the nervous dog and glanced out the kitchen window. The snow had quit falling a couple of hours ago, and now all looked peaceful and serene outside, with even a partial moon peeking through the clouds to illuminate the snow and making it light enough to see for quite a distance. The dog whined again, and as senseless as it seemed, Maggie felt that she too was concerned for Leah's welfare.

"Maybe I should just drive on out there and make sure everything's all right," she said out loud. She looked down at Lizzie. "Want to go for a ride, girl?"

Immediately the dog began wagging her tail. Maggie smiled. It was probably silly, but she knew she wouldn't sleep a wink tonight if she didn't. She thought about leaving a note, but Spencer was gone for the night anyway. She considered calling her mother, but felt certain Audrey would be asleep by now, and she didn't want her to worry unnecessarily. Besides, she would take her cell phone, just in case. Then remembering Leah's warnings about preparedness, she bundled up and even thought to grab a spare blanket for her car, just to be safe. She tossed a few cookies in a plastic bag, then she and Lizzie took off into the snowy night.

She drove slowly and with caution, marveling at the wondrous beauty of the snowy night all around her. It was a dramatic scene of varying shades of blues and purple and black. The main road had been freshly plowed and seemed to present no hazards, but when she turned onto Jed's road the plowing ceased. Still, it seemed okay; her tires had adequate traction, and even as the road began to climb and curve, her front-wheel-drive seemed to be holding to the road just fine and she didn't feel it was unsafe to continue. Now she could see the faint tracks of tires ahead of her, filled in with several inches of snow, and she suspected they belonged to the pickup. She imagined Leah snug in bed right now, and felt silly for making such an effort to check up on her. She knew she'd have to slink away with her tail between her legs for being so paranoid. Maybe she could simply spy the pickup in the drive, then sneak quietly back home. But then again what if something was wrong inside the house? No, she decided, she would not rest tonight until she saw Leah face to face, even if it meant humiliation.

Then, just as she slowly navigated a sharp, uphill curve, Maggie spotted reflector lights off to the left. She turned on her bright lights and slowed down to spot Jed's pickup hanging diagonally off the road and facing toward her. It must've spun out of control and become stuck in the deep rut next to the road, but at least there appeared to be no real damage. Just the same, her heart began to pound as she parked her Volvo. Leaving the engine running for Lizzie's sake, she leaped out of the car and ran over to see if Leah might possibly still be inside.

The pickup's front window and hood were completely coated in snow, and it was at such an angle that Maggie could barely reach to open the cab door on the driver's side. Then she ran around to the other side to find the passenger's door more accessible. Finally she was able to jerk open the snow-encrusted door. Leah was slumped across the bench seat, wearing only blue jeans and a lightweight jacket. Not even any hat or gloves. And she was not moving! Maggie quickly climbed into the pickup and cradled Leah's head on her lap. Her heart raced furiously as she spoke to her with urgency, "Leah! Are you okay?" The old pickup's interior was as cold as ice. "*Leah!*" cried Maggie, tears forming in her eyes. "*Leah, speak to me!*"

Twenty-Three

aggie pulled off her mittens and set her hand in front of Leah's nose to feel for breath. It seemed to be there but it was ever so faint. Maggie had quickly grown cold, and suspected by Leah's cool skin temperature that her problem must be hypothermia. She took off her own wool cap and thrust it onto Leah's head, and then did the same with her mittens and her thick, down-filled coat.

"Come on, Leah," she spoke loudly as she pulled her to a sitting position. "Wake up!" She gently shook her and wondered if she might possibly be able to carry the lifeless girl over to her car. "Come on, Leah!" she yelled now "You've got to wake up!" And slowly Leah began to respond. She opened her eyes and looked at Maggie as if in a daze, then finally she spoke.

"Maggie?"

"Good girl," said Maggie. "Now, come on. We've got to get you out of here. We've got to get you to where it's warm." She quickly pulled Leah out of the pickup and tried to help her stand with her arm wrapped tightly around her waist. "Come on now, honey. Try to walk. Let's get you into my car." Somehow they managed to stumble across the road,

Maggie tugging and pulling. Finally they reached the car, its motor still faithfully running. Lizzie watched with interest from the backseat as Maggie opened the passenger door and folded Leah inside, taking a moment to buckle her in and wrap the blanket all around her legs and feet. Then she ran around to the other side and climbed in herself, shaking from fear and cold. She cranked the heat up to high.

"Now, hang in there," she said as she tried to mentally calm herself in order to drive. "I'm going to do what Jed would do," she continued to speak, as much for her sake as Leah's. "I'm going to pray as I drive." She put the car in gear, but before she began to move, Lizzie hopped into the front seat and cuddled down upon Leah's lap.

Maggie glanced at the dog in surprise. "Good girl, Lizzie. Share some of that body heat with her." She thought she saw Leah smile just slightly.

Maggie decided to proceed on up Jed's road. She knew his house was only a couple miles away from where they were, much closer than her own house, and the fastest way to get Leah inside and warm. "Dear God," she prayed out loud, "please help Leah. Help her to get warm. And please, help me to drive safely." Although she could feel the heat blowing out of the car's engine like a furnace, she continued to shiver herself. "Dear God, help Leah to get warm," she prayed again as she slowly navigated the curving road that continued climbing upward. Suddenly she wondered if she were a fool to attempt this drive. Perhaps she should've turned back, but then she would've had even more distance to cover on this mountain road. Finally, after what seemed hours but was actually less than ten minutes, she recognized the dark shadow of the building that had once been their church looming straight ahead. She followed the road behind it past Jed's shop and on toward the little cabin, hoping to see warm lights glowing from the window. But all the buildings were dark. Leaving the car running, she ran on ahead to turn on some lights, but after fumbling with a couple switches, she realized that the electricity must be out and inside the cabin was cold. She ran back to the car and positioned it so her headlights would shine right into the front window of the cabin. She quickly located and lit kerosene lamps, so handily positioned she supposed that losing the power might not be such a rare occurrence out here. Then she wadded up newspaper and stacked kindling in the woodstove, pushing the couch up close to it. She searched the small cabin for quilts and blankets, placing them near the woodstove to warm. Just as soon as the kindling began to flame, she carefully placed some bigger logs on it and then went out to get Leah.

She opened the car door, and Leah looked at her with wide, frightened eyes. "Maggie," she whispered hoarsely, "I was so scared."

Maggie eased her from the car and helped her into the house, Lizzie obediently following at their heels. After settling Leah on the couch by the now-crackling fire, she piled the blankets and quilts up around her.

Then she turned to Lizzie and opened the covers. "Want to join Leah?" As if she understood, Lizzie hopped right up and snuggled close while Maggie tucked them both in. "Keep her nice and warm, old girl."

Maggie found a plaid woolen jacket hanging on the door. It smelled like Jed. She put it on and went back outside, for what she hoped would be the last time tonight, and turned off her engine, remembering to bring her cell phone back inside with her. Without wasting a moment, she went into the little kitchen area and thanked God for the gas stove sitting in the corner. She thought she'd seen a large propane tank at the side of the house last summer. She lit a burner and quickly filled the teakettle with hot tap water, wondering if Jed's water heater might also be gas powered.

Then she went to check on Leah, who was sitting up now stroking Lizzie's silky ears, her eyes still wide and dazed. "How did you know to come for me, Maggie?" she asked in a dry whisper. Maggie gently rubbed her warm hands over Leah's. The young girl's hands were white and delicate and reminded Maggie of the lilies in the springtime, but they felt as cold as death. Maggie shuddered.

"I called to check on you, leaving a message for you to call me back." Maggie looked fondly upon her. "When you didn't, I began to feel a little concerned, so Lizzie and I decided to take a little ride out in the snowy night."

Leah shut her eyes for a moment. "I'm so glad you did."

Just then the teakettle began to whistle. Maggie went over and stirred a packet of instant cocoa into a big green mug, topping it off with a little cold milk from the refrigerator, then brought this back to Leah. "Here hold this to warm your hands and then drink it slowly." Then she reached down and pulled off Leah's lightweight leather boots and gently rubbed her cold feet, holding them close to the fire for warmth.

"What happened, Leah?" she finally asked. What she really wanted to know was why hadn't Leah immediately climbed from the stranded pickup and walked on to Jed's place. It was less than two miles and couldn't have taken much more than an hour or so to get there. Surely a good hike would've been better than freezing in that truck!

Leah took another sip of cocoa and Maggie was relieved to see the color slowly returning to her lips. They had been a pale shade of blue when Maggie had first discovered her. "It started snowing real hard on my way home," began Leah, "but I was driving pretty careful—or so I thought. And then suddenly the pickup just started to swerve." She took another sip of cocoa. "That's when I jerked the wheel...I know you're not supposed to...but I just couldn't help it. And the pickup went into a spin...and ended up...well, you saw it." Her lip began to quiver.

"I can understand how that might happen," said Maggie soothingly. "I know everyone says when you lose control that you're supposed to steer right into the direction you're sliding into, but what if you're heading right smack into a tree? I'm afraid I would jerk the wheel too."

"Well, take it from me, it doesn't help anything."

Maggie patted her hand. "Are you feeling any warmer yet?"

Leah nodded. "Thanks, and Lizzie is helping a lot too. I didn't think I'd ever be warm again." She finished off her cocoa.

"Let me get you some more cocoa," said Maggie. "You lean your head back and rest a little."

She went over and made them both a mug of cocoa this time. After taking a few minutes to find some crackers and cheese to go with it, she returned to Leah. "Here, you must be starving. Munch on these for now and I'll see if I can find some soup or something to heat up for you." She tried to call home on her cell phone, hoping to leave a message on her answering machine just in case anyone was worried in the morning, but she discovered she was out of range, probably due to the mountains. She picked up Jed's phone again, but it was still dead. Well, no one even knew she was gone tonight, so no one would be concerned. And they would simply drive back home in the morning. She found a can of chicken noodle soup and began to heat it on the stove. Then remembering the Christmas cookies, she made one last dash to the car to get them. It had begun to snow again. She stamped her feet and shook out Jed's coat when she got in the house.

"Is it snowing again?" asked Leah in a fearful voice.

"Yes. Just lightly. We'll be fine in here with the fire going. Don't worry."

She arranged the hot soup with more cheese and crackers on a tray and took it over to Leah. "Okay, Lizzie, maybe you should hop down now." She patted a rug next to the fire and Lizzie obeyed. "You're a good old dog," said Maggie as she arranged the tray next to Leah. "Old Arnold would be proud of you, girl."

Leah smiled down on the dog. "I wish I could keep her, Maggie."

"Well, why not? Would Jed mind if you have a dog out here?"

"No, I'm sure he wouldn't. But you know I'm at work all day and…"

"Why not take her with you to work? She'd be good company. I remember when I was in England a lot of shop-keepers kept their dogs with them in their shops. Of course, the dogs were always rather sedate and well mannered. I don't know that anyone would want a dog like Bart with them." Maggie laughed.

"Then you don't mind if I keep her?" asked Leah incredulously as she dipped her spoon into the soup.

"Not at all. I think she's been missing you."

After Leah had finished her late supper, Maggie gave her some of Audrey's cookies. She'd purposely brought a couple of the wilder ones decorated by the boys. "Spencer and Daniel went a little nuts frosting these," she explained.

"They're great."

"I'm curious, Leah," began Maggie, "about what happened after Jed's pickup spun out of control." Then she glanced at her watch. "Although it's getting pretty late. You may want to get some sleep."

"No, I don't feel tired right now. And I want to tell you what happened. After I realized I was stuck in the ditch, the snow was coming down so fast that I was afraid to get out. It was dark outside and like a blizzard, and I thought for sure I'd get lost. So I decided it would be better just to stay with the truck and wait."

"Of course," said Maggie. "I forgot about how the snow had been coming down so hard earlier. By the time Lizzie and I got up there all was quiet and calm."

"Anyway, I thought I'd keep the engine running to keep the heat on. I had almost a whole tank of gas, but…" She made a sheepish face. "I hadn't thought to dress real warmly this morning. Pretty dumb, huh?"

Maggie just shrugged. "We all make mistakes. I'm sure you won't do *that* again."

Leah shook her head. "With the engine running, it seemed like exhaust fumes were coming into the cab. I wondered if I might've gotten the tailpipe stuck in the snow. I saw that once on a movie or something."

"Yes, and the truck was at the right kind of angle for that to happen."

"So, I turned off the engine and got out and made my way to the back end. It was buried in snow. I dug and dug and never found it. I ended up losing my gloves in the snow, and by then I was so cold I had to get back inside."

Maggie nodded. "And then you were probably afraid to leave the engine running?"

"Yeah. I'd let it run a little with the window open. Then quickly turn it off and wind the window up real fast. But it wasn't working. Finally, I left the window up. I just kept getting colder and colder. And then I must've fallen asleep."

"That's what hypothermia does to you."

Leah nodded sadly. "I was so scared. But I did think to pray, Maggie, and that made me feel a little better. I figured if I died at least I'd go to heaven."

Maggie smiled. "Well, it must not have been your time."

"I thought you were an angel when I first saw you. Thanks for coming."

"It was the only way I'd get any sleep tonight. You know what a worrier I can be sometimes."

"I'll bet you're tired. Do you want to go back home, Maggie?" asked Leah, a trace of fear in her dark eyes. For the first time, Maggie noticed how much she looked like Jed. In amazed wonder, she just stared at the girl for a long moment. In that same moment a strong maternal love rooted deeply in her heart, and she knew no matter what happened between her and Jed she would always love Leah as a daughter.

"No," said Maggie. "I'm not going anywhere tonight."

Leah smiled in relief while Maggie removed the dishes and tray. She returned to stuff several more pieces of wood into the woodstove.

"If you push in that handle on the side of the stove, it will burn longer," said Leah. "It's a damper, and there's enough wood in there right now to last for most of the night."

Maggie pushed in the handle, and then turned to Leah. "I think you should sleep right here by the fire tonight. Will you be comfortable on that couch?"

Leah smiled and snuggled down into the blankets. "Yeah, it's fine. I'm finally getting warm. You can have my room if you like, Maggie. It's the one to the right of the bathroom. It used to be Jed's when he was a little boy."

"Okay. Is there anything I can get for you first?"

"No, I'm fine. And thanks again, Maggie, for everything."

"I'm just glad you're all right," she said, her voice choking a little. "Now sleep well, okay?"

"Okay. Good night."

Maggie straightened up the little kitchen, then, taking a moment to place a glass of water on the table next to Leah, she paused to watch Leah and Lizzie. Illuminated by the orange light of the gently flickering flames showing through the woodstove's glass door, she could see that both of them were sleeping comfortably. Then she took a quick, hot shower in the tiny bathroom, admiring the handsome wooden shelving that was obviously the workmanship of Jed. She wrapped herself snugly in a dark plaid robe she felt certain must belong to him. Going into the little room that belonged to Leah, she realized that this was where she had ripped the blankets from the bed during her initial rush to get everything together in the cold, dark cabin. And so she went off in search of more bedding. After unsuccessfully looking in a tiny linen cupboard, she decided to check Jed's room. She carried her kerosene lamp in there to light the way, feeling very much like an interloper, a trespasser, yet she had no intention of freezing tonight, and she felt certain that Jed would not want her to freeze either. His room, only slightly larger than Leah's, was neat and orderly, with a four-poster bed in the center made from hand-hewn pine logs.

The bed was topped with a handsome patchwork quilt and matching pillows made from a variety of plaid flannel fabrics in shades of mostly red and black—very woodsy and cabinlike. It occurred to her, and not for the first time, that Jed had good taste. But before she removed the bedding, she was drawn to a massive dresser against the wall below a window. It too seemed to be the handiwork of Jed Whitewater. She ran her hand across the smooth top, admiring the grain of the wood in the soft glow of kerosene light. A number of framed pictures adorned the top of his dresser—all in unusual handmade frames which she was sure had also been made by him. There was an older photo of two people, a handsome Native American couple dressed in clothing that suggested the forties or maybe fifties. The woman was pretty with her thick dark bangs curling over her forehead. And she looked amazingly like Leah. The man, tall and dark, appeared very serious and there was something about the mouth that reminded her of Jed. No doubt these were his parents. She set the picture down and picked up another. This was more recent, a shot of Jed and Leah together, taken at the Harvest Party that had been held in her own barn not that long ago, although it seemed like a lifetime. Even this morning seemed ages removed from her now. Somehow being out here in Jed's cabin, cut off from the world in many ways, made her feel as if she had traveled in time. She wasn't sure if she'd gone forward or back, but it definitely felt like an entirely different dimension. Something about being out here made all the problems that had been plaguing her in town seem small and insignificant. She sighed and set the photo back down. Just as she did so, another caught her eye. This one was in a lovely frame made from white birch bark branches, and the face she found in it was her own. She stared in wonder at this photo. She was wearing a white shirt and khaki walking shorts, along with a healthy tan, and was standing on top of what looked like a high ridge with mountains off behind her. Apparently she hadn't been aware that a photo was being shot, for her expression was completely candid. In her eyes was a faraway look, almost dreamy, but with just a trace of sadness. Suddenly she remembered that day vividly. Shortly after arriving in Pine Mountain, she, Buckie, Kate, and Jed had taken a vigorous hike—it was almost too much for her. She had still been dealing with her grief over the loss of Phil at the time, thinking about how he would have loved seeing all the beauty up there. Buckie had been snapping pictures right and left for a magazine story that she'd written, and obviously he'd taken this one of her without her knowledge. Somehow Jed had gotten hold of it, had it enlarged, and made a frame for it. Indeed, a beautiful frame—as if the photo, or the person in it, was of some importance to him. Silent tears began streaking down her cheeks. She wasn't sure if it was just the result of a highly emotional evening...or seeing this. But they were good tears. Tears of relief. And somehow she knew all would be well. Instead of removing the bedding from Jed's bed, she simply climbed in and soon fell asleep. A deep and restful sleep.

Twenty-Four

The next morning Maggie awoke relaxed and refreshed. She smiled as she looked around her, seeing Jed's room, his things, illuminated by the morning light. She stretched luxuriously on the flannel sheets and suddenly realized the cabin had grown quite cold during the night. She jumped out of bed and slipped into the main room to see that the fire in the woodstove had dwindled to a small pile of red coals. At least Leah appeared warm and was still sleeping soundly. Lizzie looked up as Maggie placed some sticks of kindling on top of the coals, remembering to pull the damper back out (she could learn to be a mountain woman too!) and almost immediately their fire was revived. She stood close to the woodstove, absorbing its heat and wrapping Jed's bathrobe more tightly around her. As the flames began to strengthen and grow, she added more logs. Yes, she could get used to this sort of simplicity.

She returned to Jed's bedroom to dress and to put everything back into place. She considered laundering the sheets, but without electricity she'd probably have to use a wash tub and scrub board and she wasn't willing to be *that* much of a mountain woman! Then she tiptoed into the kitchen and hunted around until she found an old-fashioned coffeepot that could be used on top of the gas stove. She finally figured out the contraption and got it all set up over the flames, then she began to search for something to eat for breakfast. It was after eight o'clock, but she was in no hurry to get to work today. Clyde would already be printing the paper, and she would only be starting to work on next week's special Christmas edition. She shook her head in disbelief. Could it be that Christmas was only a week away? And yet, she felt no real stress or worry at the thought. Somehow being out here in Jed's cabin was like being in another world. And part of her wished she could just stay out here forever—living the simple life.

"Hey there," called Leah from the couch. "Is it morning already?"

"Yes. Did you sleep well?"

Leah climbed stiffly from the couch. "Yeah, I think I must have, especially since I don't remember a single thing since I said goodnight." She picked up the water on the table by the couch and quickly downed it. "I'm thirsty."

"Come have some orange juice," urged Maggie. "I'm fixing us some breakfast right now, then I think we had better head into town before someone sends out a search party."

Leah drank the juice, then looked at Maggie. "Would you mind very much if I stayed at your house—just until Jed gets back?"

"Of course you can stay at my house. You can stay for as long as you like, Leah. You know that."

She smiled faintly. "Yeah, I guess I know...I'm just not sure why." She set down her empty glass and her smile faded. "Maggie, there's something I really need to tell you."

Maggie flipped the bacon over and looked up. "What is it?"

"I need to apologize." Leah sighed loudly. "This isn't easy, but I suppose it'd be best just to get it out. And if you hate me when I'm done, well, then it'll be all my fault anyway." She looked directly at Maggie. "You see, I have been really, really jealous of you because of Jed. I know it probably sounds pretty stupid and totally selfish. But I was afraid that he loved you more than he loved me. I mean, he'd actually loved you longer—even before I came along. And it was no secret that he didn't even really seem to like me very much right at first—"

"He liked you," defended Maggie. "He's always liked you."

"Well, you know—he was all worried that I was a bad influence on Spencer and stuff like that. I knew all about it then, I just didn't realize at the time that he was my father. Anyway, when he found out he was my father, then it did seem like he really loved me. But still not as much as he loved you..."

"But those are two totally different kinds of love, Leah. I don't know how you can even compare one to the other. It's like apples and oranges—both good and special in their uniqueness. The way I love Spencer is just...it's just unexplainable. I mean, I'd love him no matter what he did, and I'd probably even kill to protect him if I had to. That's just the way a parent loves—"

"Not all parents." Leah's eyes grew dark now, the edges brimming with tears. "Not *my* mother."

Maggie turned down the flame beneath the bacon and moved closer to Leah, putting an arm around her shoulders. "Oh, honey, I'm so sorry about that."

Tears began to trickle down Leah's cheeks. "You know, sometimes my mother would just take off—even when I was really little. She'd just run off with some guy for a few days, or weeks. Someone she *said* she loved, even if he was just a big, stupid jerk." A little sob broke inside of her. "She always loved her men more than she loved me."

"I understand why you felt jealous, but you must know by now that your father's love is very different than your mother's. Jed would never, *ever* leave you—not for *anyone*." Her eyes also filled with tears. "I know that for a fact. He's very protective of you—almost to a fault. Oh, Leah, he loves you so much. He would never in a million years hurt you. You must know that."

"I do." Leah swallowed hard.

"Then what's the problem?"

"I wasn't so worried about Jed." Leah looked down at the floor. "I was worried about you."

Now the tears began to flow down Maggie's cheeks as well. "Oh, Leah, I would never hurt you either. Honestly, I wouldn't. I mean, I admit I was getting a little irritated at you because I thought perhaps you were trying to push Jed and me apart—"

Leah looked into Maggie's eyes. "I was!"

Maggie nodded. "I know that now. But, somehow it just doesn't matter anymore. I don't really know how to explain this very well, but last night when I was watching you sleep, and I was so relieved that you were okay, well, something happened inside me. I mean, I've always really loved you...you have to believe me. Ever since that first day when Spencer brought you home last summer...but last night, I was watching you, and I suddenly felt like...well, like I couldn't love you a bit more if you were my own flesh and blood daughter."

"Really?"

"I mean it. It was that strong sort of mother-bear-emotion that you'll never understand until you have a child of your own. But I had it, Leah. I swear, I did. I still do. I think, last night, I adopted you as my very own daughter whether you like it or not. And even if nothing ever comes out of my relationship with Jed—other than just good friends—I want to stick by you forever." She sniffed. "I want to be a grandmother to your kids. Can you understand that?"

Leah nodded and broke into a big, watery smile, then the two hugged, long and hard. Finally they stepped apart, and Maggie reached across the counter for a nearby box of tissues. "Here you go."

Leah wiped her nose. "So, I guess that means you forgive me too?"

"Leah, mothers *always* forgive their children." She thought about that for a moment. "Well, okay, at least this one does. And if you don't believe me, just ask Spence—he's tried me enough times to know."

"I do believe you, Maggie. But I'm still sorry I was such a little brat about all this. To tell you the truth, it's pretty embarrassing. It actually felt horrible being mean to you. I was really starting to hate myself."

Maggie grinned at her. "I guess that makes me feel better. It did seem a little out of character for you—it sure didn't seem like the Leah I thought I knew."

⌒

After a leisurely breakfast, with Lizzie finishing off the table scraps, Maggie drove them all carefully back into town. About six more inches of snow had accumulated over night, bringing the total snowfall to nearly a foot. Maggie asked Leah to call Audrey on the cell phone as soon as they were within range.

"She wasn't even worried," said Leah, after hanging up. "She just thought you'd gone to work early this morning."

Maggie laughed. "I guess we both could've been lost all night and no one would've even have noticed—or at least not right away."

She dropped Leah and Lizzie at Jed's shop with a promise to bring them back some lunch, then stopped by the newspaper office to explain what had happened last night and to check on things in general before she went back home to put on fresh clothes. "I'll be back in after lunch," she promised Abigail as she fingered through the mail.

"Good grief, girl, after all you've been through, I think you should just take the whole day off," said Abigail sagely. Then she looked at Maggie curiously. "Although, as strange as it sounds, you actually look more refreshed and relaxed than you have in the last few weeks."

Maggie sighed happily. "I feel better too. Something about being up there in the cabin was like having a little mini-vacation of sorts."

"Pretty wild one, if you ask me, but if that sort of thing agrees with you, maybe you ought to do it on a regular basis."

"No thanks," said Maggie. "At least the part about rescuing hypothermia victims. Now as far as staying in a cabin out in the snowy woods, I just might have to give that idea some thought."

᧤

For the next few days, Maggie got everything in line to publish a very special *Pine Cone* Christmas edition. Scott rounded up enough miscellaneous photos from the past year's activities to make up a two-page collage of town happenings. And they specifically steered away from any negative stories, which of course meant not a single word about TS Development. And that was despite the fact that both Rick and Greg made a personal appearance to complain in livid color about the paper's biased coverage of the wetlands issues, even suggesting it was the newspaper's fault that Pine Mountain Estates was being investigated in the first place. Maggie listened quietly to them without commenting one way or the other, then she handed each man a candy cane, wished them a very merry Christmas, and graciously showed them to the door.

The Christmas edition would also carry the uplifting story of how Barbara Harris was donating a church building to the town, and how Michael Abundi had been invited to pastor their congregation, though the official announcement wouldn't come until Sunday. The Christmas edition was coming along so well by Friday afternoon that Maggie suggested that after next Monday they should all take the rest of next week off and simply enjoy the holidays.

"I can do you one better than that," added Clyde, winking at Abigail and Gavin. "What Maggie doesn't realize is that we usually don't publish our next newspaper until after the New Year. Which means I don't want to see anyone in here until the first Monday after that."

"Actually, you guys won't be seeing me for another two weeks after that," added Scott.

"That's right," said Maggie. "I'm letting him take his two weeks of vacation time early this year—for his honeymoon."

Before Maggie left the office on Friday afternoon, Gavin pulled her and Clyde aside. "I wanted to let you guys know that Stan called me today. He looked over all the information I faxed him yesterday. He said he doesn't see any reason not to look into this whole thing more closely. But then he said," and Gavin chuckled, "that the only obstacle at this point might be the actual physical layout and appearance of the land we're considering."

Maggie laughed. "Boy, is he in for a pleasant surprise!"

"Good job, Gavin," said Clyde.

"Thanks, but we've only just begun," said Gavin soberly, although Maggie felt pretty sure she could see him glowing as a result of his uncle's rare praise—the first positive word she'd ever heard Clyde send in his direction.

"I know," said Clyde, "but it's a good start." He glanced to Maggie and placed a finger over his lips. "But still, mum's the word."

"Got ya. When will Stan come to check everything out, Gavin?"

"The first weekend after the New Year. I've got it all set up." Gavin looked uncomfortable for a moment. "Do you think we could do this at the expense of the development or the paper or something? Even though I sold my SUV, I'm running a little short on funds."

"Of course, son. Did you think I expected you to fund this entire operation from your own pocket? Remember this is my investment, not yours. You're just the hired help." Clyde studied Gavin, then added, "For now, anyway."

Gavin looked relieved and smiled at his uncle. "Stan's bringing his family for three days of skiing and vacation. I'll personally try to show them a good time and hopefully they'll fall in love with the small-town charm here. Maybe one evening we can meet with the two of you for dinner at the hotel."

"Sounds like a plan, Gavin," said Maggie. "Just let me know. There's so much going on in the next couple of weeks, I might need a reminder by then."

⁓

Maggie, Audrey, and Spencer spent Saturday preparing for Christmas and the upcoming wedding, with Leah joining in that evening after work.

"The shop was so busy today," she said as she bit into a piece of pizza that Maggie had thrown together for a quick dinner. "I think Jed's going to be really pleased. A lot of the sales were just small items, like towel racks and picture frames, but it's amazing how quickly they start to add up."

"That's great," said Audrey. "Everyone in town should be pleased with the traffic. I had to wait for five minutes to get a cup of coffee at the Window Seat this morning."

"Yeah, but all these tourists present another problem too," complained Spencer.

"What's that?" asked Maggie.

"No one wants to take any time to go snowboarding. Sierra is so busy at the deli that she can't get away, and, of course, Daniel can't go anyway. Then you wouldn't even take me up there today."

Maggie laughed. "But I promised if you helped me get those guest rooms ready that I'd take you tomorrow afternoon, now didn't I?"

"How's your physical therapy coming?" asked his grandmother. "Are you still doing those exercises to get your foot nice and strong?"

"Yeah, only about ten times a day! Pretty soon my injured foot will be in better shape than the other one!"

"When do Jed and Michael get home, Leah?" asked Audrey. Maggie hadn't really told her mother all of the details about spending the night at Jed's cabin with Leah, but she knew her mother had noticed the change in their relationship.

"I think they're finished with the show today, and probably will get home tomorrow, unless they decide to stay longer. I left Jed a note explaining that I'm staying back here for the time being."

"Only for the *time being?*" complained Spencer. "Why don't you just stay here for good? Then we can all do music together, and Mom can take you to work with her, and we'll just be one big happy family." He gave her a cheesy smile.

Maggie had to chuckle. "That's nice, Spence, but it's Leah's decision. She knows she's welcome here."

"Yeah, who knows?" said Leah. "I might just stay a while. Maybe at least throughout the holidays." She glanced at all the festive preparations going on around them, then took another slice of pizza. "After all, this is a pretty happening place to be, and I sure can't complain about the food."

∽

That night, Maggie, immersed in a new novel recommended by Elizabeth, was reading long past midnight when she was startled to hear a vehicle pull into her driveway. She looked out her bedroom window to observe a large truck with its lights on below, and suddenly realized it was Jed dropping off Michael. She quickly threw on her thick chenille robe and slippers and dashed downstairs, opening the door in time to greet the two men.

"Sorry to disturb you," said Jed as he handed Michael his bag, "but we were so homesick we decided to hotfoot it back home today."

"You're not disturbing me," said Maggie. "I was already awake. But I just wanted to let you know that Leah is staying here. And I didn't want you to be alarmed when you saw your pickup off the side of the road near your house. She had a little driving mishap, but she is fine, and I'm sure your pickup is okay too."

Jed walked up toward the porch with a look of concern etched into his features. "She's really okay then?"

"Yes. She's perfectly fine." She looked down from the top step to see his smooth, handsome features illuminated by the porch light. She wanted to just stare at him, to drink in his presence, but she forced herself to look away, watching as Michael unloaded some things from the cab of the truck. "She said your shop has been really busy this week."

"Good. But if Leah's fine, why is she staying here?"

"I think she was lonely. Would you mind very much if she stays a few more days, maybe through the holidays even? She just mentioned this evening that she might like to. And, by the way, Gavin hasn't been staying here for over a week now. He found his own place in town."

His brow remained somewhat puzzled. "Sure, Leah can stay wherever she wants to." Then he turned to Michael, who was approaching the porch with several bags and looking very sleepy. "Hey, Michael, maybe you'd like to come back and stay with me again?"

"Yes. I like your cabin, Jed. It is much more like what I am used to at home. I sometimes feel lost in these big houses."

"Well, then, I guess we'll see you later, Maggie," said Jed, lingering a moment as Michael climbed back into the truck with his things.

"Did you have a good show, Jed?" she asked, longing to prolong this encounter.

"Yeah, surprisingly so. Thanks for asking."

She took a breath then said, "I missed you, Jed."

"You did?" He seemed genuinely surprised.

"Of course. I've been missing you for weeks now."

His eyes began to glow warmly and he moved toward her, now standing on the first step of the porch. "Well, the truth is, I've been missing you too. And I've been wondering if we could get together and talk some things over."

"I don't know why not. I know I have some things I need to say to you." She smiled down on him.

He stepped up another step and now looked directly into her eyes. "And there's one thing I need to say right now, Maggie." He reached over and touched her arm. "I need to tell you I'm sorry for being so horrible that day in your office. I don't even know what got into me, but will you forgive me?"

"Of course, but I said some pretty harsh things too. Will you forgive me?"

He nodded and continued looking right into her eyes. "I've been giving everything a lot of thought, and I think there has to be a better way to deal with all this. I don't want to hurt Leah, but I can't stand to be apart from you any longer, Maggie. Do you think we could find some time to get together and talk about all this...about us?"

"I sure hope so!" Her heart felt like it was actually fluttering and she couldn't think of anything else to say.

"I'll call you tomorrow and we'll talk." Jed sounded hopeful.

"By the way, have you got any plans for Christmas yet?"

"None that I know of."

"We want to invite you and Michael over. We've already got Barbara Harris and Leah all lined up. We felt pretty sure you guys might like to join them."

He smiled. "Now, that sounds like a perfect plan."

"And my brother and an old friend of mine are coming too."

"I'd like to meet them." His voice was so warm, so gentle. *This* was the Jed she knew! It was all she could do not to run down the steps and throw herself into his arms, but she held onto the cold wooden railing, controlling herself.

"Well, then you will."

"I think it's pretty late, and I'm sure Michael's getting cold in the truck."

"Yeah, you better go. See you in church tomorrow?"

"That's right! Tomorrow's Sunday. Michael is looking forward to making his acceptance announcement from the pulpit. Isn't that great news?"

"Yes, almost like a miracle. I was so pleased. Good night, Jed."

"Good night, Maggie."

She felt like she was floating on air as she walked back up the stairs to her room. Perhaps this would be a wonderful Christmas after all. One way or another, she felt certain that it would.

Twenty-Five

Maggie remembered Sunday morning that she had promised to take Spencer up to the ski resort (to snowboard for the first time ever!) directly after church. She quickly explained this to Jed, suggesting that it might be the best plan as Leah hadn't even had a chance to really talk to him yet. This would get Maggie out of the picture for a while, which might be handy. He somewhat reluctantly agreed to this line of reasoning, but quickly promised they would talk as soon as possible.

She spent the first hour watching her poor son fumble and stumble on the bunny hill. It seemed he spent more time getting up than actually standing on his board. She felt sorry for him, but figured this was some sort of strange rite of passage that he must pass through, although more than once she suggested he look into lessons. But each time he adamantly refused insisting that he would get the hang of this on his own. Finally, when he splattered to the ground just as they were contemplating trying out the chairlift, she discreetly questioned the rope-tow operator, a young man she'd seen in town a few times, about whether he knew of anyone who gave snowboarding lessons.

He glanced at his watch. "You're in luck. I'll be starting a boarding workshop at two o'clock and I still have a couple spaces."

Maggie turned to Spencer, who'd managed to get to his feet and awkwardly slide his way over to her. "Hey, Spence, this guy gives snowboarding lessons, do you think you might—"

"Oh, man," he exclaimed. "Sign me up!"

She looked at him in surprise. "Okay, sure."

After taking care of the lessons, they took a quick lunch break in the big log structure that served as the main lodge. It was full of skiers and riders (as Spencer called the snowboarders), but everyone seemed to be in holiday spirits and no one minded the long wait in line. Just before two o'clock she and Spencer went back outside and parted ways.

Maggie then rode the lift up by herself and enjoyed several relaxing runs down the slope, suddenly free and unhindered after all those stop-starts that had been required as she had waited for Spencer to get his "snow legs." Hopefully a couple hours of instruction would improve all that for him; she knew how badly he wanted to develop some control before any of his friends, especially Sierra, saw him on the slopes. He'd been such a good sport about the whole thing, laughing at himself each time he fell and hardly complaining at all. Fortunately his healed foot seemed well protected by the large, sturdy boots and hadn't troubled him a bit.

Just before taking what she supposed would be her last run of the day, Maggie paused on the top of the hill to appreciate the full mountain view. Planting her skis and leaning into her poles, she surveyed the thick blanket of white all around, spotted with dark evergreens. The trees' boughs were charmingly weighted down by rounded clumps of collected snow, almost as if they were hands holding snowballs. It was all so incredibly beautiful. And off in the distance, but appearing so close it almost seemed she could touch them, loomed the various peaks of majestic mountains along the

Cascade Range. She breathed deeply of the cold, fresh air and sighed with happy contentment. Life was good!

She knew she had learned a valuable lesson in the last week, and yet she had not yet attempted to put the whole thing into actual words, for it almost seemed too big to wrap her mind around. But it had to do with simple things like peace and contentment and trusting God. Even today, when Michael had shared from the pulpit, the gist of his lesson seemed like a bright beacon of hope, pointing directly to these very same things. Somehow, he had managed to push through confusion and clutter and cut right to the heart of the matter, pointing out how, as you pass through every trial and challenge and hardship that life presents, the most important thing was to surrender your spirit to God—and to trust him with your whole heart.

Maggie brushed a strand of hair from her eyes and looked up to the clear, blue sky above her. Certainly, she couldn't understand all this yet, and perhaps her mind would never get it completely down. But somehow she suspected that her heart would. She breathed a prayer of deep thanksgiving as she started her descent down the slope, sailing with grace and abandon, and thinking that no matter what lay ahead, with God's help she could face anything.

She found Spencer waiting at the bottom of the hill with a big grin on his face. "Want to take one more run before they shut down the chairs, Mom?"

"Sure, if you're you up for it. I thought you might be all worn out by now."

"Nah, I'm fine. And I want to show you something."

By the time they reached the bottom of the slope, she couldn't believe how greatly he'd improved. He only fell twice! And even then he recovered himself so quickly, hardly losing any momentum at all as he pulled himself from the snow to an upright position on the board and continued.

"That was fantastic, Spence!" she exclaimed. "Did the instructor sprinkle you with magic dust or something?"

"No, he just gave some good tips, and it all started to sink in." He shoved his hat to the back of his head and wiped his brow. His face was flushed from both excitement and the exercise. "Want to get a soda before we head for home?"

"You go ahead. I want to check on something and then we can meet at the car." While he headed to the snack bar, she slipped downstairs and quickly purchased him a season lift pass as an early Christmas present.

∽

Jed and Maggie tried several times to get together on Monday, but everything was so busy with the paper and last minute holiday preparations, plus Jed had his shop and was trying to fill some rush orders, that between the two of their schedules it was impossible to schedule anything for more than a few minutes. Maggie honestly reassured him that she wasn't the least bit worried, and that when the time was right, they'd work it out and get together. Town was so packed with tourists and shoppers that she figured Jed had better make the most of these eager holiday customers. It wouldn't be long until this mad rush quieted down some, and there would be plenty of time to talk then.

On Tuesday she decided to avoid the additional traffic in town by staying home and helping Audrey get things ready for their soon-to-arrive Christmas guests. Besides, she told herself, she was supposed to be on something of a vacation right now, which she probably needed far more than she realized.

The Christmas edition of the *Pine Cone* came out Wednesday as planned, and she sat by the fire in her library carefully examining each page. All in all, it was a paper to be proud of. Scott's collage had turned out to be charming, and the stories felt positive and uplifting. Even Greg and Rick should find no fault with *this* paper!

Spencer, afraid he might forget all that he learned about snowboarding, talked her into returning to the ski resort again on Thursday. She agreed to go up for the afternoon, but only if he helped her thoroughly clean the kitchen and then put fresh sheets on the beds in the guest rooms. He had this all done long before noon. And after she parked her car in the ski resort's crowded parking lot, she turned to him and handed him an envelope containing his surprise Christmas present.

"A season pass!" he cried happily when he realized what it was. "Now I can come up anytime I want—or anytime I can get a ride. Thanks, Mom! You're the best!"

"So, tell me Spence," she said as they walked through the packed snow toward the main lodge. "Are you glad we moved up here now?"

"Are you crazy?" He threw back his head and laughed loudly. "Of course I am!"

She had decided to pass on skiing today, choosing to remain by the fire in the main lodge while Spencer practiced his snowboarding. She'd brought along a novel to keep her company, but instead found herself people-watching and chatting with various friends from town. All in all, it was a very relaxing afternoon. Yet, as much as she appreciated this leisurely moment, she was also starting to look forward to having the pace pick up when Barry and Rebecca showed up. Even now she found herself making a mental list of last-minute things she would do tomorrow morning before they arrived in the afternoon. As she was making this list, it occurred to her with some alarm that she had not gotten Leah a Christmas present yet. She had done the bulk of her gift shopping during the time when Leah had been holding her at a cool distance, and had probably subconsciously blocked her from her mind. Well, it certainly wasn't too late to get something. She wondered what Leah would like—it needed to be something extra special.

That night before bed, Maggie remembered the ring her mother had given to her on her sixteenth birthday, something of a family heirloom. It had belonged to her great-grandmother—the one who'd come over from Italy almost a hundred years ago. Maggie had enjoyed the ring during her high school and college days, but hadn't worn it for years. She opened an old jewelry box she'd had since childhood and picked up the ring wrapped safely in a piece of flannel. The band was of gold, formed to look like a delicate vine with a ruby set like a flower in its center. It probably wasn't terribly valuable, although she knew it was worth something, but its real value to her was in the family history, and those memories of wearing it during the irreplaceable days of stepping into adulthood. She pushed the ring onto her finger and discovered it was slightly tighter than she remembered, then, afraid it would become stuck, she quickly pulled it off and set it on her dresser. Tomorrow she would discuss her idea with Audrey.

⌒

The house seemed to spring into action the moment Rebecca and Barry burst through the doors. The lights seemed brighter, the laughter giddier, the music merrier. After a delicious dinner of Audrey's famous homemade ravioli, Rebecca suggested they all take a walk outside to enjoy the moonlit snow, a walk which quickly escalated into a robust snowball fight and ended up with them building the biggest snowman Maggie had ever seen. They situated their masterpiece right before her front porch, and Spencer even had to go fetch a six-foot stepladder so that he and his Uncle Barry could place the head on the very top. Maggie donated her old mittens and scarf, and they christened the snowman George, proclaiming him their official holiday doorman. Then they all trooped inside for cocoa and cookies.

"You guys are like a bunch of little kids," said Audrey happily as she dropped mini marshmallows into their cocoa cups and added candy canes as stirring sticks.

Barry gave his mother an affectionate squeeze. "Yeah, and doesn't that make you feel about twenty years younger too?"

She smiled at him. "As a matter of fact, it does."

They visited around the fire in the library until late. Then Spencer broke up the party by announcing that everyone had to go to bed in order to rise early the following morning (Christmas Eve day) so that they could get to the slopes as soon as the lifts opened.

"Jed said we might close shop early tomorrow and join you guys," said Leah.

"I can't wait to meet Jed," said Rebecca. "I've heard so much about him." She winked at Maggie.

"So have I," said Barry.

"What do you mean?" asked Maggie. "I've never even mentioned him to you."

Barry glanced over to Rebecca. "A certain little bird told me."

Maggie nodded knowingly. "Can't even trust my best friend, can I?"

"What do you mean?" complained Barry. "Are you trying to keep something from your little brother?"

Suddenly Maggie felt uncomfortable, hoping that Leah wouldn't be taking any of this the wrong way. "There's really nothing to keep from you, Barry," she said quickly. "Rebecca and I email a lot, and sometimes I tend to go on and on about silly things. You know how that goes."

He shook his head. "Unfortunately, I never seem to have time for such pleasures. The only email I send and receive pertains to business, and by the time I'm done with that I don't even want to correspond with anyone."

"You sound like a real grump," teased Rebecca, her blue eyes sparkling in a way that caught Maggie's attention. Could it be there was something going on here that she hadn't noticed earlier?

"All right, you guys," warned Spencer, pointing to the mantle clock which was now pushing close to midnight. "Stay up all night if you want, but you sure better not complain when I start getting you all up early tomorrow morning. Now, I am going to bed!"

That broke up the party, but Rebecca followed Maggie into her bedroom. "I hope it was okay to tell Barry about Jed," she said apologetically.

Maggie waved her hand. "Oh, it's fine. I just didn't want to make too much of it with Leah around. We've just gone through a thing where she was feeling kind of threatened by our relationship, and she and I are doing so well now that I don't want anything to mess that up."

"She seems like a very sweet girl."

"She is. And she's been through a lot in her life already. But anyway, I think it's all going to work out fine. Things have even seemed better between Jed and me."

"So you've given up all that back-burner business now?"

"Well...not exactly."

"Oh. But you and Jed are seeing each other again?"

"Well, not exactly...but sort of. We talked briefly a few days ago. And everything seems to be working out. I'm not worried." Suddenly Maggie wanted to change the subject. "So, Rebecca, what do you think of Barry these days? He's really grown up, hasn't he?"

Rebecca laughed uncomfortably. "Yeah. I'd forgotten how attractive he is, and now even more so with age. You guys and your dark Italian good looks." She poked Maggie in the arm.

"You're not looking so shabby yourself, Rebecca. And if I'm not mistaken, I saw my little brother checking you out pretty carefully tonight."

Rebecca rolled her eyes. "Now don't start this, Maggie. You know it'll only lead to trouble. Let's all just enjoy being together and let it go at that."

The two old friends continued to talk into the wee hours of the morning. Maggie knew her son would be alarmed, but it was so fun to visit and catch up on the past several years. She promised herself she'd rise early and Spencer would be none the wiser.

Twenty-Six

Somehow everyone managed to rise early on Christmas Eve day, and after eating a quick breakfast actually prepared by Spencer, they headed up for the slopes. It was a perfect day with fresh powder and blue skies, and Spencer delighted in showing off his new snowboarding skills to Rebecca and his uncle, only falling occasionally. Rebecca skied with Maggie for the first part of the day, but after lunch she and Barry (both higher-level skiers) decided to attack the more challenging slopes. Then, just as Maggie and Spencer were waiting in the lift line, they heard a girl's voice calling out Spencer's name, and they turned to see Leah, carrying a snowboard and jogging toward them in clunky boots and what looked like a brand-new snowboarding outfit. "Hey, Spence, want to give me a lesson?" she asked eagerly, then she held out her arms as if to model. "Jed gave me an early Christmas present. He got all this in Seattle."

"Cool." Spencer smiled broadly, holding his chin with pride. "I'll teach you *everything* I know." He glanced over to his mother. "And that should take about five minutes."

Maggie laughed. "Don't believe him, Leah. He's actually pretty good on that thing. I'm sure he can get you going just fine."

"But we had better start on the bunny hill," said Spencer wisely.

"Mind if I ski with you, Maggie?"

Maggie turned in surprise to see Jed right behind her. "I didn't know you were up here. Did you close the shop early today?"

He nodded. "It's been so busy that at this rate I'll run out of merchandise before New Year's. So Leah and I decided it was time to take a break and start celebrating the holidays." He waved as Leah and Spencer took off toward the bunny hill. "So, do you mind if I join you?"

"Not at all, but you should know that I'm not a real hot dog skier. I tend to ski very carefully, kind of like an old lady."

He smiled warmly. "Suits me just fine."

On the ride up the mountain they chatted congenially, without actually discussing their relationship specifically. Maggie felt slightly relieved by this, for it seemed they needed a few minutes to warm up to each other and to connect again. She inquired about his trip to Seattle and he told her about some accounts he'd begun to set up with a couple of big Northwest furniture firms, all with the understanding that orders would be placed and filled on an individual basis. "I don't want to feel like I need to hire more help too soon," he explained. "I'd like to do all the work myself, at least for a while."

When they skied down together, Maggie could tell by Jed's form and control that his expertise level was far above hers, but he kept pace with her the entire way. At the bottom, she suggested he might like to look for Barry and Rebecca and join them on a more difficult slope.

He studied her face. "Are you trying to get rid of me, Maggie Carpenter?"

"No, not at all. I just thought—"

He pushed a strand of hair from her face. "Sometimes you think too much."

"You're probably right."

On the next chairlift ride, Jed told her all about how Leah had confessed to him about her close call with hypothermia that night. "I don't even know how to begin to thank you, Maggie."

"Thank me?" She turned and looked at him, trying to gauge his expression halfway hidden beneath his goggles. "I *love* Leah, Jed. I thank God that I found her."

He smiled then. "I think he was looking out for both of you. By the way, it was generous of you to give her the dog. She's been good company for her at the shop."

Maggie swallowed hard, wondering how or even if she should say this, but somehow she wanted to make it clear. "Jed, I want you to understand that my feelings for Leah stand alone. I have loved her since she first came to live with us. And even if you and I were to permanently part ways, I would continue to love her just as fiercely as I do now. Does that make any sense?"

He looked slightly surprised by her intensity, but as it was time to unload from the chair, he could only nod and say briefly, "I understand."

On the next ride up the mountain, Jed told Maggie that Leah had confessed something else to him. "She admitted that she was trying to come between us, Maggie." He seemed uncomfortable. "I just couldn't believe that she would do something like that."

Suddenly Maggie felt defensive of Leah. "But you must understand how it all relates to her mother—and how all those men took her away from Leah. She didn't want to lose you too, Jed. She was afraid that I would take you away from her. I understand all about that now, and I have completely forgiven her."

"She told me that you had. And I have too. I'm just trying to understand the whole thing. I guess it makes me feel kind of foolish for being taken in by it."

Maggie smiled at him. "Jed, I hate to tell you this, but I'm afraid you've got a lot to learn about women."

He grinned. "Well, I'm looking forward to some really excellent instruction from both you and Leah."

After that run, they checked on the two kids. Leah said she was ready to try a run on the beginner lift. Maggie encouraged both Jed and Spencer to accompany her on the three-person lift, explaining that she was just about skied out for the day (not wanting to admit to her son that last night's late chat session with Rebecca was starting to take its toll on her). She asked if he could catch a ride with either Jed or Barry, and then she headed on home to help Audrey with preparations for the evening's get-together.

⌒

For Christmas Eve dinner, Audrey and Maggie served a buffet for their boisterous guests. Everyone was in good spirits, but they steadily became more subdued and relaxed after their full day of skiing. After singing carols and then listening as Michael read the story of the first Christmas, the good food and the warmth from the fire began to catch up with them. It wasn't long before eyelids started growing heavy and people began to turn in for the evening, promising to meet first thing in the morning to exchange gifts and share in Audrey's traditional Christmas brunch.

Maggie wrapped one last present before collapsing onto her bed and sleeping soundly and dreamlessly. To her surprise, she awoke early the next morning and slipped downstairs before anyone else had stirred. She puttered around soundlessly, straightening up from last night, then she started a big pot of coffee. She took a hot cup and went to sit in her parlor, taking time to enjoy the quiet of the morning in her festively decorated home, with beautiful scenes of snow right out the window. She sighed in happy contentment. This is what life should be like always—snuggled up in a warm house, surrounded by loved ones, sharing good food.... Heavenly.

Soon the house bustled with people and activity, and it wasn't long before Spencer and Leah urged everyone into the parlor to sit around the Christmas tree. And then they began to hand out gifts to everyone. Shouts of excitement and "thank-yous" were heard around and about the room as people cheerfully opened presents. Maggie was keeping an eye out for Leah and the small box wrapped in gold foil paper. Finally, she saw her opening it. Leah quietly stared at the contents for a long time before she read the small note tucked inside.

Then she came over to Maggie with tears in her eyes and wrapped her arms around her and whispered, "Thank you, Maggie. You have no idea how much this means to me. I promise I will treasure it always—in exactly the same way that I'll always treasure you." Then she stepped back and slipped the ring on. "It even fits!" She held out her hand and admired it. "It's beautiful!"

Audrey joined them, placing a gentle kiss on Leah's cheek. "Since you're a part of our family, it only seemed right for you to have this."

Maggie went into the kitchen to take the cinnamon rolls out of the oven and make a fresh pot of coffee, humming happily to the Christmas music playing softly in the background.

"Thanks for the pocketknife," said Jed. She turned in surprise to see him standing in the doorway with his hands behind his back, as if he'd been watching her for a few moments. "It's a very handsome piece of work."

She smiled. "It reminded me of you."

"I'm not very good at wrapping...but I wanted to give you something."

She wiped her hands on a towel and stepped over to him expectantly. Then he pulled out a small wooden box and handed it to her. It was intricately patterned with various colors of inlaid wood, and looked perfect for a few choice pieces of jewelry.

"This is absolutely beautiful, Jed," she breathed, examining the delicate pattern with appreciation. "I assume you made it, but it hardly seems possible." She was afraid to open it, afraid to appear as if she thought something should be inside. But she didn't want him to think that the lovely box wasn't enough in itself. For it surely was.

"Go ahead and open it," he said with a smile.

Almost afraid to breathe, she did, but the beautiful box was empty. It was lined with a layer of fragrant rose-colored cedar. She held it to her nose and inhaled deeply. "Lovely."

"Remember?" he asked.

She smiled. "Of course. And just for the record, I no longer think that it's a waste of wood."

They both laughed, and the brief uncomfortable moment passed. Had he known she'd wondered if there was something else? She hoped not. She didn't want to seem like one of those women who always wanted more. Really, she didn't. She was completely happy with life just as it was. Content. She was perfectly content!

Twenty-Seven

*B*arry and Rebecca joined Maggie and Spencer for one more skiing day after Christmas, and the following day they prepared to depart. "I just can't believe the life you guys live here," said Barry with a frown as he loaded their things into his car. "It's just not fair."

"Not fair?" exclaimed Maggie, hoping for his sake to play down what she considered to be a perfectly wonderful life. "We live out here in the sticks with little more than weather and small-town gossip to entertain us while you two have all the glamour and glitter of city living. I'll bet that you're already planning some fantastic big-city New Year's Eve celebration."

Rebecca laughed sarcastically. "I'm not even going to honor that with a response."

"Oh, come on, sis," urged Barry. "Admit it, you've got it pretty sweet here."

She smiled sheepishly. "Okay. Well, I happen to like it, but it's certainly not for everyone."

He shook his head. "I don't know. I might like to give it a try someday..."

She grabbed his arm. "Are you serious, Barry? What about your fancy job in that prestigious international design firm?"

"Lots of designers are moving off-site to work these days. Ever heard of the age of computer technology?"

"You *are* serious!"

He shrugged. "I don't know. But you should know as well as anyone that big-city life ain't all it's cracked up to be."

Rebecca nodded sadly. "Amen. I hear you, brother."

"You two!" laughed Maggie. "Five minutes back in your old stomping grounds and you'll be singing a different tune."

"I suppose," said Rebecca unconvincingly, "but Barry's right. You guys do have it pretty sweet here. I'm trying not to be too envious."

Maggie shook her head in wonder. "So tell me the truth, Rebecca, would you honestly trade your law career in L.A. to become a small-town attorney?"

"Maybe..."

Maggie vigorously hugged them both. "Well, you both know you'd always be welcome here!"

Just then Audrey hurried out the front door, carrying a basket of provisions for their trip back. Maggie decided not to get her mother's hopes up with any word of the previous conversation. Goodbyes were said, promises to phone and email more often were made, then Barry and Rebecca drove away, pausing to wave from the car at the end of Maggie's driveway.

"You know, honey," said Audrey as they walked back into the house, "I think I might've seen a little spark passing between those two."

Although she'd thought the exact same thing herself, she just laughed, saying, "Nah. It must've been your romanticist's imagination, Mom."

∽

The following days passed in a whirl as Maggie worked furiously to get every detail in order for Scott and Chloe's wedding. With the winter tourist season in full swing, the town was hopping with business. Chloe was trying to make the most she could of this traffic in her little shop and Rosa and Sierra were busier than ever in the deli. Maggie saw this as her opportunity to repay her dear friend for all her previous kindness as she attempted, with Audrey's help, to carry as much of the load as possible. Abigail eagerly helped too, glad to participate in this greatly anticipated event.

Somehow by New Year's Eve all was in place for the wedding. Sam had spent the entire day at Maggie's house, setting up chairs, tending to the horse and sleigh, and even polishing the brass faucets in all the bathrooms. Rosa and Sierra came over just after the lunch hour to tend to the final food details. Then Clara and Abigail arrived in mid-afternoon with beautiful fresh flowers. All traces of Christmas, save the greens and white lights, had been removed from Maggie's house. Instead, it was transformed into what reminded Maggie of a fairy princess house, with delicate white roses, white candles, and white organza ribbons trailing everywhere mixed with the dark forest shades of evergreen and ivy. The transformation was nothing short of miraculous, and when Chloe arrived at four, she oohed and awed over everything. Maggie had invited Cherise to come and give the bride the full beauty treatment (although it wasn't a part of her regular business, Cherise was well known in Pine Mountain for giving the best herbal facials, and now she was thrilled to have the opportunity to participate in this exciting event). Besides, thought Maggie, perhaps it would help keep her mind off her own situation with Greg.

⌒

By seven o'clock the guests were all seated, and the ceremony began as planned shortly thereafter. To Maggie's relief, both of Chloe's parents had shown up. Chloe's mother, now seated in the front row, wore an expensive black gown, which Maggie hoped wasn't a reflection on her attitude toward this marriage. Cherise had tried to assure Maggie that many people wore black to evening weddings these days—sometimes even the bridesmaids! Sierra looked lovely and grown up in a tea-length vintage gown of moss green as she slowly came down the stairs, accompanied by her brother Max in a dark brown suit. Scott stood next to Michael (who also looked quite dapper in his neat black suit). When Scott had told her that he planned to wear an old tuxedo that had belonged to his grandfather during the forties, she thought he'd been kidding. But now, seeing him looking so handsome, albeit nervous, in a well-preserved satin-trimmed suit, she knew it had been a perfect choice. All these unique touches, combined with Chloe's wonderful dress from the turn of the century, created a surprisingly elegant and dramatic ambiance to the whole affair. Maggie suspected that Chloe's parents were somewhat impressed with what this young couple had managed to pull off so quickly and with very little expense, all things considered. Now everyone rose to their feet as Chloe and her father gracefully proceeded down the stairs, a recording of Bach's *Jesu, Joy of Man's Desiring* playing softly in the background. Chloe looked absolutely radiant with her red curls heaped on top of her head with a few loose tendrils curling delicately over her shoulders.

All in all it was a beautiful wedding, and Maggie noticed both of Chloe's parents daubing monogrammed handkerchiefs to their aristocratic noses. Midway through the touching ceremony, Maggie's eyes had met Jed's. He was seated next to Leah and across the room from her, and he looked unusually handsome in a dark tweed sports coat over a charcoal turtleneck sweater. His eyes seemed to lock onto hers as Michael continued to speak eloquently of the biblical meaning of marriage, and Maggie felt her own eyes mist over and blur as the couple repeated their promises to one another. Then finally, the ceremony ended and the crowd began to move about, congratulating the newlyweds and steadily escalating into a more effervescent mood appropriate to a joyous New Year's Eve celebration. Rosa had hired several high school girls to help in the kitchen and serve food so that all the guests were free to mingle and enjoy the festive atmosphere.

After the cake was cut and numerous congratulatory toasts made, Scott and Chloe prepared to make their exit, thanking everyone for everything, and wishing all a very happy New Year. Then Sam, wearing an old-fashioned top hat and scarf, proudly escorted the surprised newlyweds onto the front porch where an elegant sleigh, complete with brightly glowing kerosene lanterns, awaited them. The driver helped the couple into the sleigh as birdseed and well wishes were tossed their way. And then everyone waved and cheered as the harness bells began to jingle and the sleigh slowly cut across the meadow and on toward the road where a car awaited. People trickled slowly back into the house, but Maggie remained on the porch a few minutes longer. Entranced by the sight, she wanted to paint a picture of this magical evening in her mind before she rejoined the cheerful and noisy crowd. As she entered the house and worked her way through the rooms, she tried not to conspicuously search for Jed, and yet each time she spotted him, he seemed engaged in some lively conversation with someone else. Well, that was okay. She was just happy to see him here, and glad to see he was having what appeared to be a very good time.

Just before midnight, Maggie felt a light tap on her shoulder and turned to see Jed smiling down on her. "Care to take a walk?" he asked, holding her long winter coat all ready for her to slip into.

"I'd love to." She allowed him to help her with her coat, and then lead her to the backdoor. There by the back porch was the sleigh again! The driver nodded knowingly to Jed as he opened the tiny door. Jed helped Maggie aboard and then he climbed in next to her, tucking the thick wool blanket all around both of them. With the soft jingle of harness and bells, the sleigh took off into the snowy night.

She felt her face smiling brightly in the cold winter air. "What a perfectly wonderful idea, Jed. Thank you so much for thinking of this!" She turned happily to him. His face, illuminated by the lantern's golden glow, was smiling too.

He reached over and took her hand. "Thank you for joining me, Maggie." He slipped his arm around her shoulders. "I wanted to do something romantic for you. I think I'm still trying to make up for being such an unwitting idiot during the past few weeks. Anyway, I worked out the details for the sleigh with Sam. It seemed like the perfect way to get a moment alone with you."

Happily, they rode together with only the sound of bells, the muffled rhythmic thump of hooves, and the metal skids slicing over the frozen snow. Then after a while, Jed spoke again. "I had a reason for planning this little midnight ride," he explained, his voice sounding just slightly uncertain. "It's probably not going to make a whole lot of sense...but I think you know me well enough...well, you'll understand that I don't always do things in a traditional sort of way. Plus, as you said yourself, I have a lot to learn about women. So, if I'm doing this all wrong, please feel free to set me straight." He looked directly into her eyes with an almost pleading expression.

She nodded, trying to encourage him, and at the same time comprehend what he was talking about. As far as she was concerned, they were all right now. There was nothing more to be said about what had transpired between them. Jed was completely forgiven, and she looked forward to what was ahead for both of them.

He cleared his throat. "You see, there was something that was supposed to go with your Christmas present last week..." He reached into his pocket with his free hand. "I know this might all seem rather sudden to you, and I don't want you to think that I haven't given this thing plenty of thought. Because the truth is, I hardly think about anything else." He sounded so unsettled and nervous that suddenly her heart began to beat wildly. She was filled with a strange hope and what seemed a wild expectation. Surely this *wasn't*...surely it *couldn't* be!

"Maggie Carpenter, I love you more than I have ever dreamed was even possible, and I feel that I cannot live my life without you. Would you please do me the honor of becoming my wife?"

It was!

She just sat there in speechless and silent shock. Jed Whitewater was actually proposing to her! Why had she not seen this coming? Then she looked straight into his eyes and saw a flicker of worry there, and suddenly knew her pause was giving him some serious cause for concern. She realized just how difficult this whole thing must be for him—and perhaps this was why he had done it in what seemed like a slightly abrupt (albeit intensely romantic) fashion.

"Of course, I'll marry you!" She threw her arms around him, and he began to laugh.

"You will?" His voice sounded incredulous.

"Yes, I will! I just thought you would never ask!"

"You didn't?" He held her back and looked into her eyes, then smiled shyly. "I guess I'm not very good at this sort of thing, but I thought I was sending you all kinds of signals."

She laughed heartily. "Well, like I said, Jed Whitewater, you still have an awful lot to learn about women."

He gently touched her cheek with his hand. "I'm sure you're right about that, Maggie. I can't believe how dense I've been about so many things. That's just one of the many reasons I need you in my life. You help me to see things differently."

"I could say the same about you, Jed."

Then he slipped the ring onto her finger, and it fit perfectly. She held it up to the light and examined a simple yet elegant solitaire set into a smooth band of gold. "It's incredible, Jed. I love it. But when did you get this, and how did you know the size of my finger? It's all so amazingly fairytale wonderful!"

He smiled. "Well, I've known almost since I met you that this day was coming. I know it must sound crazy to you, but something in my heart clicked almost from the moment we

304 ⌒ Melody Carlson

met. I didn't even quite believe it myself, at first." He touched the ring on her finger. "I very carefully traced a ring you left sitting in your kitchen window sill when we were cleaning up after Thanksgiving, and I bought this while I was in Seattle. I loved its elegant simplicity—it reminded me of you." He smiled warmly down on her, then tenderly gathered her into his arms and kissed her for a long and incredible moment where the rest of the world seemed to spin totally away. When they finally pulled apart, she heard a series of loud explosions and looked up to see colorful fireworks lighting up the night sky and reflecting softly in the snow below.

"Wow!" she exclaimed breathlessly. "I always knew that every time we kissed I'd see fireworks, but this is truly amazing!"

He laughed happily. "Happy New Year, Maggie!"

"Happy New Year, Jed! Somehow, I feel certain it's going to be the best year ever!"

About the Author

Melody Carlson is an award-winning author of more than 40 books, from novels to children's stories, including *Homeward* and *King of the Stable*. When not writing, she enjoys skiing, hiking, and boating. Melody lives in Oregon with her husband and their two sons.

Harvest House Publishers

For the Best in Inspirational Fiction

Linda Chaikin

TRADE WINDS
Captive Heart
Silver Dreams
Island Bride

A DAY TO REMEMBER
Monday's Child
Tuesday's Child

G. Roger Corey
Eden Springs

Melody Carlson
A Place to Come Home To
Everything I Long For

Lori Wick

A PLACE CALLED HOME
A Place Called Home
A Song for Silas
The Long Road Home
A Gathering of Memories

THE CALIFORNIANS
Whatever Tomorrow Brings
As Time Goes By
Sean Donovan
Donovan's Daughter

KENSINGTON CHRONICLES
The Hawk and the Jewel
Wings of the Morning
Who Brings Forth the Wind
The Knight and the Dove

ROCKY MOUNTAIN MEMORIES
Where the Wild Rose Blooms
Whispers of Moonlight
To Know Her by Name
Promise Me Tomorrow

THE YELLOW ROSE TRILOGY
Every Little Thing About You

CONTEMPORARY FICTION
Sophie's Heart
Beyond the Picket Fence
Pretense
The Princess